Angel of Retribution

Also by Anthea Cohen:

Poisoned Pen (1996)

Featuring Agnes Carmichael

Angel Without Mercy (1982)
Angel of Vengeance (1982)
Angel of Death (1983)
Fallen Angel (1984)
Guardian Angel (1985)
Hell's Angel (1986)
Ministering Angel (1987)
Destroying Angel (1988)
Angel Dust (1989)
Recording Angel (1991)
Angel in Action (1992)
Angel in Love (1993)
Angel in Autumn (1995)
Dedicated Angel (1997)

ANGEL OF RETRIBUTION

Anthea Cohen

Constable · London

First published in Great Britain 1998
by Constable & Company Limited
3 The Lanchesters, 162 Fulham Palace Road
London W6 9ER
Copyright © 1998 Anthea Cohen

The right of Anthea Cohen to be
identified as the author of this work
has been asserted by her in accordance
with the Copyright, Designs and Patents Act 1988
ISBN 0 09 479200 3
Set in Palatino 10 pt by
SetSystems Ltd, Saffron Walden, Essex
Printed and bound in Great Britain
by MPG Books Ltd, Bodmin, Cornwall

A CIP catalogue record for this book
is available from the British Library

1

Agnes gently stroked the brown hen's outstretched leg; it trembled a little in her hand. The five others walked about in the nice enclosure she had built for them. The brand new hen-house smelt pleasantly of creosote. Out of the six battery hens she had brought home with her, rescued from the most horrible prison she had ever seen, four had improved. The raw, featherless places on their necks, made by the bars they had to stretch through to reach their food in the battery, were healing. They were walking about, pecking in the grass of their generous new living quarters. Two, one of which she now held in her hands, were slower to recover and, being Agnes, she was more interested, more passionately determined to bring those two back to a normal hen's life than the others. She placed the one in her hands on the grass; it made a much better effort to walk, limping, one leg perhaps maimed for ever by what it had been subjected to. She noticed the feathers were growing slightly on the bare parts. Well satisfied, she got up.

Two eggs had been their gift to her. She thought of the farmer filling the troughs with food, without emotion, without pity, and as she carefully closed the hen-house door behind her, she thought how easily she could put him in a battery, just head and shoulders protruding, and pour in the food until he was dead. Oh, it was his living, she realised that, but to make your living off cruelty, discomfort, suffering ... She shook herself as if to shake off her thoughts, which were depressing. She crossed the well-kept lawn to her house. The early spring weather was not yet encouraging the grass to grow.

Agnes' life had changed in the last eighteen months. Bill's sudden death in America had been a great blow to her, and she had blamed herself for not being with him. Sometimes she went, sometimes she didn't. This time, as he was only going for a few days, she had decided to stay at home. When they had told her, she felt part of herself had disappeared. The flat in Rutland Gate and the house in the Isle of Wight became repugnant to her, too full of memories. The house on the Island was still for sale. Rutland Gate had sold almost at once and here she was in Sussex, in the house she had bought. Not really a house, Rose Cottage was a marrying of four small farm labourers' cottages. The joining had been well done. The little building, low and cosy-looking with white-painted outer walls, thatched roof and rather small cottage windows, was nothing like any house Agnes had ever lived in. It had done something already to comfort her, to help her start a new life.

'Mac, it's not your dinner-time yet.' Agnes sat down on the small settee and Mac, a bit stiff now – he was eleven – managed to get up beside her. His high excited bark was the only sound in the house. Agnes could feel the warmth of his small, now rather fat little body. She put her arm round him and thought of Bill. She missed her husband, though he had not perhaps been the love of her life – someone else had been that, and death had robbed her of that love too. Agnes got up: that way, those thoughts, they triggered depression, depression.

She decided Mac could have his dinner and she went into the kitchen, closely followed by the tap, tap, tap of Mac's claws on the wooden floor. Depression was not far away though. She went out into the back garden through the kitchen door, leaving Mac eating his Pal with his usual enthusiasm.

From her back garden, unlike the front, she could see both her neighbours. The ones to the right, quite a way away, partly hidden by shrubs and trees, were Mr and Mrs Merrill. They had asked her in for pre-lunch drinks when she had moved in three months ago. The house Agnes judged as phoney, though to do it justice it did not pretend – and neither did the Merrills – that it was old. Indeed, Edwin Merrill proudly boasted that he had had quite a lot to do with the building of the house. He was also proud of the beams, which ran the length of the sitting-room ceiling, and the diamond-paned windows.

'My husband was a master builder, you know.' Mrs Merrill offered Agnes a cigarette which she declined. 'Almost an architect, people used to say.'

He was a portly, short man, balding. They both seemed utterly self-centred and boring. She had asked them back after a week had gone by and hadn't altered her opinion.

'How can you manage in such a jinky little room?' Agnes was to learn that Pansy Merrill called everything small 'jinky'. Agnes wondered if she meant 'dinky'.

'Oh, very well. Living by myself I don't need much room.'

Pansy Merrill nodded.

'There's only Mac and I.' She had tried to lighten the atmosphere. 'Have you any children?' she asked.

There was what dear Bill would have called 'a pregnant silence', then: 'A son, we have a son.' Pansy Merrill looked almost pleadingly at her husband who got up and went over to the window.

'You can just see our house, Mrs Turner,' he said.

'Oh, a son. How old is he?'

Pansy twisted her rather large and, Agnes thought, vulgar diamond engagement ring. She looked toward her husband and then replied in a rather lower voice, 'He's nineteen next week. Nineteen. His name is John, just John. We've always liked plain names, haven't we, dear?'

Her husband had lighted a cigar without asking Agnes' permission. 'John was a good name until our son got it.'

Agnes could feel the tension between them like an electric current.

After that they had left, not even acknowledging Mac who, in his usual friendly way, had greeted both of them, tail wagging. The residual smell of Edwin Merrill's cigar was pleasant to Agnes. Bill, after much persuasion from Agnes, had given up smoking cigarettes and had turned to the occasional cigar. The almost sweet smell reminded her of him. In the bookcase that stood against one wall of the sitting-room was a row of Bill's books. It had taken him some time to get noticed by television companies, and later a film company had shown interest. On one dreadful visit, a mugger in New York had ensured that smoking would not kill him. A knife had done that.

The Merrills had gained a black mark in Agnes' estimation because they had not left until twenty to two. If asked to drinks she always watched the time; if it was for a pre-lunch drink she said goodbye at about quarter or ten to one. Some of her old friends did not bother with lunch, just dinner at night when their husbands came home from the office or wherever. Bill had always looked forward to his pre-dinner drink when he came home in the evening, which Agnes would have poured when she heard his key in the lock. Then dinner. Bill had almost resented being asked out to dinner, he preferred being at home. Agnes cooking, feet up, happy . . .

Agnes felt her eyes prickling. She went into her neat 'jinky' kitchen to prepare her lunch, but loneliness had driven her appetite away. She made herself a cup of soup and stood in the doorway. Mac was rolling on his back in the middle of the lawn. The spring was just showing now. The crocuses were over. Part of the garden, the part near its boundary, was already tangled with wild garlic leaves. In the middle of the tangle two white hyacinths stood like candles. Agnes wandered across the lawn, but the flowers were not yet giving out their delicate perfume.

Agnes was not attempting to plan the garden until she had found out what it already held. She had moved into her new house when snow was around. Bill had died in New York when the customary rotund Father Christmases were ho-hoing along Main Street. Why is it, she thought, that death is so much worse at Christmas? The following Christmas, or just after, Agnes had moved into Rose Cottage. Away from Rutland Gate. When she drove the Porsche away from that square of houses, Mac by her side, she had realised she was having to start again. What now? She remembered how an old song had suddenly belted out from the cassette, left in by mistake probably. 'Alone Again Naturally.'

The house on the other side of Agnes' cottages was surrounded by a brick wall over six feet high. The wrought-iron gate revealed only a rather weedy path, shrubs both sides, badly in need of pruning; an arbour of tangled, also unpruned roses cut off any view of the garden behind it.

The little one could see of the house above the wall looked rather like a wedding cake – at least the top of one. The white walls were long unpainted. A solid white balcony ran round the house in front of the bedroom, or anyway the upper, windows.

This too looked neglected. Green moss spotted the surface of the white balcony here and there, making it look rather like a painting by Utrillo. Agnes, whenever she passed the house, had to pause a little, walk more slowly, peep in the gate. Occasionally, when she was taking Mac on his bedtime walk, there would be a light in one of the upper windows, but so far she had never seen any of the occupants, and only once had a car been parked outside. Agnes could not but be curious about the house. After all, they were her next-door neighbours, though rather far away. One day, however, she was to meet one of the occupants of the house in rather strange circumstances. At least, strange in their outcome and a sudden request.

It was a Friday morning, the day Agnes drove to her hairdresser. She was very particular about her hair and had tried two while she had been in Sussex: the one in Lewes had met with her satisfaction. Her hair was turning a little grey now. Agnes had a dread of getting and looking old. She had always, since her nursing days, used moisturising creams, hand creams, body lotions. Now, at fifty-seven, she still took great care with her make-up. Bill had loved the way she dressed, loved the perfume – Joy – she always used, and now, even though he was gone, perhaps for his sake, she still took the same care. This day, her hair appointment day, she had been a little earlier than usual giving Mac his morning walk. She had to keep encouraging him to walk a little more quickly, but the early morning smells in this pleasant, almost carless lane were enticing. Just before she reached the iron gate she heard it squeak open and a figure emerged. Although it was a fine morning the person had on a long mac, buttoned from the neck to mid-calf. The macintosh was made of a shiny material and cut straight, like a dressing-gown with no belt at the waist.

'Good morning.' Agnes ventured the greeting. She felt the girl might not want to be greeted at all. Her eyes turned suddenly and met Agnes'. They were blue, blue as the sea and the sky on a fine, sunny, summer day.

'Oh, isn't he cute.' She bent down to pat Mac's head. His tail as usual was wagging in delighted greeting. As she bent, her hand, long, thin and white, emerged from the black sleeve of her curious coat, then the wrist. Mac, oblivious of his muddy paws, jumped up. She put out both hands to rub his ears. Both wrists were bandaged. Neatly, as if done by a professional. A nurse, a doctor? Her eyes met Agnes' again. This time she was no longer smiling as she had at first at the dog. She looked embarrassed, confused.

'Have you hurt your hands? Don't let Mac make your bandages dirty.'

'Bandages?' The girl withdrew her hands, slid them back up the arms of her coat.

It was Agnes turn then to feel embarrassed. 'I'm sorry, I thought . . .'

'You live in the cottages?'

Agnes nodded.

'They are pretty, cosy. Our house is big and cold. It's called High Hurlands, look.'

She went round Agnes and pulled a piece of board out of the shrubbery just inside the half-open gate. It was rotting wood, but just visible on the surface was painted in green the word 'High'. The rest, presumably 'Hurlands', was broken off. 'It's all like that.' The girl smiled again. 'Broken, I mean. I must go.' She threw the piece of the home name back into the shrubs. 'Goodbye,' she said and took a few steps, then turned. 'My name's Amanda. Can I come and see you one day?'

'Of course, Amanda. My name is Agnes. Agnes Turner.'

'I know.' The girl said it almost triumphantly.

'Oh, right.' Agnes felt slightly disconcerted. She took her diary from her pocket and tore a page out. 'Have you a pen?'

The girl shook her head. 'Just tell me, I'll remember.'

Agnes repeated her phone number twice. The girl thanked her then turned her back and continued on her way, her ankles slim under the long coat, her surprisingly high-heeled modern black shoes and black stockings looking to Agnes rather ridiculous on the grassy, slightly muddy verge of the road.

Agnes turned too. The girl was walking quickly and drawing away from her. Inside the cottage, Agnes put down fresh water for Mac, fed him his small breakfast, changed her shoes and went out again, locking the door behind her.

In the hairdresser's, under the drier, she thought of the girl, the bandaged wrists. Would she come to see her? Agnes half hoped she would, half hoped she wouldn't. The cut wrists might mean she wanted counselling and Agnes had long given up counselling anybody.

2

A week passed and Agnes had not heard from the blue-eyed girl, no telephone call, neither had she encountered her on her early morning walks with Mac. The red car, however, several times during the week was parked outside the gate.

Agnes had acquired a daily woman and was hoping to employ the gardener who was coming to see her this morning at eleven. Both had been recommended by a Mrs Beaven who ran the only shop in the little hamlet between where Agnes lived and Lewes. The shop was about a mile and a half away from Agnes' cottage, and it made an ideal walk for Mac, as it could be approached through the fields.

Mrs Beaven had suggested Mrs Tracy, a very good cleaner and honest as the day, according to the shopkeeper. The gardener got a rather different recommendation. 'Bit crusty and know-it-all, if you know what I mean, Mrs Turner.' Agnes though she would take a chance and interview the crusty one. She didn't relish the idea of coping with the garden by herself. She didn't mind pruning a few roses and shrubs, although she knew she was no expert, but digging, mowing and edging the rather large lawn at the back and smaller ones in the front would, she felt, be a bit much and would probably give her backache.

'None of these gardens have ever been much, miss,' Will Nelson, as he had introduced himself, said with some contempt. He persisted in calling Agnes 'miss' though she had three times told him her name was Mrs Turner.

'How do you mean, Mr Nelson, none of these gardens?'

'Well, High Hurlands, this place and the Merrills'.'

Agnes protested mildly. 'The Merrills' garden is very nice – tidy, full of flowers in the summer, I am sure.'

'Yes, flowers all right. Busy Lizzies and African marigolds. Park stuff, not country garden stuff.'

Agnes visualised the picture and rather agreed with him. Her suggestion of a wild, overgrown end to her garden with cottagey flowers and nesting boxes appeared to meet with his approval, as did the chickens in a roundabout way.

'Rum lot of birds you got there,' he remarked.

'Yes, they are rescued from a battery. I'm getting two more,' Agnes said with some determination.

Mr Nelson – Will – looked at her, his face red and chin stubbled, his cap pulled backward on his head, his hair grey and brown to match the beard, his eyes, grey and screwed up against the spring sunshine, twinkling at her. 'Oh, so you're one of those ladies. Well, you'll probably get rats, there's a few round about.'

Agnes took this to be approval. 'Yes,' she said, 'I'm one of those ladies. Come in and I'll make us a coffee.' He followed her into the house. 'Then we can talk terms.'

They had 'talked terms' and how many mornings a week and where to buy some roses. Will Nelson was just finishing his coffee and large wedge of cake when the telephone rang.

'Excuse me.'

Agnes answered the one in the hall, just outside the kitchen door. It was the blue-eyed girl.

'Oh, Amanda, how nice. I thought you had forgotten.'

The arrangements were made for the girl to come for coffee or a glass of wine the next morning. Agnes put the telephone down and came back into the kitchen.

'That's Amanda.'

'That Amanda girl from up High Hurlands?'

'Yes, I met her out the other morning, in the road just coming out of her gate.'

Will slurped the remainder of his coffee dregs, fingered up the four or five sultanas that had fallen out of his cake. 'Thanks, see you Tuesday then, we can start on the path.'

Agnes agreed. 'And the pond,' she added, smiling. She wanted a pond in the wild part of her garden to encourage frogs and water creatures. 'You know Amanda, then? What is her surname?'

'Holstein – funny name. They'd let her out, had they, else she'd got out on her own?' For some reason Agnes did not want to encourage her new gardener to gossip. 'Mixed up with a boy, that Merrill boy – broke up now.'

Agnes watched him walk down her front path. He was short and fat; he looked like a gardener, she thought and then wondered exactly what she meant. What did a gardener look like anyway, Capability Brown? She was glad the girl Amanda was coming tomorrow and realised she was beginning to feel a trace lonely. The place was not ready yet to start asking her London friends to stay. She looked forward to a visitor.

She thought of Will Nelson's remark as she washed up the coffee cups. They had let her out? What did he mean? Then she thought of the bandaged wrists, of the Merrills' reaction to the mention of their son. Interesting. High Hurlands was interesting too: the weedy-looking path and arbour which was all one could see, the moss-spotted and in part peeling white paint of the fascia. Had the girl parents? Had she a history of attempting to harm herself? Had the boy, John Merrill . . . ? She stopped herself. There was enough to think about with the various small alterations she was having done to her own house – no point in getting mixed up in other people's problems.

Mac gave his usual high, sharp bark. The front door bell. Agnes hurried to open it.

'Come about the tank, Mrs Turner.'

Outside the gate was a white van: 'Hattsell: Plumber and Heating Engineer.'

'Come in,' she said, thinking, Why do they have to come at lunch-time? Never mind, she would have to make a meal this evening. She waited while Mac gave the man his enthusiastic greeting.

'Welcome a burglar, he would,' said the plumber, giving Mac an affectionate rub.

Amanda was a little early, and apologised as she hesitated outside the door when Agnes opened it.

'No, it doesn't matter a bit, do come in.'

The girl came in rather as if she felt she was entering a trap and the door might close and lock behind her. Agnes noticed she had on a red pullover, the sleeves of which came well over her wrists. Her dark green skirt was well cut; the high-heeled shoes of a week ago had been replaced by brown lace-up brogues. She looked curiously old-fashioned.

'What a pretty house.' Amanda looked around her as she sat down in the middle of the settee.

'Thank you. I haven't done much with the decorations or altered much at all. In fact nothing.'

'It's lovely to see a proper fire.' Amanda held out her hands towards the fireplace, where the flames licked around the logs Agnes had thrown on just before her guest arrived.

'Are you warm enough, Amanda? The heating isn't really working very efficiently yet.'

'Yes, yes, thank you.'

The girl appeared shy, uncertain. Agnes tried to lighten the atmosphere a little. 'The plumber said Mac would welcome a burglar rather than see him off!' she said.

The girl nodded. 'He's friendly, that's why. He wouldn't understand a burglar.' The girl patted the cushion beside her on the settee and Mac immediately struggled up to sit beside the girl.

'He's not really allowed on the furniture,' Agnes said and the girl immediately lifted the little dog down.

'Oh, I'm so sorry, Mrs Turner, I didn't mean to, I wasn't thinking.' She looked so guilty and remorseful that Agnes almost wished she had let Mac stay there.

'Don't worry, he was just taking advantage of your kindness. I'll make us some coffee.'

'Thank you, can I help?' the girl asked, half rising.

'No, no, I'm afraid it's instant. It won't take a minute. I hope you are not used to real coffee.'

Without waiting for an answer, she went into the kitchen, divided only by a door from the sitting-room. There were contradictions about the visitor that interested her. Her clothes were old-fashioned, yet her hair was not. Two strands hung down each side of her face, while the rest had been done in a rather incompetent French pleat. The hair was blonde but the roots were already showing their true colour, a mousy brown.

Agnes put the tray of coffee down on the small table between the settee and the wing chair where she seated herself. She noticed as she passed the coffee to Amanda that the girl's hand trembled.

'Are you feeling all right, Amanda?' she asked as the girl put the cup and saucer down with a little clatter.

'Oh yes, quite all right, thank you. It's just that I will feel better after I have told . . . after . . . you know. You see, you may not want to . . .' She paused, stirred her coffee and sipped it, her blue, blue eyes looking straight at Agnes over the rim of the cup.

'May not want to – what do you want me to know?'

The girl put her cup down. 'You were a nurse, weren't you, long ago?' Mrs Beaven at the shop told me, so I knew you'd know, well, you'd guess. My wrists, I cut them.' Agnes waited. 'He killed my horse, my pony Magic, so I killed him. I had to, didn't I? Then I thought I'd be better dead. I see the shrink all the time, but he doesn't know, he doesn't help me.'

'Who did you kill, Amanda?' Agnes asked.

'John. John Merrill.'

'John Merrill, but I thought . . . ?' Agnes remembered the electric silence between husband and wife when they had mentioned their son John, but they hadn't said he was dead. She leaned back in her chair, assuming a relaxed air, trying to calm the girl opposite her whose agitation seemed to be growing.

'I knew I could tell you the moment I met you in the lane. I knew you'd understand, your little dog and everything.' She drank more coffee. 'May I have a biscuit?' Agnes had brought a plate of biscuits in with the coffee.

'Please do.'

Amanda took a bourbon. 'These are my favourites,' she said, smiling. She bit through the biscuit with strong, rather large white teeth.

'Why not begin at the beginning and tell me all about it, Amanda?' Agnes was not sure if she wanted to hear the story or not, but her curiosity was aroused. Was John Merrill dead, missing? Had the girl . . . ?

'Yes, I'll tell you. I'd like to.' Amanda put the half biscuit back on the small plate Agnes had passed to her. 'You won't tell anyone, will you, what I'm going to tell you?'

Agnes shook her head. 'No, I won't tell anyone, Amanda,' she said, not knowing how much these words were going to mean.

Amanda got up and went across the room and shut the sitting-room door, came back, sat down again in the middle of the settee. The blue eyes met Agnes' and this time they were full of tears which she did not attempt to wipe away. She looked down. 'It was like this, Mrs Turner.' She clasped her hands tightly together so that the knuckles were showing white. 'It was like this . . . I had to do it, Mrs Turner. I had to do it.'

'Do what, tell me what you had to do?'

'I had to kill John, anyone would have after what he did to Magic.' She stopped, covered her face with both hands. 'He was so lovely, Mrs Turner – he was twenty-eight, that's a good age for a horse, but he was, well, he loved me, he was mine, he knew he was mine, he was older than me.'

Agnes could hardly hear what the girl was saying. She left her chair, went over and sat down beside Amanda, drew the girl's hands down away from her face. 'I can hardly hear what you are telling me, Amanda. What happened to Magic?'

The girl looked up at her, her eyes wide, her face distorted. 'He cut Magic, with a knife, down the side of his neck. There was blood everywhere.'

'You were there, when he did it, Amanda?'

'Oh, I'm not telling it right.'

'No, start at the beginning,' Agnes suggested.

The girl exhaled in a long, long sigh, took a crumpled tissue from the pocket of her jumper, wiped her eyes with it, and then looked down and began to tear it into little pieces. As she tore it into smaller and smaller pieces, she told her story, stumbling, hesitating, sometimes stopping altogether, but as Agnes managed to piece it together, she became more and more horrified.

Apparently Amanda had been in her bedroom listening to music. She blamed herself for this because otherwise she would have heard Magic make a noise, heard the stable door click, but she didn't. It was only when the animal made a really loud, distressed sound that she switched off the music and listened. 'Even then,' she sobbed, 'if I hadn't stopped to listen, to check, I might have saved him.' She had run downstairs, out through the back door, round to the stable. Too late. Magic was down, blood all round him, and a man was standing over him ready to strike the fallen animal with the knife in his hand: John Merrill. It had been moonlight. When he had seen her, he had dropped the knife and turned to run. He was dressed all in black, black jeans, black shirt, thick gardening gloves. Amanda had picked up the knife and chased him to the gate. It was open, but just by the rose arbour he tripped. There he had lain, struggling to get up. The grassy path was wet with dew, slippery.

'I gripped the knife hard, Mrs Turner, and I struck him, cut him, just like he had done to Magic. I cut the side of his neck.' She paused, looked towards the small window as if she could still see, still savour, the scene. 'Then I stuck the knife in him, in the back, between his shoulder blades. He didn't make a sound.'

'Was there no one in the house, your mother, your father?'

Amanda nodded. 'They were in there, looking at the telly. My father is very deaf, they have the sound on loud.' She kept on nodding, as if to corroborate her own words, and suddenly Agnes wondered if the whole story was a fabrication or lie. But the horse, it would be easy enough to find out if a horse had been killed.

'What did you do then?' she asked. 'Where is the body?'

The girl had stopped crying now. She looked different, more composed. 'That was the hardest part of all, and that's why I had to come and see you. When you bought the cottage, I knew I had to come and see you.'

'Why me?' Agnes asked with real curiosity.

'Because the body is in your garden, Mrs Turner. It's in your garden.'

'In my garden? How could you manage . . . ?'

Amanda shook her head. 'It was difficult and it began to rain. John is – was – a thin, weedy . . .' A look of contempt came over her face. 'I dragged and dragged, a car came by.' She suddenly laughed. 'I was terrified, but it didn't see me – us. Anyway, it didn't stop, or even slow down.'

'Why did you laugh then, Amanda, at the thought of that terrible task of dragging, dragging a body up the lane, round my house? You must have taken it round my house. It's not in the front garden?'

Amanda shook her head. 'No, I dragged and dragged. I was sweating.' She stopped. 'I would like some more coffee, Mrs Turner.'

'Of course.' Agnes picked up the cups. At the door she turned. 'Then, will you show me where you put John Merrill, Amanda?'

'Yes, I will, but I'm thirsty, all that talking. I don't usually talk a lot.'

When Agnes came back with two steaming cups, the girl had got up and was standing by the window, looking out on to the front garden. She turned as Agnes came into the room.

'Most people wouldn't think I had enough in me to do such a thing.'

'Wouldn't they?' Agnes put the cups down on the table.

'My brother, Guy.'

'Oh, you've a brother? You didn't mention him.'

'No, I don't like him much. He's everything, I'm nothing.'

Agnes sat down. She was longing for the girl to show her the body, if it were there. 'Come and have your coffee.'

They drank in silence. The girl finished her coffee first, then jumped to her feet. Agnes stood up. 'Come on, Mrs Turner. I'll show you.'

Half-way across the damp, winter-worn grass, Amanda paused and suddenly gripped Agnes' arm. 'He'll be all rotted away, won't he?' She swallowed and stood, eyes wide, looking towards the end of the garden where the beginnings of the wild garlic grew. A shallow incline divided the garden from the field which stretched away, flat and empty. Agnes had not yet explored that incline, it was muddy and wet. The end, she had visualised as the border of her wild garden where she would throw seeds of wild flowers, make it a place for small animals to hide in. She drew the girl forward, not answering her.

'I mean, it's three months ago he killed Magic. He will be all, you know, gone into the earth, won't he?'

Agnes shook her head. They reached the little incline where the garden ended in a ditch. Tangled dead grass and brambles from last year, just nature's rubbish, but no body. No decomposed corpse, no bones, no clothes or shoes, no sign that Amanda's story was true.

'Well?' Agnes turned and faced the girl who still leant forward, peering into the flat brownish-green mass of dead leaves and thorny stumps that had, perhaps, held last year's blackberries. 'Well, where is he?'

Amanda straightened up, and pushed back her hair. 'He couldn't have been alive and . . . he couldn't have, Mrs Turner.'

'What about his mother, his father, they would know if he was dead. They would have searched for him.'

The girl shook her head. 'No, no, no. You don't understand. They wouldn't have anything to do with John. Ask them, ask them.'

She started to run up the lawn, round the house. Agnes walked quickly after her, but did not feel any great urgency to argue with her guest, so when she entered her front garden she picked up Mac, who obviously thought it was walk time again. He had been asleep in his basket in the kitchen. Agnes heard the girl's running steps, then heard the iron gate slam. She walked back to the house, closed the front door behind her, put Mac down.

In the garden shed she found an old broom. She returned to the end of the garden and started to poke amongst the debris, behind the growing garlic. Nothing. The girl was deluded. Perhaps she took drugs, hallucinated, imagined the whole thing. Still, Agnes felt curious enough to try and verify a few things. Had there really been a horse called Magic? She could ask. Was John Merrill really missing? Certainly his parents' reaction to her asking about her son had been rather odd. Could a girl so slender and unathletic-looking drag a body and hide it somewhere else – not in this garden, but maybe somewhere in the lane? If nothing else, it was intriguing, interesting.

Agnes went back into the house. Life was suddenly moving again, things to do. Maybe it would all come to nothing, but Agnes felt stimulated. One thing she was sure of, she had heard of these ghastly men who injured, killed or mutilated horses, donkeys. If she ever got to know one, she knew exactly what she would do. Meanwhile, as always, when life was becoming a shade more exciting, she mixed herself a brandy and ginger ale. She sat down at the kitchen table, raised her glass to Mac, who had returned to his basket and was sitting up looking at her with bright brown eyes. 'Here's to finding out, Mac,' she said and sipped her drink. For after all, the thing Agnes loved most was knowing things that other people didn't know. Finding out and, if necessary and possible, dealing with them in her own particular way.

As she sat there she plotted, then got up and went to her bedroom. She carefully sorted through her headscarves, neatly packed, one on top of the other, in the top drawer of her low serpentine-fronted chest, a piece of furniture which had cost her rather a lot of money, and a piece of which she was very fond. One scarf, which she did not particularly like, was exactly right. The mixed colours, green and red, could easily have been worn by Amanda. She would call on the white house up the lane. 'I believe your daughter left this behind when she came to coffee with me,' she would say, though of course she did not know if her visitor was 'a daughter', whether there was really a mother, father, living there. The house looked, from the road, as if no one was in charge of it. Anyway, it would be very interesting to find out. She took the headscarf downstairs and put it on the little table that stood just inside her front door. Agnes decided to take it tomorrow, or the next day, leaving Mac behind in case there were cats in the house. She looked forward to the visit. Then there were the Merrills to cope with. Ask, tactfully, about their son. Had they not seen him for three months? Where was he? A lot to do, a lot to find out. Agnes began to get her lunch ready with more appetite than usual.

As she cooked, she wondered about the horse. Was Magic a figment of Amanda's imagination? Had he really died in that field behind the white house? What, if so, had they done with the body? A big task. Had they buried it there in the garden, or had it been carted off to some knacker's yard? Poor, poor creature. Still, what had Amanda said? He had been twenty-eight, older than the girl herself. Maybe the animal had had a good and comfortable life. That thought comforted her a little. Agnes was, as always, more concerned about an animal than any human. They were so vulnerable. So much at the mercy of human cruelty and exploitation. That thought reminded her it was time to feed her chickens.

3

It was two days before Agnes had any time to start on the problem of the mystery of the missing corpse. She intended to search about in the fields, next to her fenced-off and hedge-protected little garden. Some things, however, were solved during the everyday routine of two very full and busy days.

'How is Mrs Tracy doing, Mrs Turner? I do hope you are getting on well?'

This question Agnes was glad to be able to answer in the affirmative. Mrs Tracy had already proved herself to be a treasure. She cleaned well, was reasonably quiet and, very important, got on well with Mac.

Mrs Beaven had also recommended Will Nelson but luckily she did not, on that particular day, ask about him. Will was undoubtedly a good and knowledgeable gardener but 'obstinate' was his middle name. Agnes had suggested that one hedge should be replaced by a variegated privet just, she had thought, to make that side of the garden a little lighter. 'Birds won't like it – won't nest in variegated rubbish,' he said. The wild end of the garden he agreed with. Bluebells, primroses, he also knew a good deal about grasses and had promised to bring more seed. He had suggested two buddleia to attract the butterflies. Every other part of the garden – front and back – everything, he argued about. The middle beds, the roses, the borders. Most of the arguments he won because Agnes had to admit her knowledge was very much less than his, and every gardening book she brought out to show him was greeted by a sceptical look and a 'That's what they say.' At present they were arguing about a clematis. Agnes pictured her font door wreathed in *Clematis viticella*. 'Ruin the bricks,' he said.

One or two things regarding High Hurlands, though, Agnes had been able to sift out from the general chat in the little shop and in her garden. Mrs Beaven knew all about poor old Magic.

'It was terrible, terrible. I did see him once. He was a big white horse and poor Amanda, well . . . in my opinion, she'll never get over it. She heard it, you know, saw the man running away.'

'How dreadful! Did she recognise him?'

'Oh, no, he got away. Someone, maybe him, had done a donkey, in a field near Lewes, but the donkey was stitched up by the vet and got better. It was all in the paper, the local one. Those Holsteins are funny people though, aren't they?'

An unknown waiting customer had chimed in – rather, Agnes thought, to Mrs Beaven's annoyance. 'What's that to do with the price of potatoes?' she snapped. 'They pay their bills.'

'Yes, but I mean, you never see them. They're like hermits.' The stranger would not be put down. 'Well, that poor girl nearly got put out of her mind by the death of that poor horse.'

Agnes broke in: 'What did they do with the body, the horse's body?'

Another woman had entered the little shop. 'He had long hair, right down his back, right down his back, so they say.'

Mrs Beaven smiled at her new customer. 'That's rubbish. People just said that to try to put Guy Holstein in the picture, make people think he did it.' She turned to Agnes. 'People will say anything to make a story, and nobody likes young Holstein.'

'Why is that?' Agnes was determined to squeeze every bit of

knowledge from the assembled customers, which had now grown to four. Nobody seemed to mind waiting, as long as the talk and rumours went on, and it was obvious too that the topic of the mutilated Magic was still very fresh in people's minds, although the incident had happened three months ago.

Mrs Beaven answered Agnes' almost obliterated question. 'Poor Magic, he was carted away, I suppose. Don't think anyone saw it though. Perhaps they buried him in the field, could have done.'

Agnes was about to leave when the third customer, who had mentioned the long hair, gave an impressive sneeze. 'I've got a cold – can I have some tissues? It's not rubbish. He is odd, that young man Guy. What a name! Real guy he is, too.' She sniffed, reached for the box of tissues, paid and left.

Mrs Beaven shook her head. 'She's right in a way. They are all a bit queer, but whatever she says, I believe they all loved Magic and wouldn't have hurt him. Poor Amanda really did have a sort of breakdown.'

Agnes had left Mac with Mrs Tracy, so she hurried home. There was no need to worry about Mac though. He had taken to Mrs Tracy the first day she had arrived. Mrs Tracy had not been very informative about High Hurlands. She came by car from some distance away, and affairs in her own village were naturally of more interest to her, although she had been horrified at the poor animal's, as she put it, 'murder'.

Will Nelson though had plenty to say. He had in his youth been a groom, and horses and ponies had been his life. 'I'd do the bugger in if I caught him. Pardon the language, miss.' But he had little to add in the way of real information, though he did confirm the sniffing lady's remark in the shop that 'the man, according to young Amanda, had long hair'. Agnes was a little puzzled by this, as Amanda's description had been of John Merrill, short-haired and dark-suited. That the girl had had a nervous breakdown might make her mind play tricks on her.

More ideas and subsequent arguments with Will Nelson, and later with the decorator, and a visit to a nursery for bedding plants had filled Agnes' day. Two or three walks with Mac past the white house had elicited no sign of life. Agnes was getting a little bored again when something suddenly happened to arouse her interest: another invitation from the Merrills, this time for dinner and to meet, Mrs Merrill explained on the telephone, another of Agnes' near neighbours. Agnes hoped it might be the occupants of High Hurlands. She accepted and again put off her visit to Amanda's house. She wanted to gather all the information she possibly could before she met the girl again. Something told her it would not be the Holsteins she would meet at the Merrills' – it would be an entirely new couple.

Agnes took special care with her appearance before going to dinner at the Merrills'. She had accepted few invitations since Bill's death, even when she had been in London. Her friends had tried to persuade her. 'Agnes, you must make an effort. Come out with us.' To dinner, to lunch, to meetings. But she began to hate going out without Bill. Even on the occasions when she had not accompanied him on his trips to America, she had usually stayed at home, refusing dinner or cocktail party invitations.

She put on a beautifully cut grey dress with an almost demure white pique collar. The sleeves came just below the elbows and she clipped on her diamond and gold filigree bracelet. A present from Bill, a jewel that had figured large at the time – which now she so bitterly regretted – when she had been unfaithful to Bill. Not that he ever found out, though he so nearly had, so very nearly.

She stood back from the dressing-table and looked at herself critically. She was conscious of the lines around her neck, not too visible perhaps to a stranger, but very visible to her. Her hair, in spite of its grey streaks, was beautifully cut – straight, short and shining. 'Not too bad, old girl,' she said to her reflection. She added a little more perfume to her wrists. Joy. Always Joy. She could not remember ever wearing anything else and again her thoughts drifted back to Bill, dear Bill . . .

The Merrills' front door opened, almost before she pressed the bill. Mr Merrill greeted her, almost too effusively. He put his hand on her arm and drew her into the well-lit warm hall, took the light coat she had thrown around her shoulders and hung it up. In the sitting-room were two guests, a man and a very attractive, dark-haired woman. They were standing, as was Mrs Merrill. Agnes felt for some reason that she was entering a totally artificial atmosphere, that she was being introduced to these new people for a definite reason. She tried to banish a feeling of caution and shook hands with the two, introduced by Mrs Merrill as Mr and Mrs Greenham, Violet and Ivan.

'Christian names are so much easier, and quite the thing these days, aren't they?' Mrs Merrill said. 'I'm Pansy and my husband is Edwin, mostly we call him Ed though.' She giggled a little.

'I'm Agnes, Agnes Turner.' She felt she must join in the exchange.

'Do sit down.'

Ed Merrill began to dispense drinks and the atmosphere became more relaxed. Ivan Greenham lit a cigarette after politely asking Pansy Merrill for her permission. The normal questions were asked about the drinks: 'Ice and lemon?' 'Soda in your whisky, Ivan?' Agnes got the impression that the Merrills were used to entertaining; while in the hall she had heard, muted noises coming from what she assumed was the kitchen area, which was why, apparently, Mrs Merrill did not continually leave the room to check the kitchen.

Conversation waxed and waned.

'Do you like your new home, Agnes?' Mrs Greenham, Violet asked.

'Oh, very much. It was in very good order. I have had very little to do.'

'Yes, the Brownlees were very devoted to the place. I don't remember quite why they left, do you?' Violet looked towards Pansy Merrill. She was the youngest of the little company. Her black curly hair was long and luxurious, and she looked much younger than her husband. Agnes thought she detected a hint of mischief in her eyes as she asked this question.

Pansy Merrill seemed upset. She got up. 'I'll get some cheese biscuits.'

She left the room and Violet Greenham came across, sat close to Agnes, put her hand up to her mouth as if to guard what she was going to say, to keep it from the two men, who anyway had gone over to the bar to replenish their drinks. 'Pansy always says she doesn't know why the Brownlees sold the cottages.'

'Does she know then?' Agnes sipped her gin and tonic, feeling only a mild interest.

Violet looked at the men as if she wanted to be sure they wouldn't hear. 'It was their son John. I never got to the bottom of it, but the Brownlees took against him for some reason, and there was a terrific row. John's a real bastard. Even though he is my nephew, I don't like him.'

'Your nephew?'

'Yes, Pansy and I are sisters. Didn't you realise?' She laughed loudly. 'How do you think we both got these awful names?' Pansy had come back into the room with a little dish of biscuits. 'Agnes did not know we are sisters, Pansy.' She laughed again, her rather high, loud laugh. 'We've another sister who lives in Cornwall, called Lily, wouldn't you know.'

'And where is John, there son, now?' Agnes asked, this time with real interest. After all according to the girl Amanda, he had been stabbed to death.

Pansy heard her. 'John. Oh, John's on a business trip.' She touched her husband's arm. 'Dinner's ready, Ed. Will you open the wine?'

'Sure.' He left the room and the others followed him into the dining-room.

The dinner was excellent, a seafood hors d'oeuvre followed by lamb chops, peas, baby carrots and roast potatoes, then a chocolate mousse and coffee. The wine was not to Agnes' taste. She wondered if it would be tactless to ask for the name of the cook, decided it would be, so turned the conversation to John, thinking at the same time that she would take her dinner guests out to a hotel in Lewes rather than hire a cook.

'And what business is your son in, Mr Merrill?'

He leaned back in his chair, patted his stomach, looked at his wife. 'Very nice, my dear. Hope you have had enough to eat?'

They all assented, and praised the food, the cooking. Then he answered Agnes' question. 'Prospector and financial adviser.

Same as I was.' He seemed immensely proud of himself and, by his attitude, was proud of his son.

'I expect he has to travel a good deal.'

Pansy spoke this time. 'Yes. We haven't seen him for three months. Not even a card to his mother, or a telephone call.' Her lips trembled.

Violet leant over and took a chocolate mint from the green box on the table. The movement diverted Agnes' gaze from Pansy to her sister, who closed one eye in a long sustained wink for Agnes' benefit, which on their rather short acquaintance made her feel slightly uncomfortable.

They all moved back into the sitting-room. Pansy Merrill brought in fresh coffee and her husband handed round liqueur glasses of crème de menthe, Agnes most loathed liqueur. However, she took one and sipped it with as good grace as possible. She was determined now to proceed with, and not let the company divert her from, her little bit of research. She started casually, after Pansy Merrill had at last settled beside the new tray of coffee.

'I hear there was a nasty incident when Amanda Holstein's horse was mutilated and subsequently died. That must have been very upsetting for everyone round here?'

'Oh, very.' Violet spoke up readily enough. She sipped her green liqueur. 'Some people are sick, aren't they? There was a donkey mutilated about a mile away. It didn't die, poor thing, but only thanks to the vet, I believe. And a horse near us, that was badly cut about and sexually – '

She was obviously about to go into further details, but her husband broke in. 'My daughter's pony is in stables, reasonably near the house. We've had an alarm installed, but if I caught anyone harming that animal I'd kill the bugger.'

'Darling, no need for that language.'

Violet had interrupted his flow, but Agnes sympathised with him. 'Have the police any idea who could be responsible for such vile behaviour?' she asked.

Everyone shook their heads and replied in their own manner. Merrill waved his cigar in the air. 'No idea, expect they think it's someone local. Knows his way about the place, you know.'

'Some have seen him. Medium height, short hair.' Violet's contribution. 'But that could be anyone.'

Greenham finished his liqueur, made a slight grimace that led Agnes to think he felt much toward the sweet liquid as she did. 'One farmer near us caught – or rather didn't catch, but frightened away – a man from his field where he keeps a couple of horses. Said he had a distinctive type of pullover on. Bottle green with what he thought was a horse's head on the breast pocket, but it had been fairly dark. He could have been mistaken.'

'Hardly a thing a horse mutilator would wear,' Agnes suggested.

'Oh, I dunno. John's got a pullover like that, hasn't he, dear?'

'No, he hasn't.' Agnes felt Pansy had retorted a shade too quickly. 'John's is pale blue.'

The conversation turned to other subjects. Agnes tried mentioning Amanda and High Hurlands but got little feedback. Either no one was interested in the house, when the house had been built or the inhabitants, or they did not wish to become involved in talking about it. There was one quick remark, however, so quick that Agnes almost missed it: 'Oh, they're all mad in High Hurlands, mad as hatters.' The remark came from their cigar-waving host. Agnes' 'Oh, why do you say that?' was lost in the general chatter as a game of bridge was suggested then quashed because there were five of them; another card game, pontoon, was decided upon. Agnes was no card player and said she must leave because of Mac, a lame excuse which was greeted with cries of 'Oh, what a shame,' and 'Oh, you should have brought him with you.' However, with thanks and goodbyes, Agnes managed to escape. Not before she had heard Ivan Greenham remark, 'Nice-looking woman that,' which pleased her.

She walked slowly down the lane, glad to be in the fresh air. She was a non-smoker, and the cigarette smoke from Violet Greenham and the clouds of cigar smoke from her host had begun to irritate her. The trees stirred in the breeze. It had rained while she had been in the Merrills' and the sweet smell of earth and wet grass was pleasant. Mac greeted her with his usual excitement and she snapped on his lead and walked the opposite way, along the grass verge. Two lights shone from the upper windows of High Hurlands. There might have been lights in the downstairs windows, but the wall made it impossible to see. As she passed, she thought of that great animal – Amanda had told her Magic was seventeen hands – friendly and trusting, being done to death by someone so evil. And at the same time she thought of John Merrill, if it were he . . . or was he already dead? If he was responsible, she hoped he *had* been slashed to death – but by Amanda? It seemed unlikely. She must talk to the girl again. She decided that she would take the headscarf back tomorrow, no matter how busy she was.

4

'I won't be long, Mac.' Agnes always said this to the dog when she left him. She laughed at herself for doing so. Did Mac understand? Mostly she thought he did and that all animals understood far more than we gave them credit for. When she said this to Mac he always dispatched himself to the kitchen, got in his basket, and then sat there looking at her. She felt, if he could answer, he would have said, 'Well, see you are not too long then.'

Agnes was off to the Holsteins'. She had in her handbag the headscarf, supposedly left by Amanda on her visit. For some reason she felt slightly nervous about the visit. Maybe it was the remark made at the Merrills'. 'Oh, they are all mad at High Hurlands, mad as hatters.' She reached the gate leading into the weedy path, skirted the tangled rose arbour.

The garden was larger than Agnes had expected. The ill-kept lawn stretched away, she judged, almost to the boundary of her own garden though a wide stretch of undergrowth, brambles and ferns bordered the high wall. The white house, High Hurlands, now it was all visible to her, looked rather like the houses in Italy or at the base of the hill in Monte Carlo. Its flaking paintwork and walls, however, did not sustain this impression.

The day, too, did not help. Bright sunshine would probably have made the house and garden look better, but under the rather brooding, stormy, overcast skies, the whole place had a menacing, desolate, deserted look. Poor Magic.

Agnes mounted the four steps to the door and pressed the modern, rather inadequate-looking bell push. She waited. Nothing happened. She tried again. Still no answering footsteps or sound from inside the unpolished wooden front door. She tried yet again, waited and then decided to give up. She retreated down the steps and was about to walk down the weedy path and out of the gate when curiosity overcame her. A quick look round at the upstairs and downstairs windows revealed no twitching curtains, no one peering out to see if whoever had run the bell had gone. The fine rain was still falling, a spring rain, not unpleasant to Agnes, who had on a mac and thick waterproof headscarf. She continued along the left of the house, preparing to say, if she met anyone from the house, that she was looking for the back door as she felt the bell did not work. She turned the corner to be confronted with a hut, strongly built and cosily thatched. Its double door made her guess that this had been Magic's stable. She looked inside. The floor was covered with straw, clean straw, and on the far wall hung a depressingly empty hay bag. A shelf, shoulder high and stoutly built, held a numna, its sheepskin shape draped over a saddle and other tack. Sad, sad, sad, she thought, poor Magic. She hoped that whoever had done that awful thing would be caught and punished, and half wished that she could believe the girl's story of the stabbing. The courts nowadays, she felt certain, would never pass a sentence long enough or harsh enough to suit her feelings as to what should be done to such a person.

Round the back of the stable was more field bordered by a high wall. This wall was similar to the one in the front of High Hurlands that hid the house from her view as she walked Mac. All the walls round the house were in surprisingly good repair. Glancing again at the house, she crossed the path of the field that led to her own garden. She was curious to know if any of her house could be seen from the slight rise in the grass mound nearby. She stood, peering over. Only her roof was visible, nothing else. She was rather glad that she was not overlooked.

Agnes was about to go back to the house and have one more try, perhaps knock this time, when, in turning round, her glance took in a patch of brambles and nettles in what looked like a ditch. They were dry and dead now, but ready to start growing again. Indeed little shoots of new spring green could already be seen, but it was not those small buds and shoots that caught her eye. She descended the grassy mound, one more quick glance back at the house – nothing. For as she drew nearer, what she had suspected at the top of the little grass mound proved to be quite correct. From out of the tangle of green, towards Agnes' right, something was just visible. A well-polished black shoe. The toecap was wet and clean. Luckily in the cold wet weather she was wearing thick gloves. She parted the brambles almost four feet along the ditch away from the shoe. The material she revealed was soaked and looked darker than it probably was. She did not want to see the face, so went no further, only parted the rotting greenery a little more. The darker stain on the chest could be water or blood. Agnes tried to remember Amanda's description of her knife thrusts, but could not do so. She straightened up. There was no smell, yet Magic had been killed – was it three months ago? Surely if the man in the ditch was John Merrill . . . ? Perhaps the cold weather and the fact that the body was in the open air had preserved it. So Amanda had been telling the truth, or maybe she had been . . . Perhaps this muddy ditch was someone else's grave.

On impulse Agnes returned to the house. This time she would knock, rap hard, on the door. Perhaps Amanda's father was in, only her father – hadn't Amanda mentioned that he was deaf? What to do about the body? Agnes as usual was intrigued by the fact that she knew the body was there, who it was, or might be, and no one knew that she possessed such knowledge, her very favourite situation. Agnes smiled to herself as she rapped with her fist on the door of the house. Rat, tat, tat. At last she had made someone hear. She heard footsteps crossing the floor inside.

The man who opened the door was good-looking in what Agnes thought of as a military kind of way. White hair, with a slight wave in the front, white moustache, neatly clipped, about five feet seven, rather short.

'I'm sorry, I didn't hear the bell.'

'I've called to see Amanda. Is she in?' Agnes raised her voice just a little.

'Oh, yes, do come in. She's in her room, playing music I expect, she doesn't go out much since . . .' He stepped back and opened the door wide. 'Please come in. Would you perhaps be Mrs Turner from the cottages? Rose Cottage, that is?'

Agnes nodded. 'Yes, she came and had a coffee with me.'

'Did she tell you about her horse, Magic?'

Again, Agnes nodded.

'It upset her badly, made her ill in fact. I'll call her.'

He crossed the hall. The parquet floor was well polished and there were some rather nice rugs scattered about. The hall smelled of wax polish; the banisters, too, shone. The inside of the house did not match the outside but then, Agnes thought, she had only so far seen the hall.

Amanda appeared at the top of the stairs. 'Hello, Mrs Turner, Agnes. How nice to see you.' She ran lightly down the stairs. 'Come into the sitting-room. It's nice of you to call.'

Agnes opened the handbag on her lap, took out the headscarf. 'You left this behind when you came to see me.' She unfolded the square of material.

'It's not mine, Agnes, but it's pretty.'

'Oh, it's the same colours as your jumper and skirt, I thought it must be yours.'

'No. I wish it was.' Amanda fingered the scarf.

'Well, do have it. It must be one of mine I'd forgotten I had.'

Amanda was pulling the scarf through her hand, loosely. She looked up. 'Oh, may I really have it? Thank you.'

Her father's head and shoulders appeared round the door. 'Would you like a drink of anything – tea?' He looked slightly harassed.

Agnes looked at the girl beside her. 'Tea would be lovely,' Amanda said. 'Thanks, Daddy.'

'Did you say your brother's name was Guy, Amanda?' Agnes was interested after her discovery in the garden. All the family interested her. Had the girl's brother killed the man in the ditch? Had her father? Had her story about her stabbing the man herself been just a fabrication, the result of her shock on finding the horse dead or dying, or the result of her breakdown? Could she have dragged the man to the end of the garden, put him in the ditch by the wall? Certainly an easier feat than what she had claimed to Agnes. What had made her lie, say she had dragged the body all the way to Rose Cottage? Perhaps it had not been a lie, perhaps she believed that was the way it had been. Agnes wondered how the police had missed the body – but why should they search for a body around a mutilated, dead horse? Who knew John Merrill was there? Amanda's father, her brother, her mother? Who knew he was there, silently rotting away – if indeed it was the Merrills' son?

'You're very quiet, Mrs Turner.' Amanda broke into Agnes' silence. She started, then smiled. She had been staring out of the window at the field, thinking, almost forgetting the girl, where she was.

Mr Holstein came in with a tray on which were two mugs, a sugar basin and a small jug of milk.

'There you are,' he said, smiling as he placed the tray on a small table beside them. 'Your mother's just come back. She'll come in a minute, wants to meet Mrs Turner.' He backed out of the room.

'Mum's a bit nervy. I mean, always has been, before Magic and that.' Amanda handed Agnes the yellow mug. 'Sugar?' Agnes shook her head. They were both silent again. Agnes felt tense, sipped the hot tea. The liquid burned her mouth but for some reason she wanted to leave. Perhaps it was the knowledge of the dead man outside in the ditch. She had a certain strange feeling that she was the only person who knew he was there, but that was, of course, ridiculous. Somebody had put him there.

Agnes realised Amanda was talking about the garden, about her brother, about Magic. Agnes was wondering, was there anyone she should, could tell? Certainly not the police. John Merrill had got what he deserved and no one should suffer for it. Magic had suffered enough and Merrill had, she supposed, died in the same way as Magic, by the knife.

'I do hope they have looked after you, Mrs Turner. Oh, mugs, Amanda. Couldn't you manage cups and saucers?'

Amanda's mother, Mrs Holstein, was short and plump with the perfect peach-like skin that plump women seem to be blessed with. She looked a little younger than her husband.

'Oh, please don't worry.' Agnes stood up to greet her. 'I came to bring back a headscarf which I thought Amanda had left when she came to see me.'

'And she has given it to me, isn't it pretty?' The girl unfolded the headscarf and showed it to her mother.

The sun suddenly appeared, making the room much lighter. 'I would have to shop in the rain,' said Mrs Holstein. 'Now the sun has come out when I'm safely home.'

Agnes got up. 'I must go. I've left my little dog Mac alone at home and he will be complaining.'

'We have no animals now. I expect you heard . . .'

Mrs Holstein and her daughter accompanied Agnes to the front door. 'Yes, indeed, and I am so sorry.' Agnes must have said it with the conviction she felt because she noticed as she said goodbye that Amanda's eyes had filled with tears. Agnes took the girl's hand in hers. 'Try not to grieve too much, Amanda. You told me he was twenty-eight and I am sure he had a very comfortable and happy life, unlike what some poor horses and ponies have to put up with.'

Amanda turned and ran up the steps and away.

'That was a lovely thing to say to her, Mrs Turner. She has taken it so badly, and if you had seen the poor creature's injuries!'

'I hope the person who did it dies in much the same way, Mrs Holstein.'

Amanda's mother looked at her for some seconds before she answered. 'You really mean that, don't you?'

'Oh yes, I really mean that, I assure you.'

Agnes walked away down the weedy path, turned and waved to the woman, who called out just as she was about to become hidden by the tangled rose arbour, 'You must come and have a meal with us soon, Mrs Turner.'

Agnes called back a 'Thank you, I would love to,' then went through the iron gate, closing it carefully behind her.

5

'I want a variety of colours, but predominantly yellow.'

Agnes was buying polyanthus in a nursery not far from her house. The girl who was picking out the plants for her was outstandingly pretty, her full lips pursed in concentration. Her eyes were grey and carefully mascaraed. She looked up at Agnes, holding in each hand a small pot of polyanthus. 'The yellows are a tiny bit different. Some are a bit darker. Did you want the primrosy ones, or these?' The one in her right hand were a shade darker, but bigger. Agnes chose the paler ones, six pots. The girl arranged them with the other plants Agnes had selected in a flat earth-stained box they could use to carry them home in the Porsche.

'You've been vey patient,' Agnes remarked as they made their way back to the car.

When she saw the car, the girl stroked the bonnet. 'A Porsche. I've always dreamed of having a Porsche.' She laughed. 'Not much chance though.'

Agnes smiled as she unfolded a newspaper to cover the passenger seat ready for the box of plants. Mac was in his special compartment at the back of the car. 'Oh, I don't know. You might marry a very rich man and he will give you a Porsche for your wedding present!'

The girl pulled a face. 'No, my boyfriend John, he knows about money, he's a financial adviser – whatever that means.'

Agnes felt her interest quicken and tried to think of another question that would not look too pointed. She need not have bothered. The girl volunteered further information. 'John lives near you.' She knew Agnes address because she had ordered a particularly scented rose from the little nursery.

'Really? What was his name, or should I say, what is his name?'

'Merrill, and you might just as well say "was". He hasn't phoned me for ages. He's been north for months, or so he says.'

'So he says?' Agnes turned from closing the passenger door of the car.

'Well, when he first went, he telephoned me every other night, but I haven't heard a word from him...' She paused, as if thinking over the time. 'Yes, it's nearly three months, a whole three months, more perhaps.' She pouted. 'I don't care all that much, he's a bit weird.' The girl nodded. 'Jealous. If I spoke to another boy he'd go ape. Silly like that.'

Agnes got into the car. 'Well, thank you again. If I want more plants, and I probably will, I'll ask for you. What name shall I say?'

'Sally, that's me. Sally Winters.' She waved as Agnes drew away.

Agnes put out a hand to steady the box of plants as she turned out of the nursery and into the lane. Well, she thought, if it was John Merrill in the ditch – and she was pretty sure it was – Sally would have a long time to wait for a telephone call. A little frisson went through her. She certainly knew something. Something quite momentous that a great many other people did not know. Agnes wondered, did Guy, Amanda's brother, know about the body in the ditch? Did her mother and father know? Had Amanda really stabbed him? Agnes decided to ask the Merrills for drinks. It wasn't her turn to do so, but she suspected they liked going out and were not invited out a great deal. Should she ask the Holsteins as well? She thought a bit about that, but by the time she had arrived home she had decided against it. Just John's parents would be enough at the moment.

The invitation to drinks was readily accepted by the Merrills. Agnes had added, 'If your son is home do include him in my invitation, should he like to come.' Agnes felt the irony of this. But she felt absolutely no sadness, no grief, for the human body in the ditch. It was pretty obvious, pretty certain, that it was the body of Magic's killer. But she had to admit that she was relying on the word of an apparently unstable witness. Had she really stabbed the man, and was it really John Merrill who lay, hidden, dead?

She had not steeled herself to look at what was, after three months, left of the face, and anyway she could not have identified it because she had never seen John Merrill. Maybe he was alive, would turn up at her drinks party, then she would know the girl was confused in her story.

Agnes also rang the Greenhams, but they regretted they already had a date in Lewes with some friends. Their regret sounded genuine and Agnes agreed to their request to ask them the next time she had a party.

Now, as she planted the polyanthus, making a splash of welcome colour, she hoped she was not putting them in too early and that the frost would not get them. She was glad the Merrills were coming; she wanted to find out as much as she could about their son and the stabbing of Magic. Agnes was unaware that she was to learn more at the little shop near her home, that afternoon – things that would change the direction of her efforts to find out more about Magic's killer, or at least make her realise that maybe there was more than one despicable vandal on the loose.

Before she set off with Mac for the little countryfied shop Agnes, always methodical, made a short list of things she wanted to get. The shop was to Agnes interesting, because Mrs Beaven seemed gifted in stocking things that one often forgot when buying at the supermarket in Lewes. Agnes wanted an extra pint of milk, some brown sugar and – something she always preferred to get at the little shop – a particular brand of dishcloth.

Mrs Beaven greeted her with her usual wide smile and intimated with a little nod that she would soon be finished with the present elderly lady customer who was busy picking out, penny by penny, five pence from a purse which would hardly allow her rather arthritic fingers entrance. Agnes wandered round the tiny shop, Mac pottering behind her. Birthday cards. These, Agnes thought, were a very sensible item to stock. Nice ones, too. She picked out a horse's head, beautifully pictured. It was a chestnut, but its direct, trusting gaze made her think of Magic and any other of the horses that had been attacked.

Mrs Beaven had several items of news to tell Agnes after the departure of the elderly customer. 'Old Mrs Dewhurst, did you know her, Mrs Turner, lives down the lane by Swainston's farm?' Agnes shook her head but this denial did not deter Mrs Beaven. 'Well, she's dead. Died in her bath, seventy-eight, poor old thing. Wasn't found until the next morning, all waterlogged she was.' Agnes made suitable sympathetic noises. Mrs Beaven had more to tell. 'Oh, and that Mr Clark, keeps the battery hen place, along by the old pigsties. Fell down in his battery shed. Hit his back on something and broke it. He's paralysed from the waist down.'

'Oh, I'm so glad. I hope someone is looking after the chickens.'

The little shopkeeper looked shocked by Agnes' remark and then her lips curved in an 'in spite of herself' smile. 'I know what you mean, give him a taste of not being able to move about like his poor birds. I won't buy eggs from him, even though he lives so near.'

She handed Agnes the pack of brown sugar and carton of milk, put the birthday card in a paper bag to keep it clean and handed Agnes her change. Then, speaking almost in a whisper: 'Another horse and a donkey. The horse is up at Marshall's stables and a donkey, cut up and a broom stick stuck in you know where – horrible – it died. Well, had to be put to sleep. The horse is all right.'

The description of the injuries made Agnes feel quite sick. 'But I thought . . .' She stopped herself, but in her mind she saw again the body under the brambles in the next-door garden. Why was he there? Who else was guilty?

She walked home almost in a dream. Two things she was determined to do. Go to the stables where the horse had been injured and then to the place where the donkey had been so cruelly treated, and after that, to the Clarks' place to get two more of those maltreated birds. If she had good luck she might discover something that would lead her to the person who was doing these wicked things, and she had her own way of dealing with evil-doers. She would not hesitate to use her powers. It might be young offenders who were doing these dreadful, cruel things to vulnerable animals. The magistrates who gave them light, almost non-existent punishments – community work, fines – were almost excusing the young thugs just because they were young, as if that fact was in itself an excuse for their crimes.

Somehow, Agnes did not think, according to what she had read about other cases of horse mutilation, that this would involve the very young. As far as she could remember, it had been older men who had been suspected and, in some few cases, caught. Once her small party was over she would start her investigations.

The Merrills arrived slightly early. Agnes was caught out by not having the ice cubes decanted from the refrigerator. She seated her guests then went into the kitchen and tried to get the ice out of the tray by running water over it. The ice cubes made their slight cracking noise as they hit the stainless steel of the draining board. To her annoyance Pansy Merrill appeared in the kitchen doorway.

'Oh, I'm sorry, I said to – '

Agnes knew she was going to apologise for being early, so forestalled her. 'I meant to get these out before but it's so much warmer I was afraid they would . . .'

'Melt.'

'Well, they do.'

Agnes felt the disjointed conversation was slightly mad, so changed it with perhaps too much abruptness, but she hated and was not used to acquaintances coming into her kitchen. 'You didn't bring your son? I was hoping to meet him.'

Pansey Merrill's face collapsed into a despondent grimace. 'No. It's over three months. It's too bad of him not to write or phone, but he's done it before, for longer even.'

Agnes put the ice bucket on a tray and the two women walked into the sitting-room, Agnes noticing as she walked behind her guest that the dress she was wearing was much too tight and showed the layers just below her shoulder blades that her bra failed to encompass. This, for some reason, pleased Agnes.

Edwin was standing looking towards the Holsteins' house, rather as he had on the last visit to Rose Cottage. 'They never get asked anywhere – live the life of hermits.' He drew on a cigarette, made a round mouth and let out small rings of smoke.

'Amanda rather liked our John,' Pansy Merrill volunteered.

Agnes was surprised but tried to answer casually. 'And did your John like Amanda?' she asked, placing the tray of drinks on the table.

'Well, yes, I think he did, but they used to argue a bit.'

'What about?'

Agnes passed the drinks around. Edwin Merrill answered. 'That damned horse. John said it was ridiculous keeping it on, past its shelf life, so to speak. Not ridden or used in any way. Cost them about six hundred a year.'

Pansy broke in then. 'Our John's a trained financial adviser, Agnes, he knows about these things. Edwin can't bear to see money wasted.'

Agnes thought about the body in the ditch and decided, if it was their son, he well deserved to be there.

'Then Magic was killed by this vandal, so it all worked out.'

'And was John here to comfort Amanda?' Agnes asked.

'No, he'd driven off that night to avoid the traffic jams. He liked to drive at night, well, it was evening really. He went in to say goodbye to Amanda and drove off. He'd said goodbye to us.'

Where was the car? Who had driven that off? Someone – maybe the man who was now on the rampage again with the donkey and the horse? Then again, if the man in the ditch was not John Merrill, there would have been, maybe, no car to drive away. In that case, too, was Amanda self-deceiving or had she, having stabbed the man in the back, never seen his face as she had dragged and rolled the body to its hiding place? It was intriguing and it was exciting.

Agnes was so preoccupied she suspected she had not been a particularly good host and her guests left early. But she had managed to elicit the information that John Merrill did not use a company car: Edwin had helped him buy a 'handsome green Volvo'. 'Cost him a bit,' Edwin had boasted. But in his son's trade, which, before his retirement, had been his own, you needed a good substantial-looking vehicle to make the clients feel that they were on to a good thing. A man who knew his way about the complicated financial world. Well, Agnes felt that was right.

After they had gone Agnes walked about her little garden, thinking, thinking. She felt she would like to talk to Amanda again, but before that she would go and see the chicken farm and bring home two more chickens.

The next day Agnes drove to the farm where the donkey had been tortured and eventually died. The field she had to cross to get to the small cottage was stony and ill tended. There was no sign of a shelter, or even a shed. Agnes knocked on the door with her knuckles as there was no bell. There was a long pause, then the door was opened.

'Yes?' The woman peering through the crack of the door, which was opened about six inches, was very old, her face lined and white, the eyes red-rimmed, the lips blue and thin.

'Your donkey, I believe it was killed?'

The door was opened a little wider. The woman pushed back the hair that fell forward each side of her face. 'Yes, you from the papers?'

Agnes shook her head. 'No, I'm not from the papers. I just heard about it and I came to say I was sorry.'

The door opened wider. 'Oh, well.' The old lady seemed to hesitate, then slipped back. 'Better come in then,' she said. Agnes followed her.

The room they entered smelled fusty and was piled with clothes. A coal fire gave out a good deal of heat, adding to the general stuffiness.

'Why do you care about Molly, I mean?' The woman slumped down in a chair. Agnes moved a coat from a hard chair and sat down.

'I care about all animals. I want to find out who did it.'

The woman shrugged. 'I was asleep. I never heard anything till I heard her braying – just light, it was.' She leaned back against her chair. 'Had a stick shoved up her and cut about. I got the vet. Took her off. Could do nothing, so . . .'

'Were you fond of Molly?' Agnes felt herself grieving for the maltreated animal.

The old woman looked thoughtful. 'Fond of her?' Agnes realised that 'fond' meant little to her. 'She was my husband Fred's. He had her for years. He's dead three years. Molly missed him, I fed her regular. Vet didn't charge me. Police came but I couldn't tell them owt.'

Agnes got up. 'So you didn't see or hear anything?'

'No. The bobbies looked round though.'

'Did they say anything?' Agnes felt she was trying to walk through a vat of treacle. The old lady did not react to questions, or to anything. Maybe, Agnes thought, it was because she was so old.

'No, well, not much, found some car tracks, so the bastard came in a car. May he rot in hell.'

Agnes almost jumped at the sudden vehemence and feeling in the voice. She turned back from the door. 'We'll find out who did it,' she said.

The old woman shrugged. 'And what will they do to him?' she said, then: 'I'd push a stick up his arse till he died of it.'

Agnes suddenly took the blue-veined hand in hers. 'So would I like to do just that.'

She left the cottage and walked across the field and got into the Porsche. As she started the car she realised her eyes were wet with tears. For the donkey or the old woman? She wasn't quite sure.

Marshall's stables next. She loved the purr of the Porsche as it drew away from the edge of the field and the wheels gained the smoother surface of the road. But even as she drove purposefully along toward her destination, she could not forget the old woman's red-rimmed eyes. We never really know the other person, never can gauge, not correctly, how they are feeling, she thought, and hoped as she drove that Molly had died easily.

Marshall's stables were as different from her last venue as chalk from cheese. The stables stood in a neat row, some horses looking out of the open top halves of their doors. A girl with long hair was sweeping the yard in front. Agnes parked in the lane leading up to the yard and got out of the car. The closing of the Porsche door alerted the girl who straightened up, turned round and pushed the long fair hair behind her ear, revealing a small gold ear-ring.

'Can I help you?'

Agnes walked carefully over the wet stones. 'You had a horse mutilated here. I was so sorry to hear it.'

The girl eyed her suspiciously, 'Yes, we did. You from the press or the police?'

'Neither. The horse Magic, next door to me, was killed, cut up, three months ago. I would like to find out who did it. He was twenty-eight years old, deserved a peaceful death, a loved pet.

The girl's manner changed. 'I'm sorry about that too. What's the matter with the man? Why does he want to hurt such lovely creatures?' She leaned the broom against the wall. 'Come and see Maisie. She wasn't too badly damaged by that . . .' She left out the last word.

Maisie thrust her head out of her stable, answering the girl's call. Her ear and the side of her head were bandaged. She backed away when she saw Agnes.

'She's still a little nervous, can you wonder?'

'Who's this?' A man's voice interrupted them.

'This is the owner, Miss . . . ?' She looked enquiringly at Agnes.

'Turner, Agnes Turner.'

'I'm Eric. Eric Marshall. I should keep away from Maisie. She's still a bit jumpy.'

The girl blushed as if she had been reproved.

'Your Porsche?' he asked.

Agnes nodded. 'I must explain,' she said. 'The horse next door

43

to me was knifed to death three months ago. Just an old, much-loved pet. No longer ridden, even.'

He nodded. 'Was in the paper, the local paper. Now the low life has started again.'

Agnes agreed. 'Was there anything, anything in the way of a clue as to who he was?'

They started to walk back towards the Porsche. The man shook his head. 'Nothing. Oh, except the car. Someone, a farm-hand going home from work, saw a car. Says it was green, even thinks it was a green Volvo. But considering the bad light and his knowledge of cars, the police were pretty sceptical.' He smoothed the bonnet of Agnes' car. 'Lovely job.'

'Thank you, and I hope you won't be cross with your stable girl for letting me see Maisie.'

Eric Marshall laughed. 'Stable girl? That's my wife,' he said.

It was Agnes' turn to blush. She turned the car and drove away, leaving him standing there still smiling.

As she drove to the battery to call for her chickens, she decided she would bring four from that hell, not two. She had room enough. 'A green Volvo, a green Volvo.' She remembered Edwin Merrill's words. 'I helped him buy a green Volvo. You want a substantial-looking car to impress the clients.' Had the farm labourer been right and if so, who had been driving the green Volvo? Who indeed? Agnes remembered too the look of fear and mistrust the bandaged horse Maisie had shown in her brown eyes as she, Agnes, had drawn near her. Would the poor creature ever regain confidence in anyone again? Agnes knew little about horses. Perhaps they forgot very quickly the sting of a whip or even the thrust of a knife. She hoped so. Humans let them down so frequently and they forgave. She hated to watch those slender legs being forced over high, impossible-looking jumps. The Grand National was abhorrent to her. Asking too much of the animal, screaming encouragement. Ignoring falls, as long as the money was won.

Returning home with Mac after his short morning walk past High Hurlands, Agnes met Amanda just coming out of the gate.

She banged it shut behind her, not bothering with the latch. The red car was parked outside the house. The girl skirted the car and greeted Agnes with eagerness. Without smiling, she asked, 'May I walk with you to the cottage?'

Agnes agreed and indicated the car. 'Visitor?'

Amanda shook her head. 'Hardly a visitor, Agnes. My shrink, actually. He talks to me, then tells my parents what he thinks of my mind.' She smiled, but not a pleasant smile. 'He's wet actually. I can say anything to him, lead him up any path.'

Agnes shook her head. The fact that she was a nurse made her stick up for medicine and medical men. Doctors were still, although it was now a long time since she had worked amongst them, wise and hard-working people. 'You may think you are leading him, but probably, in doing so, you are telling him a lot about yourself.' They reached Rose Cottage. 'Do come in and let me make us some coffee, Amanda. I feel rather lonely this morning.'

With the same eagerness that she had shown on their meeting, Amanda followed Agnes. 'How nice, I'd love to.'

'Let's have it in the kitchen, mugs too – that does mark you as one of my friends,' Agnes said, snapping on the kettle.

'Yes, let's, and thank you for saying that – about friends, I mean.' Amanda said this almost shyly.

'Cream, sugar?'

'Please.'

They sat, one on each side of the kitchen table, the smell of coffee pleasant. Amanda stirred her coffee, eyes downcast, silent. It was Agnes who at last had to break the silence. 'And is he any use to you, your psychiatrist? Does he help you with whatever your problems are, Amanda?'

The girl looked up. 'No. It all started when Magic was . . .' She looked away, white even teeth biting her lower lip.

'Please don't talk about it if you don't want to, perhaps I should not have asked. I shall quite understand if –'

'Oh no, I'd like to tell you. Mum and Dad, well, it only worries them. They think, well, perhaps they think I'm mad or . . .' She paused, and stirred her spoon round and round the cup. 'Perhaps I am mad Agnes. You see, I can't remember, not properly, what really happened that night.'

Agnes was quiet, determined to let the girl say what she perhaps needed to say in her own time. She was wise enough to see that Amanda hardly knew what was the matter with her, perhaps did not understand how it was possible to block out a terrible happening. At last, after the girl had blurted out one or two remarks showing how little she could recall, Agnes reminded her of the remarks she had made about stabbing John Merrill. Dragging him round to Rose Cottage. Did she remember saying that?

Amanda almost smiled. 'Silly, wasn't it, saying it was – the body was in your garden, when I knew . . .'

'Knew what?'

'It wasn't there. The shrink says I only sort of dreamt that part. I told him we looked and he wasn't there and he said I had imagined it all. The man had run away. Well, that must be true, because if I had really stabbed him, he couldn't have driven away, could he?'

Agnes got up and made more coffee. As she replaced the steaming mug in front of Amanda, the girl looked up at her. 'Could he?'

Agnes shook her head. 'Of course he couldn't. Did you see his car?'

Amanda nodded. 'Yes. It was dark but it was his car. His father gave it to him. He was proud of it.' She sipped her coffee. 'Cars. It's all cars with men, isn't it? They both thought Magic was a waste of money. Guy said he could have a car if it wasn't for Magic.' She got up and began to walk round the kitchen. 'Sometimes I wish I had killed him, anyway.'

Agnes took the girl's hand as she passed her chair. 'We often feel we could kill someone,' she said softly. 'How many times have you heard people say, "I could kill him"?'

Amanda sat down. 'Yes, I know. There was a girl at school . . .' She calmed down a little. 'But poor Magic, all blood, and his eyes, looking at me as if he was saying "Help!" Then he was dead and I chased the two men – '

'Two men?' Agnes broke in almost sharply.

Amanda looked at her for some seconds. 'Yes, two men. Why

did I say that, Agnes? Two men. There was only John.' She buried her head in her hands. 'That's what happens when I'm talking. I say silly things. Two men?'

Agnes took the girl's hands in hers, making her uncover her face. 'Look, Amanda, you had a terrible shock. Magic, the blood, an awful scene. Why don't you try and stop talking about it, to the doctor and to your family?' She pressed the girl's hands. 'I won't say forget it, you couldn't do that, I know, but don't talk about it. It makes you more muddled.'

Amanda nodded. 'It does, it does, Agnes. But not when I talk to you. I seem to remember more.'

'Well, when you feel you want to say something that puzzles you, come here and talk to me.'

'I will, I will, Agnes and thank you so much. I think the psychiatrist muddles me. I won't talk to him any more.'

Agnes watched her walk up the path to the gate. Poor child, she thought. Confusion. The girl was still in shock after months, but 'two men' – was that the truth? Was it really John Merrill's body? Was there indeed a second man who had driven away the green Volvo? The plot, as they say, was thickening. The second man might be the one who was still torturing and killing. Agnes waved back to Amanda as she turned at the gate and raised her hand, calling out, 'Thank you, Agnes' as she did so. Mac ambled out to see what was going on.

Up at the chicken house Agnes was pleased to see the four new ones were managing to walk about and peck at the grass. One staggered a little, but did not fall down. Agnes scattered in a little grain and they all, including the four new battery hens, began to peck the seed. They must feel strange in their new freedom, Agnes thought, and she hoped they felt better, happier, if a chicken can. As she watched them, she felt they could. She thought of herself as a young girl, caged by shyness, low self-esteem, afraid. Afraid all the time of what others would think of her. What had freed her? Half a million pounds left her by an old and grateful patient who Agnes had mistakenly thought was as poor as a church mouse. Power could mean freedom, so could money, as Agnes rapidly found out. She watched the four newly rescued chickens turning their sore lacerated necks this way and that. Freedom after all was what every human being craved and every animal deserved.

Agnes wandered back to the house. The polyanthus were flourishing. Mac trotted beside her. She thought suddenly of the man in the ditch, the other side of the wall. She could not be sure if he would be found, his death investigated. What would this mean for Amanda, if the death was traced to the girl? Would the fact that she was under a psychiatrist help her accusers? Agnes wondered too if the suggested invitation to dinner would ever come from the Holsteins. She rather hoped so. She was interested to meet the whole family, especially the son Guy who seemed, according to his sister, not to have been a great lover of Magic.

6

She had not long to wonder if the invitation would materialise for the next day Mrs Holstein telephoned to ask her to 'have a meal with them', as she put it, on Wednesday evening, which was in a couple of days' time. Before she put the telephone down she said, 'You have been so nice to Amanda. She has really taken to you. She's been going through rather a bad time.'

Agnes replied cautiously, 'I gathered all was not going smoothly for her.' She thought of the body mouldering away in the ditch.

Agnes could not get it out of her head, the scene at the stables, the bandaged horse and the farmhand's remark, casual and seemingly not thought to be an important clue. Surely the police would have followed up the guess at the green Volvo? Mr Marshall had seemed casual enough about it too. Agnes decided she would go back to the stables and try to get in touch with the man who had 'thought he'd seen'.

Luck was with Agnes that evening. As she drove up and

parked the car outside the gates of the yard an elderly man came out of one of the stables. Agnes waited while he shut and locked both half-doors and crossed the paved stones of the yard near the gate.

'Yes, miss, did you want something?' His brown face was wrinkled, his eyes half shut against the evening sun.

'Yes, I wonder if you could tell me the name of the farm worker who thought he saw a car here the evening Maisie was injured.'

The man immediately looked suspicious. 'You from the police?'

Agnes shook her head.

'Papers, magazines?'

'No.' Agnes spoke patiently. 'My next-door neighbour's horse Magic was stabbed to death and I want to – '

'I tell you this much, miss, if I could corner that bastard ... Excuse me, miss.' He touched his cap in a brief apology, Agnes presumed, for using the word. 'I'd run this pitchfork straight through his guts and swing for him, I wouldn't mind.'

'I feel the same.'

'It's Jess Lewis. He lives over there, look, in that cottage.' He pointed out a small white-painted, slate-roofed house about three fields away. 'There's a road to it, rough though. He's in the far end one. Jasmine Cottage.'

Agnes thanked him.

'He's off, on the sick with his back, so you'll find him in.'

The road was rough, but dry. Agnes drove slowly along to the end and backed the car round the side of the last white cottage. It looked pretty, the white paint on the walls white as white could be, just painted by the look of it. The door was bright green with a rather cheap brass knocker. Agnes used this and the door opened at once. Obviously Jess Lewis's wife. She fulfilled perfectly the description of a farmer's wife. White hair swept back, straight and out of the way, into a neat bun at the back. She was fat, rosy, and presented a perfect picture as she stood at the door, smiling already though Agnes had not yet spoken.

In the warm kitchen, sitting in front of a small range, legs on a stool, was Jess. When Agnes stated her business, he seemed co-operative enough but not quite as certain of his facts as the stable owner had given Agnes to believe.

'Well, it was dark, you know, miss. The car looked sort of green, well, could have been, or dark blue.'

'Or black, even?' Agnes suggested.

He looked at her earnestly. 'Not black. No, I don't think black, miss.'

Agnes waited patiently. He was busy lighting a pipe. She had to pass him the matches from the table because he couldn't bend forward easily. 'You thought it was a Volvo though?' she asked.

Again he took some time before he answered. The match flared up in a long bright flame and a bluey smoke engulfed him. 'Well, my son's got a Volvo, see, and it was the same shape as his.' Agnes nodded and waited again. 'Bill, my son, he's got the same. You know, written on the back, Volvo.' The match went out and he started on the pipe again.

'And did you see it written on . . . ?'

He shook his head. 'No, I never. But it was the same shape as Bill's. I couldn't quite see.'

'Well, thank you, Mr Lewis.'

'Wish we could get him. He wants beating up.'

Agnes thanked him again and left the cottage, refusing Mrs Lewis's offer of a cup of tea.

Driving home, she tried to assess the farm labourer's certainty of what he had seen and decided that, though she was disappointed in him as a witness, at least the green Volvo had not been ruled out. Someone had driven it away from High Hurlands. If the dead man had not driven the car and was John Merrill, then who had been the driver?

As Agnes got ready for the visit to High Hurlands she was a bit uncertain what to wear. Would the rather smart black dress she had got out of her wardrobe and laid on the bed be suitable? High-heeled shoes. Or would it be a jeans and flatties affair? Mrs Holstein had not looked very formal for her shopping trip. Dress and cardigan, white plastic peep-toed shoes. But perhaps they would dress up because a guest was coming. Suddenly Agnes felt frustrated and irritated. If only Bill had not died, if only, if only. She would not be here, trying to accommodate herself to new friends, new customs. She would – they would – still be in Rutland Gate with friends who gave dinner parties, lunches, drinks parties that they knew about. Knew what people would wear, would talk about, even how much they would drink, eat. Who liked what . . .

She put the dress back in the wardrobe and decided on a burgundy trouser suit, its colour relieved by a pale tan silk shirt. No jewellery, she decided, then changed her mind and pinned on a little diamond brooch, a tiny model of Mac given to her by Bill soon after they had adopted him. Somehow Bill seemed to be very close to her this evening. Agnes gave a long sigh. 'Wish he were here, Mac,' she said to the little dog who was on her bed watching operations. He wagged his tail, but slowly. Not, Agnes felt, because he sensed she was thinking of Bill, but because he suspected she was going out. Agnes thought the fact that she had done so little going out in the evenings since Bill had died meant that on this occasion she missed him more than ever. She sprayed a little Joy on her wrist and neck, slipped into some black patent flatties, picked up her small black evening handbag and was ready.

Her usual remark to the dog, 'I won't be long, Mac,' justified his suspicions: he got into his basket, casting a brown reproachful eye at her as she went out of the kitchen door. Agnes left the hall and sitting-room lights on, partly for Mac's comfort and partly to welcome her when she came home. She locked the front door with the large old-fashioned key of which she was rather fond. She popped it into her bag and started on the short walk to the white house.

As she walked she knew she was making her mind up to ask, find out, more about the relationships between the two neighbours. The subject of Magic, she felt, must be approached subtly, with care. She already knew it had caused Amanda to have a breakdown, but her brother had probably been pleased if the horse's death had eased the family finances enough for them to buy a car, perhaps for him and the parents. They seemed to be more worried about the effect the animal's death had had on their daughter. Her last thought as she mounted the front steps to the door of the house was that she was not sure how many – if any – of them knew of the body in the ditch. She felt none of them did, or maybe one. This thought gave her power, she felt. Power to talk to them from the knowledge she possessed, but of which they were completely unaware. She shivered slightly as she waited for the door to open. They didn't know she knew and that was Agnes' favourite stance.

'Oh, good evening, Mrs Turner, how nice to see you.'

She entered the well-polished hall, smiling and ready for her own particular battle. Was it an omen? In the background she could hear music. Gilbert and Sullivan.

'Oh, that's Guy, he loves . . .' Mrs Holstein did not finish the sentence. Agnes smiled more widely: the tune, now switched off, probably because the guest had been heard to arrive, was Gilbert and Sullivan's famous 'Let the punishment fit the crime, the punishment fit the crime.' How she agreed with that, Agnes thought, as she politely refused Mrs Holstein's offer to relieve her of her jacket. The hallway felt chilly.

Agnes had no need to worry about what she would wear to the little party. Informality was the order. Mrs Holstein was in much the same attire as when she had last seen her, flowered summer frock with a rather sad-looking fawn cardigan and white plastic shoes. She was a pretty woman, her grey hair curling softly on her forehead, a touch of lipstick her only make-up. Her husband, in a grey suit with a white shirt and blue striped tie, looked equally dull. Amanda at least had youth on her side, but she was not as animated as she was when she visited Rose Cottage.

In the sitting-room Mrs Holstein brought in a tray of small glasses, filled, to Agnes' horror, with sweet sherry. She took one, sipped it, tried not to show her dislike of the sickly sweet liquid and put the glass down on a small occasional table.

'Isn't there any beer, Ma?' The voice, rough and bored, took Agnes by surprise. She had not heard anyone enter the room.

'No, dear. I forgot to get any. I think – '

'God, you would!' He turned to Agnes. 'Can you drink that

muck?' he asked. 'I'll see if there's any beer. Sometimes she forgets when she's bought it. I'll go and see.'

He padded out of the room. Agnes watched him go, realising why she had not heard him come in. His trainers made no sound on the wooden floor. His long dark hair hung past his shoulders, slightly curling at the ends. Round his head he wore a wide strip of what looked like coloured webbing. Tied at the back, it hung down over his hair. He was tall, his hands and forearms showing brown beneath the rolled-back sleeves of his check shirt. Agnes had not got a clear look at his face. When he came back he carried a six pack of beer. The outsides of the green and silver cans were covered with drips of water which spotted the table. His right hand held four large-stemmed glasses, a finger in each. He put them down with a little clatter. Then he looked up. Agnes' first impression was that he looked like a brigand. His long hair hanging each side of his face was reinforced by a large black straggly moustache. His face was as brown as his arms. He smiled, righted the glasses.

'Like one?' He looked directly at Agnes, his hazel eyes cat-like.

'Agnes doesn't drink beer, Guy.'

'Oh snobsville, aye.' He laughed, showing white even teeth.

'I like a beer now and again,' Agnes said, rather defensively.

'Right.' He pulled back the ring on another can, and a little spray of beer spattered on Agnes' face. Go well with Joy, she thought.

'You've got a Porsche.'

Agnes nodded.

'Don't suppose I could borrow it one day, just for a drive?'

'No,' Agnes said positively.

Guy Holstein laughed good-humouredly. 'Well, I wouldn't lend it to a yobbo like me either.'

He emptied his glass and Agnes took a drink from hers: the taste was fresh, clean. Anything was better than sweet sherry.

'The meal's ready. Would you like to come through?'

Agnes followed Mrs Holstein and then the others followed her. The meal was edible, straight from the microwave. There was no starter and the sweet was apple crumble with custard.

Mr Holstein said little to begin with, then started to talk about the new supermarket in Lewes.

'Kill what's left of the little shops stone dead.'

Guy broke in. He had lit a cigarette. 'Bugger the little shops, they charge too much.' His voice became high-pitched and mocking. '"Well, they can't buy in bulk, you see." Rubbish.'

'Mrs Beaven would perhaps have to close.'

'Well, would that matter?'

Amanda looked at him, then her eyes turned towards Agnes as if to say, 'You see what he's like.' To her brother she was indignant. 'She was very nice when poor Magic was ... when Magic died, kind and understanding. It would be a shame to see her little shop close.'

Guy got up, stubbing his cigarette end in the custard left on his plate. 'Back to that bloody horse again. I knew we wouldn't get through a meal without Magic being brought up.' He suddenly looked across at Agnes. 'Another beer, Mrs Turner?'

Agnes shook her head. She suspected Guy Holstein had had quite a few beers before he started on those he had found in the kitchen.

'Now, Guy, that will do. You will upset Amanda.'

Guy ignored his mother and kept his eyes focused on Agnes. 'Do you know, Mrs T., if we hadn't kept that useless animal I might have had a Porsche. Not a new one like yours, I admit, but at least a bloody car.'

Agnes looked at him, her voice low. 'Even a Volvo, eh, Guy?'

This remark roused Mr Holstein. 'John Merrill's got one of those hasn't he, Mother?'

Amanda went into the kitchen to make coffee. Mrs Holstein started to clear away the plates. There was a long silence. Guy lit another cigarette then his eyes remained fixed on Agnes' face. Agnes felt a quick stab of fear. Had she gone too far, said too much?

Amanda came back with the tray of coffee. Mrs Holstein came in from the kitchen. Guy opened another beer. They all sat down. The tension was electric. Amanda looked close to tears. Guy was smiling a sarcastic smile. Mr Holstein relapsed into a gloomy silence. Mrs Holstein, trying to rescue the situation, did her best.

'Did you have to pay a lot for Rose Cottage, Mrs Turner? Everyone said it wasn't structurally sound.'

Agnes did not answer but Guy did. 'Another of your clangers, Ma,' he said, crushing the last beer can with a strong muscular hand. He aimed it at the waste-paper basket, missed and leant back in his chair.

'Guy!' his father said. 'Don't be such a slob, pick that up.'

Guy did so, holding the crushed can in his hand above shoulder height, then dropping it with a smirk in Agnes' direction. He sat down again.

'What is your work, Mr Holstein?'

'Call me Guy, for God's sake. It's Agnes, isn't it?' He lit another cigarette. 'I don't work. Can't afford to, know what I mean? I'm not trained.' He spread his legs.

'Aren't there training schemes?' Agnes felt herself wanting to goad him. 'Do you drive, Guy, that's always a useful skill?'

'Yes, I do. Maybe I'll get a car now Magic's dead.'

Amanda left the room for a moment. 'Very sad for your sister though.'

Guy shrugged. 'Magic was no friend of mine. I don't think the thing liked me.'

Amanda had come back. 'Please don't refer to Magic as "the thing".' She stood, white-faced, in front of her brother. Agnes thought she was about to strike him.

Mrs Holstein came between them. 'Now, now, Guy. No need for that. Amanda, remember we have a guest.'

This seemed to calm both her children down. They drew apart. Guy sat down on the sofa, putting one leg up on it so that Amanda could not sit beside him. Amanda, however, turned to Agnes.

'I'm so sorry, Agnes. I didn't mean to . . . it's just that I loved him so much, I can't bear to hear Guy speak of him like that.'

Agnes took her hand. 'Look, I must go now. Mac may be barking.'

She thanked Mr and Mrs Holstein. It had been a rather weird

visit, she felt. As she said her goodbyes, Mrs Holstein was in the kitchen piling up the plates and cutlery.

'Can I help?' Agnes felt compelled to ask.

'Not in that lovely suit.' Mrs Holstein smiled at her. 'No, I'm leaving it all for tomorrow.'

'I've so enjoyed meeting you all.'

Agnes walked out of the kitchen. Mr Holstein was reading the paper. He did put it aside and got up, pressing on both arms of the armchair to lever himself up.

'Thank you for having me.' Agnes smiled at him. He was standing, bent a little forward. His son had disappeared from the room.

'Guy shouldn't have said that. Talked about Amanda's horse like he did.' He took a handkerchief from his pocket and blew his nose. 'They hate each other. Never agree. Sometimes I think he was quite fond of Magic, just said things to tease Amanda.'

Agnes passed Guy in the hall. He was shrugging on a short leather coat. 'Cheerio,' he said as Agnes passed him. She could not bring herself even to look at him and did not answer.

As she walked home she thought about his reaction to the word 'Volvo' – or had she imagined it and there had been no reaction at all? Supposing ... What a strange family. Amanda had gone upstairs, not even come down to say goodbye. Funny family.

Once home she put on Mac's lead and walked by the white house again. The lights were all out, at least upstairs. She wondered where Guy had been off to. It had been about ten past ten. Perhaps he would spend an hour or two in the local pub. It was quite a walk. Still, he had probably finished all the beer in the house.

Agnes felt suddenly tired. The whole visit had been tiring, full of tension, full of animosity, hate almost. By their rather odd behaviour, they did not entertain much. She gave Mac his goodnight biscuit, picked his bed up and carried it up to her bedroom. Mac slept in her bedroom. When Bill had been alive he had slept in the kitchen – where a dog should, Bill used to say, laughing. But nowadays she liked to have him in his basket in her bedroom, near her. When she couldn't sleep, it was a comfort to hear him. He stirred a little sometimes, or moved around in his bed. That night, perhaps because of the visit, Agnes fell asleep as soon as her head touched the pillow and, very unusually for her, did not wake until the milk cart drew up outside at eight o'clock and the sun streamed through the bedroom window.

In the morning, after breakfast, she decided to call at High Hurlands and thank them for her visit and to enquire after Amanda. Agnes was genuinely worried about the girl after her outburst last night. On the evidence of her behaviour then, Agnes felt she was capable of the violence she claimed. Agnes felt she might even confront Amanda with her own discovery of the body in the ditch.

The morning was sunny and a little warmer. Agnes left Mac with Mrs Tracy and once again set out for High Hurlands, thankful that this time she would not have to suffer the aperitifs and meal. Amanda was the only one in.

'Oh, Mrs Turner, I'm so glad to see you again. Wasn't last night awful? Guy is horrible. I hate him.'

Agnes refused the girl's offer of coffee or tea. 'Let's just take a turn round the garden,' she said smiling. 'Do you remember, Amanda, how they always said in Jane Austen "a turn round the garden"?'

Amanda looked at her blankly. 'I couldn't read Jane Austen, Agnes. She went on so about trifles.'

'Well, yes, I suppose you could say that, but you must try again.'

They strolled on. 'You can't see my house from your garden, except the roof,' Agnes remarked. She had carefully, and without apparently doing so, led the girl to the little mound that did overlook her house. 'I've been here before, Amanda,' she said. 'Do you know what's down there, in the ditch by the wall? The body.' Amanda's face was expressionless. 'But who, and is it the one you saw killing Magic? You must tell me, Amanda,' she said, watching the girl closely.

'I didn't see him cutting Magic. Magic had fallen down and I . . .' She looked at Agnes, confusion showing, wrinkling her forehead. 'I chased him and stabbed him.' She started to cry.

'Are you sure it was John Merrill?' Agnes asked.

'Yes, oh yes.'

Amanda began to scramble down the little slope, parting the brambles with her hands. Agnes watched her, then joined her to help with her gloved hands. Amanda was dragging away brambles and rotting weeds. Agnes pulled away a great tangle of growth. Between them they revealed the empty ditch beneath, slightly waterlogged and muddy, but it was self-evident as their eyes met. There was no body in the ditch. The body was gone.

'He's not there.' Amanda's face was ashen.

Agnes quickly had to think how to handle this development. She put her arm round the girl's shoulders. 'Perhaps you didn't put it there, Amanda. Remember how you thought you had dragged a body round to my garden?'

A ray of hope lit the girl's face. 'Yes, I did, didn't I?'

Agnes tightened her grip. 'You see, you were so shocked by poor Magic's death your mind got all muddled up, confused.'

The girl's trembling ceased a little. 'Yes, that's it. That's it, Agnes.' Her face suddenly hardened. 'But I did stab him, I think, Agnes. I'm almost sure I did.'

Agnes interrupted her. 'Come on, we must clean ourselves up a bit.'

As they walked back to the house Agnes decided on a course of action she was not quite sure of. 'Supposing John Merrill comes back, safe and sound. Then you will know there was no stabbing.'

The girl did not accept the idea at all. 'Oh no, he was stabbed. I saw the blood, his coat was torn at the back, I think. I had the knife. I dropped it, picked it up, it was all blood, even the handle.'

'That could have been Magic's blood,' Agnes suggested.

'No, no.' Amanda was adamant.

'How do you know all this when you are so muddled up about the rest of it?'

'That's what the psychiatrist keeps asking and I don't know. I don't know.' Amanda broke down completely, sobbing.

Agnes left the house when she had managed to comfort and reassure the girl, but she was really as confused herself now. She had no doubts that there had been a body in the ditch, no doubts whatsoever. But where was that body now? Who had moved it? It must have been done in the night when she slept so soundly. Someone had come, silently, in the night and taken it away. Someone who had put it there all those months ago. That someone could be anyone – well, not anyone, but someone who had been there the night Magic was so cruelly killed. Agnes was becoming more and more convinced that Amanda had stabbed no one that night, but somebody had and that person was ... who?

7

'But Mr Hattsell, you said you would be here at ten thirty yesterday, then today, and it's now twelve thirty.'

The plumber on the other end of the phone made another excuse and another date to do the job needed – a new kitchen sink. Agnes was determined to have a white enamel draining board, instead of the existing stainless steel one. She put the telephone down, forcing herself to do it gently instead of banging it back on its rest with irritation. She had, in her own estimation, wasted her morning, and by the time she had got lunch ready, the whole day. There were so many other things to be looked at, coped with. Painting, hanging wallpaper, a small built-in cupboard under the stairs. Carpenter, plumber, painter, decorator. Agnes could not blame their non-appearance for causing all the delay. Some of it, perhaps most of it, was due to herself. She had been in Rose Cottage four months and acknowledged that at first she had not felt at all interested in making a home. She had never been or imagined herself as a home maker. She felt so alone after Bill's death. Rose Cottage. So what? She could not summon up the interest just for herself.

Perhaps her rather reluctant meetings with her neighbours, her interest in the strange happenings, had aroused her and maybe made Rose Cottage more of a project that had to be tackled, like the puzzle of the disappearing body. Not only interest, but fury at the cruelty. She could not get the look of suspicion and distrust in Maisie's brown eyes out of her mind.

She had one or two ideas, and one took her late that afternoon to Lewes, to a garage that was an agent for Volvo. Perhaps unfortunately the salesman had noticed her arrival and immediately came forward to meet her as soon as she opened the heavy glass door.

'Can I help you, madam?' he said, his eyes on the Porsche.

'I'm not thinking of buying a car for myself, Mr . . . ?'

'Harris, Reg Harris, Mrs . . . ?'

'Turner,' Agnes replied crisply. 'What I want to see, if you have such a thing, is a green Volvo.'

'Green.' He looked down the row of shining cars. Red, white, brown, lavender. 'Yes, we have a green one, last from the end.'

They walked down the diagonally displayed row of new Volvos, Agnes realising by the time she reached the last one, how much she loved the smell of new cars. It crossed her mind as she gazed at the green one that perhaps she would change her Porsche. She had made such a good profit on Rutland Gate she could easily afford it, and the smell of a new Porsche was even better when it was your own.

'Is this the normal green for a fairly new Volvo, have they changed it at all?'

The salesman shook his head. 'Nope. Kept it the same shade, added the thick black line. Makes little difference to the appearance, but looked good in the catalogue, I suppose.'

Agnes knew he thought he might have a sale and tried to let him down as lightly as she could. 'Thank you. I'll have to think about it.' Then she turned and asked, 'Green, though – isn't that colour supposed to be unlucky?'

'That is just an old wives' tale. Nowadays, we only stock one green. Red's the colour. Lavender's not that popular.'

'But you managed to sell last year's green one. I know the owner, Mr Merrill, John Merrill.'

The man looked vacant for a second then his smile widened. 'Oh, John Merrill brought his father with him. Funny, the old gentleman didn't like green. He said it was unlucky.' He opened the big glass door. 'Up to now he's all right. Had his first service a few months ago.'

'Thank you.' Agnes left and got into her own car, thinking, as she fastened her safety belt, Up to now, he's all right? She wasn't so sure.

It was now that fate took a sudden turn in events. She was, as she motored along, still looking automatically at car colours. No green, no green. She pulled into the side of the road: the sun had come out. She pressed the button that opened the sun roof then, taking a headscarf from the compartment in the dashboard, she tied it firmly over her hair and in a double knot. Not getting her hair messed was one of Agnes' big concerns. Hers was not, and never had been, easy to control; once it was blown about it stayed blown about, did not fall straight back into the hairdresser's arrangement as in the shampoo adverts on television.

She was ready to draw out from the roadside, no cars behind, when about a hundred yards ahead a car began to edge out of a driveway – a green Volvo? Agnes could only see the bonnet, then, looking up and down the road, seeing only her apparently parked car, the driver pulled out into the road. The word Volvo was plain to see, and last year's registration letter, but the biggest surprise of all was the driver. The car was driven by the fair-haired young girl she had met at the stables. Agnes got a very good look at the girl as she scanned the road for oncoming cars. The man beside her had long hair. As the car gathered speed, he turned round to take something from the back seat. It was Guy Holstein.

It was enough. He must be the horse mutilator. But what was he doing with her, why was she driving what was, or had been, John Merrill's car? All these questions poured through her head as Agnes sat, clutching the steering wheel. She felt frustrated because she dared not follow them. Guy knew her car, he would at once recognise the Porsche. She drove slowly past the house from whose driveway the green car had emerged. It was a nice, suburban house, not spectacular in any way. On the open gate a nameplate read 'The Hollies'.

A thousand questions went through Agnes' mind as she drove home, not daring to drive at the Porsche's usual speed in case

61

she overtook the Volvo. Why was the girl, Mrs Marshall, driving? Did her parents live at The Hollies? If so, why should Guy Holstein visit them with her? On the way, she determined to force the pace a little. Perhaps go back to the nursery for more plants, ask the girl more about John Merrill.

She arrived home feeling exhausted and frustrated. Too many questions, and Agnes hated not knowing – but Mac must have his walk, she would never deny him that. She made herself a cup of tea while the little dog danced around her, his lead in his mouth. 'Yes, we are going, just give me a minute,' she said, almost sharply, to him. He looked at her, brown eyes astonished, she supposed at her unusual tone. She was immediately sorry, picked him up, gave him a cuddle, then poured him a cup of tea, or rather a saucer of tea with a lump of sugar in it, a rare treat. She snapped on his lead and decided to walk towards the shop past the Merrills' rather than go past High Hurlands, then cut through the little lane into the fields and back to her house that way. She was so glad she did, for some of the questions she was troubling herself trying to answer were to be answered on that walk.

Agnes drew to the end of the lane that went up almost beside Mrs Beaven's little shop. At the end of it, where it opened into the fields, Mac's excitement grew. This was one of his favourite walks. They very seldom met any other dog walkers and the fields were free of sheep or cattle. Mac streaked away on his short legs. He had not gone more than a few yards when a large black Labrador bounded up to him, mouth open, pink tongue lolling.

'He won't hurt him, he's only a baby.'

Agnes turned towards the voice. It was Violet Greenham. The two dogs bounded off together, Mac obviously glad to find one of his own kind and a playful one at that.

Violet Greenham was all smiles. 'I didn't think I would meet anyone I know to stroll with,' she said. 'What a sweet little chap, what's his name?'

'Mac, and yours?'

'Buster. He's only fourteen months. We lost our last one. He was sixteen, same make as this one. Decided not to have another, then, well, you know how it is.'

'Are you staying with your sister?' Agnes asked.

'Yes, the two "boys", Edwin and Ivan, have gone on a golfing weekend, they go twice a year.'

Agnes called Mac, and he came back to her at once. Satisfied that he wasn't getting too carried away, Agnes let him go back to playing with Buster.

'Pansy hates being alone, so I come down and stay a couple of nights. We quite enjoy it, having a girls' gaggle. No men around. You must join us, for a drink or something.'

'Love to. Have you heard from John yet?' Agnes asked.

'John? Oh no, he'll come back when he's ready . . . got a new boyfriend I shouldn't be surprised.'

Agnes showed her surprise. 'Boyfriend? Do you mean . . . ?'

Violet nodded. 'Yes, dear, bent as a hairpin. Upsets Pansy and infuriates Edwin. I tell them not to worry and it takes all sorts and all the stupid things you do say.'

Agnes nodded. They walked a little way in silence. Then Agnes had to ask. 'I thought Amanda Holstein was keen on him, and another girl I met said . . .'

'That will be the girl at the flower place, nursery. All covers. He's quite a good-looking lad, our John. Likes to pretend he's playing the field, girl-wise.'

'Where is he now?' Agnes asked.

'Don't know. He had a big crush on Guy Holstein, but Holstein is as straight as a ruler. John hated him for it too. Tried hard to bring him round to his way of thinking, but no go.'

Agnes took a little time to digest this. 'And did John have a boyfriend, I mean around here?'

Violet bent down, picked up a piece of a branch and threw it for Buster. His education had not gone that far though. He chased the stick, smelled it, then left it. Violet shook her head. 'Don't know. Pansy said he did, told me in confidence he did. Some farmer's or farm labourer's son over at . . .' She paused. 'Can't remember the name of the farm, but near Marshall's stables.' She sighed. 'Edwin couldn't believe it at first that his son was a poof, you know how men can't, but in the end he half accepted it. John isn't home, doesn't write or telephone.'

Agnes and she were walking slowly, giving the two dogs ample time to chase about. They came to a big fallen tree. 'Please let's sit down a minute. I'm knackered – need a cigarette.' She lit one and the smoke spiralled in the still evening air. Mac came and sat down beside Agnes and Buster rolled on his back a little way away from them.

'Bet he's rolling in something smelly,' Violet said. 'Labradors always do. By the way, Agnes, that's a lovely perfume you use.'

'Thank you.' Agnes did not divulge the name. She rarely did, in case the person would decide to go and buy some. 'Did John like Amanda?' she asked.

'No. John was bitterly jealous of her, I think, because she was Guy's sister and so was close to him. I suppose that's how John thought.'

'He must be a strange young man,' Agnes suggested.

'Strange? You can say that again, Agnes. Ivan always said he was a nutter, not just because he was gay, but somehow he was always a bit weird.'

'Do you think John could have injured Magic, Amanda's horse?'

Violet gazed at her wide-eyed for at least five seconds before she answered, then it was almost in a whisper. 'No. Do you, Agnes?'

Agnes shook her head. 'I don't know the man, Violet, I've never even seen him. I just wondered. Your husband said he was weird, a nutter?'

'Yes, but . . .'

Agnes shrugged. 'And you said he was jealous of Amanda because she was near to Guy.'

Violet Greenham brushed the bits of grain and bark from her skirt. It was after they had taken a few more steps that she looked sideways at Agnes. 'Wouldn't it be awful if he'd done it and that's why he's not getting in touch with Pansy. Oh, Lord!' They had reached the path leading up to Violet's sister's back gate. 'I wish you hadn't said that Agnes, you've given me the shivers.'

'I'm sorry, it was a stupid suggestion, it just occurred to me when you mentioned his jealousy of Amanda.'

Violet nodded. 'I know, but he was in a state.' She paused. 'But then, he always was.' She turned to leave. 'Come in and see us.'

Agnes smiled. 'Don't mention what I have said about the horse to Pansy.'

'No, of course not. See you.' She called Buster who, after a call or two more, followed her up to the house.

Agnes walked on slowly. Mac began to scamper about again. She knew what she must do. Go back to Marshall's place. That cottage across the field, Jasmine Cottage, the man with the bad back, Jess Lewis. He had talked about his son. Violet had given her the idea. A farm labourer's son. Could it be he? He would not have heard from John Merrill. Were they lovers? Two more horses had been injured since John Merrill's body had been mouldering away in the ditch at High Hurlands. Who had moved the decomposing body, and why? Agnes searched her memory. What was the name of the son, the farm chap had mentioned his son? Bill, yes, that was it. Bill Lewis. Were he and John . . . Agnes shied away from the word. Had they got a thrill from injuring horses and donkeys? Tomorrow she would go back to Jasmine Cottage. Before she drove there, though, she thought she would call on Mrs Beaven. She had to impart her inside knowledge. Agnes was sure she would not call it gossip. 'Just being well up on what goes on, Mrs Turner, it helps when you run a little shop.' She had said this to Agnes earlier on in their acquaintance. Perhaps her knowledge wouldn't encompass Bill Lewis or the young Mrs Marshall, but Agnes would drop in and put a few tactful questions.

8

The next morning Violet Greenham telephoned to ask Agnes to drop in for a drink about six o'clock that evening. 'Only Pansy and me, and do bring Mac.' Agnes accepted for herself but said she would leave Mac at home. That big boisterous Labrador of Violet's in the confines of the drawing-room, Agnes felt, might prove too much for Mac, so she would leave him alone. Besides, she could always make him the excuse for leaving if she found the conversation of the two women particularly boring.

At ten thirty the plumber arrived. He was a pleasant unpunctual young man who somehow made one feel pleased when he did turn up. Agnes trusted him to be left. He was plumbing in her washing machine, a new one, not a huge job, and then putting in a new kitchen sink.

'I'm just going to give Mac a little walk. I won't be long.'

He pushed his baseball cap further to the back of his curly fair hair. 'OK. I can finish the machine job, but I'll come tomorrow to start the sink.'

Agnes felt slightly irritated. 'But why don't you get on with it today, now you are here?'

He smiled his cherubic smile. 'No can do, Mrs Turner, got a leaking hot water tank just up the road. I promised.'

'Well, do try and turn up tomorrow.'

'Will do.'

Agnes wondered if 'Will do' meant he would come, but according to Mrs Beaven he was a good plumber, the best around. So she put on a resigned air, snapped on Mac's lead and set off for the little shop. She hoped that, as well as the purchases she felt she had to make, she would also pick up a few hints. The knowledge that more horses had been attacked was building up inside her and, as on many other occasions in her life when justice had had to be carried out – especially on someone who had hurt an animal or, in one case in her life, a child – she would not rest until she had paid that person in full for the pain he or she had caused. John Merrill had paid already by the look of it, paid with his life. Well, that was as it should be.

Mrs Beaven greeted her with her usual wide smile. The shop was empty so Agnes decided to wade straight in with her questions.

'Mrs Beaven, I need some writing paper and envelopes, but there is something I want to ask you. Rather a delicate question and please don't feel you must answer it if you would rather not, but it's to do with those poor horses that are getting hurt and killed.'

The little shopkeeper paused on her way to the shelf that held the writing paper and gave her full attention to Agnes, who leaned close to her over the counter.

'Did you know that John Merrill was, well, you know...' She hardly knew which word would mean most to Mrs Beaven and did not want to shock or offend her. She need not have bothered.

'Queer. Oh yes, I know that. We all did, I think.'

Agnes was a little surprised. 'I thought Amanda Holstein was rather keen on him, Mrs Beaven.'

Mrs Beaven, as if the sale should not be forgotten, took a pack of Basildon Bond envelopes from the little shelf. 'Blue or white, Mrs Turner?' she asked.

'Oh, white, thank you.' Agnes was not quite sure if she was being dismissed and decided to enlarge on the situation a little. 'It's not just gossip, Mrs Beaven. I am determined to find out who is injuring these horses and somehow I feel John Merrill was mixed up in the death of Magic.'

Mrs Beaven stopped putting Agnes' purchases in a white paper bag. 'Well, Amanda was keen on him, didn't realise, but why should he...?'

'What do you think of Guy Holstein, Mrs Beaven?'

The reply rather surprised Agnes. 'Well, he's a funny young man with his long hair and his talk, but I like him. He confided in me a bit.' Mrs Beaven gazed out of the doorway, deep in thought. 'I had a son, Mrs Turner. He was killed. Motor bike. He would have been about Guy's age, like him, long hair and all.' Agnes again was surprised. 'He was naughty, you know, just like Sam, my son. Going out with Mr Marshall's young wife, he told me. Said her husband was too old for her. I said, well, she married him.'

Agnes paid for her writing paper. 'Who lives at The Hollies, Purbeck Road, Mrs Beaven, do you know?'

Mrs Beaven now seemed to be getting into the swing of things. 'That's young Mrs Marshall's parents' house, The Hollies. Nice people.'

'Thank you, you've been a great help.'

Another customer came in, well timed as to their conversation Agnes thought. She left. Next call, Jasmine Cottage – hope the son might be there.

First, however, she had to check on her angelic-looking plumber's work. As she approached her gate the red car coming from High Hurlands passed her. The psychiatrist. Agnes glimpsed his face. He looked furiously angry.

Hurrying up her path, Agnes heard her name being called. It was Amanda.

'Agnes, Agnes, please wait. I want to talk to you ... I've remembered. I've remembered. I wouldn't tell Dr Gaynor. I couldn't. I couldn't. I couldn't tell Mum or Daddy. How could I now I remember?'

She was almost shouting and Agnes could do nothing but take her indoors, sit her down at the kitchen table and try to calm her down. At first she did not succeed and the girl just cradled her head in her hands and cried.

'All right, Amanda. Take your time, but I can't help you if you just cry.'

To give her a little time Agnes fed Mac, who was always more anxious to have his next meal than concerned about other people's emotions.

At last Amanda dried her eyes, composed herself and began to speak. At first nothing she said made much sense.

'Oh, Agnes, it's so tangled, all of it, so tangled and nasty. Of course I couldn't tell the wretched psychiatrist. Poor Magic lost his life because of it all. I hate everyone. Humans are horrible, including me.'

Agnes felt her irritation rising, experienced the old feeling she used to have when she was comforting a junior nurse. The hospital sister's manner came to the surface.

'Well, Amanda, all of that may be quite true but it is totally irrelevant to the facts as they actually happened. So, why not start at the beginning and try to get your facts marshalled in correct order.' She paused a moment; the girl did not speak, but at least stopped her bitter crying. 'You say you want to talk to me and I presume tell me what happened, or is this to be another emotional outpouring, which gets us nowhere?'

Amanda sat up, dried her eyes and looked at Agnes. 'You are right, Agnes, but when you hear the truth you will, I am sure, understand my refusing to discuss it with Mum and Dad or the shrink.'

'Right. Explain away.' Agnes too sat up straight, her mouth set in a firm line, and Amanda began in a way she did not expect.

'Why it all happened, why Magic lost his life, did not begin that night. It started much earlier.' One more use of a tissue, but this time not to wipe her eyes, just to blow her nose. 'Agnes, have you ever been in love, I mean so it means everything?'

Agnes nodded and as she did a pain shot through her for her own lost love.

'Well, you will understand then. I loved John Merrill – worshipped him would be a better word.' Suddenly Amanda turned from a girl to a woman. Her eyes left Agnes and shifted to the window. She paused, drew a deep breath and started again. 'I didn't know. I'm so stupid. He called at High Hurlands a lot, I thought to see me. What a fool! He put on a great act, brought chocolate, made a fuss of Magic. Mum and Dad thought it was great, romantic.' The gaze came back to Agnes. 'It wasn't me he came to see, it was Guy.'

'Guy?' Agnes interposed, hardly in surprise but to make Amanda think she was surprised.

'Yes, Guy. He was in love with Guy. That's why he killed Magic, so that Guy could have a car, but he went wrong there. Guy did moan about what Magic cost and did say that if he wasn't there he could have a car. He did say all that but I know Guy. He'd say anything, but he would never harm an animal.'

She tried to keep the tears from her eyes but a few spilled over her lids. 'When Crackers, an old wire-haired terrier, had to be put down, he was thirteen. Guy was devastated. Wouldn't show it though. Tried to act tough, always did that.'

Agnes listened to all this, her sympathy growing. 'Did Guy know John was homosexual?' she asked.

'I don't know, Agnes. I feel perhaps he didn't want to tell me. He knew, I suppose, how I felt about John. He saw how pleased Mum and Dad were, and what a fool I was making of myself.'

Agnes put out a hand and covered Amanda's hand. 'I don't think you were – how could you know?' She pressed Amanda's hand. 'Try and forget all that for the moment and tell me about the night Magic was killed.'

Amanda covered her eyes briefly and then went on. 'I've told you some. I was in my room listening to music. I didn't hear anything until Magic . . .' She looked away for a moment, then blinked her eyes determinedly and resumed. 'I ran downstairs then, out of the door and round to the stable. Magic was down, sort of lying. He was alive, I'm sure he was alive. There was John Merrill, a knife held near Magic's neck. He plunged it in. I couldn't scream. I wanted to. John saw me. He threw away the knife. It landed almost at my feet. I picked it up and stuck it into John, I think his back or his side. It went in easily, but he got up. "You bitch," he said. "You bitch. I did this for Guy." Then he turned and started to run for the gate, I suppose.' She did weep a little then. 'Poor Magic. He was dead. I thought of that horse Sefton – in Hyde Park, wasn't it? That man had saved him, held the vein together. I tried but I couldn't find where the blood was coming from – anyway, he was dead.'

Agnes squeezed the girl's hand a little harder. 'Then?' she asked.

'While I was still trying to stop Magic's bleeding, Guy – at first I couldn't think who it was, I was so muddled.' She thrust back her hair. 'Guy picked up the knife, it was beside me then, and chased after John. There was a sort of scream and a clang of the iron gate, then a little while went by, only a minute or maybe seconds, I don't know. Then Guy came back, dragging John. "Help me, Amanda," he said. We dragged the body to the ditch near the wall. Guy pulled back the brambles, rolled John down, pulled the tangle of brambles and dead weeds over him and then we went back to Magic. Guy stroked his head. "Bastard. Queer, bloody bastard," he said. "Call the police. Say nothing, only that the man ran away."'

Agnes listened. She was drawn towards Guy, who had acted as she would have done, but the picture that Amanda drew, the dead horse, the blood, the body. No wonder the girl could not tell her story to a doctor, or even her parents.

'What happened then, Amanda?'

The girl let herself relax a little. 'I heard Guy drive away – in John's car, I suppose. There couldn't have been another car there, could there?'

'You called the police then?' Agnes asked.

'Yes, I went into the house, told Mum and Dad about Magic, stabbed by an unknown man who ran away.'

Amanda swallowed. The hand Agnes still held was damp. 'Are you thirsty?' she asked.

Amanda nodded. 'It's talking too much, Agnes, but I feel so relieved to have been able to tell you, someone I could trust. Mum and Dad would have never understood. Well, I mean, perhaps they would have understood, but in some ways, I don't think I would have been able to convince them that John didn't want me. He wanted Guy.'

There was silence in the kitchen, broken only by the clicking of the kettle when it at last boiled. The pouring of water into the teapot, the gentle clatter of cups on to saucers and spoons on china. Agnes brought the tray to the table. In silence again, both waited till the tea drew a little, then Agnes poured a cup each and passed one to Amanda. She sipped the warm liquid, looked up at Agnes.

'Thank you, that's nice, Agnes,' she said.

Agnes had waited before answering Amanda's remark. 'Yes, I can understand your difficulty.'

'You asked me if Guy knew John was after him rather than in love with me. I don't think he did at first, but he did when he stroked poor Magic's head. He did then.'

'The police came?'

Amanda nodded. 'They were good. I made a statement. I lied. I said the man had a knife. I picked it up and gave it to them.' Amanda smiled a little for the first time. 'That was clever, wasn't it?' My hands were covered in blood, so it went all over the knife. "Don't touch it, miss," one of the policemen said, but of course it was too late.' She sipped more tea. 'No one knew, Agnes. John Merrill went off that night, up north he told his parents, and he's never got in touch, but then he does behave like that. He stays at home for ages and then takes off. They think he's done that now.'

'Where do you think his body is now?' Agnes asked.

The girl looked curiously uninterested. 'I don't know. Guy will see to it, it's over now. Magic is dead, John is gone.'

'Tell me about Guy. Did he keep the car?'

'What car, Agnes?' Amanda looked puzzled.

'John Merrill's car.'

The girl shook her head. 'I don't know. It must have gone somewhere, mustn't it?' Again this strange lack of interest.

'Yes, it must. Has Guy got a girlfriend, Amanda?'

Amanda avoided Agnes' questioning eyes. 'I don't know, Agnes, really I don't.'

Agnes thought of the green Volvo coming out of The Hollies, driven by the fair-haired wife of the owner of Marshall's stables. But even as she thought of it, Amanda's next remark suddenly blew some of her theories sky high.

'Well, he did like Lyn Marshall. Her husband runs Marshall's stables. But once when I teased him about her, I met them together once, he said it was because she had a nice new car and he liked driving it. Sometimes she let him. It was a Volvo, green. Just like John Merrill's. Now poor Magic is dead and won't be an expense any longer, maybe he will get Dad to buy him a car of his own. I know he'd love to have a sports car, red he always said.'

Amanda got up from the table, went across the kitchen and began to fold back the pictures of the large calendar of cat pictures, her back to Agnes. 'Agnes, can I ask you something?'

'Yes, of course.'

There was a long silence before the question came. 'I really loved John and if I had tried, you know, really tried, do you think I could have changed him, made him love me instead of Guy?'

Agnes felt her reply could be pretty positive. 'No, I don't think so, Amanda, I truly don't think so.'

The girl sighed, dropped the last cat picture down and into the correct month. 'No, I don't expect I could.' She came back to the table, but did not sit down. 'I guess it doesn't really matter that he's dead then, does it, or who killed him or where his body is – not to me, anyway.'

Agnes saw in her mind a sudden clear picture of the man stabbing the dying horse. 'No, I don't think it matters at all,' she said.

Amanda's face cleared. 'I'm going now, and thank you for listening. I knew I could trust you, Agnes.' She bent and kissed Agnes on the cheek. 'I won't tell any of what I have told you to anyone else. I'll just let them see I feel better.' She smiled a real smile this time. She looked younger, prettier.

Agnes did not get up but watched the girl as she walked away. She felt that the responsibility for the whole affair had been placed solidly on her shoulders. Now her task was to find the man who was still at large, maybe the man who had partnered John in some of his vile doings: hurting, killing, maiming animals that had done nothing to them. She would go to Jasmine Cottage again tomorrow. She felt there was a link there somewhere, and also she had to find John Merrill's green Volvo. Where had Guy hidden it? Had he used it to take away the body in the garden to protect himself or his sister? Agnes felt she had to know.

Agnes was tied to Rose Cottage for nearly four days. The new kitchen sink was put in and the kitchen painted and colour washed. She was pleased with it. It was not quite right yet, but almost. The angelic plumber had turned up, and so had the heating engineers. The other rooms were beautifully decorated by the previous owners, to Agnes' taste. All this work done lulled her into a false sense of security. She blamed herself when two more horses were attacked and slashed about the neck and withers, in the same field, on the other side of Lewes. These matters, she felt, were more, far more, important than her own affairs.

The fifth morning, a day off from the workmen, Agnes felt she must pay the promised visit to Jasmine Cottage. She was not sure, as she argued with herself again and again; there was no valid reason for connecting Jasmine Cottage or the parents or son who lived there with any of these evil doings. But the fair-haired girl, Guy Holstein, the farm labourer and his wife, Marshall's stables and the ghastly sexual nature of the injury to the donkey, why did it all knit up in her mind?

9

Agnes' car was due for a small service and a valet the next day when she arrived at the garage in Lewes that dealt only with Porsche cars. She looked round the forecourt as she got out of the car. A rather battered blue Mini Cooper was parked near the road.

'Could I hire that for the day?' she asked.

The mechanic turned from getting into her car to drive it into the service area. 'We can let you have something better than that, miss,' he said.

Agnes shook her head. 'No, I want something like that, just for the day.'

'It belongs to one of our clerks, but I'll ask her.'

He disappeared through the big glass doors of the car showroom. He was soon to come out again.

'Yes, Julie says OK, as long as it's back by five for her to go home in.'

'Yes, it will be back by then. I'll pay her for hiring it when I get back.'

He handed her some keys. 'Well, miss, I told her we've only got a Porsche as surety, but I think that will cover it.'

Agnes laughed, and got into the little blue car, which seemed unbelievably small and yet comfortable. Long ago she had learned to drive a Mini; it was rather pleasant to be in one again.

Agnes was not quite sure of her reason for deciding not to take the Porsche to Jasmine Cottage, or even why she was going there again. Violet Greenham's rather vague careless remark about John Merrill's knowing, or even having an affair with – how had she put it? – a farmer or a farm labourer's son ... Could that be the son of the labourer at Jasmine Cottage, the one who was suffering with his back, the one who had seen or might have seen, the dark-coloured car that looked like the one owned by John Merrill? Agnes felt almost as muddled as Amanda. If those two men, John Merrill and Bill Lewis, had been the ones injuring horses, one of them was now dead. Had Bill Lewis teamed up with someone else? And where was Merrill's green Volvo and his body? According to Amanda, if at last she had got over the shock of her beloved Magic's death to remember more clearly the events of that tragic evening, it had been her brother who had dragged the body to the ditch, and John Merrill who had done the slashing.

On the way to Marshall's stables and Jasmine Cottage, Agnes stopped at a newagent's and tobacconist's to buy a pack of pipe tobacco and a small box of chocolates. She had liked the couple at Jasmine Cottage and thought a little gift might act as an excuse for calling again. She was also considering calling at the stables to see if Mrs Marshall, the good-looking young blonde, was there. She would like to have a word with her about Guy – a rather touchy subject, she realised, if the girl was really having an affair with him. She wanted to see a less nervous reaction from the horse Maisie: Agnes hated any animal to be nervous of her, to expect harm or hurt from her. She had rescued so many in her time. The horse's sideward, suspicious glance had lived with her.

She did not regret her choice of car. The little blue Mini seemed to fit in better with the farm and farm cottage than the Porsche had done. As she drove up she could hardly believe her luck. At the end of the little row of cottages, attached rather inadequately to the end wall of Jasmine Cottage, was a very dilapidated barn with what was left of a thatched roof. In it was a black car, not a Volvo, but a Metro. Certainly its shape did not in any way resemble a Volvo as the occupant of Jasmine Cottage had suggested, but it was at least a dark-coloured car and perhaps meant that the owner of the car, John Merrill's friend or lover, might be at the house. She was glad she had bought little gifts. They would make a perfect excuse for calling again and would perhaps prevent the couple from thinking that she had simply come to ask more questions about the injured horses.

Agnes shut the door of the Mini with some difficulty and attempted to lock it, but without success. She pocketed the keys and made her way once again to the door of Jasmine Cottage. For some reason her heart beat a little faster as she heard footsteps inside in answer to her knock. The same trim little woman opened the door.

'Oh, Mrs Turner, I didn't recognise your car when it drove by the window.'

Agnes explained briefly that her own car had needed attention. She had not allowed for the fact that her visit would coincide with tea-time. A white cloth covered the table; on it were bread and butter and a large jar of what Agnes guessed by the handwritten label was homemade strawberry jam, plates and an array of cups and saucers, large cups.

'Please have tea with us. This is my son Bill.' Mrs Lewis indicated the young man sitting opposite at the table.

'Hi.' Bill raised his hand but made no attempt to rise to his feet. Agnes tried to assess him. From what she could see, he looked short and burly. His hair was cut close to his head; his face was smooth and well shaven. As he stirred his teacup she noticed on his forearm the words 'The world is sick'. This she rather agreed with. His shirt was navy, unbuttoned at the neck. His eyes were small and brown and reminded Agnes of hard little pebbles; his fingers were fat, his hands and wrists podgy.

Agnes handed the tobacco to the boy's father and the chocolates to his mother. They both seemed surprised but pleased and Mrs Lewis murmured the obligatory, 'Oh, you shouldn't have.' She poured tea for Agnes into a cup she had just fetched from the dresser. 'Have you got any further about the poor horses?'

Agnes shook her head. 'No, alas, nothing,' she said, accepting the cup of strong looking tea, but at the same time watching for any reaction from the young man seated next to her.

'Oh, it's awful, isn't it. Who would want to do a nasty thing like that? All that blood and everything. Ugh!'

Agnes felt he was over-reacting. His words, the turn of his head, the movement of the free hand, were so typical. Agnes had met many homosexuals in America when with Bill in 'film land'. Some had become friends. She found it easier to be friendly with them than Bill had. Was this John Merrill's lover? Were they responsible for the injuries to the horses? There was no reason why they should be, except the one Agnes had heard. Jealousy on John Merrill's part of Amanda's nearness to Guy, brother and sister. John, Bill and Guy Holstein. One, Guy, having perhaps clandestine meetings with Marshall's wife, the other two . . . ? She suddenly asked the question she had really been determined not to ask.

'Do you know John Merrill, Mr Lewis?'

He looked straight at her, put his teacup down gently into its saucer. 'Bill, please . . .' He opened his eyes wide. 'I certainly do know John Merrill. I certainly do know him. Some friend, he is. Haven't heard a word for four months.'

His father spoke up. 'That's the bright man who advised you about – '

'Shut it, Dad, he's a financial adviser.'

'Not to advise about doing the unemployment down, though!' His father began to sound heated and his mother interposed.

'Now, you two – you've learned your lesson, though, Bill.'

Bill slurped the rest of his tea. 'Off his trolley, John Merrill, right off his trolley. Got the hots for a chap who couldn't stand him, so took it out on . . .' He did not finish, then: 'I liked him, though, in spite of him being – well, I liked him.'

'That will do, Bill! Button your mouth, this lady doesn't want to know stuff like that.'

'Oh, I thought you said she was interested in the horses?' He turned to Agnes. 'Nothing to do with me. John's a nutter. I'm off.'

He slammed out of the front door. Agnes heard a car start up. He was gone. How much had she learned? That this man might be responsible for the horses' injuries or not. But there had been two more since John Merrill's death.

She left the cottage, followed by apologetic remarks about their son's behaviour. John Merrill and Bill Lewis – partners in crime, or not?

On the way back, she called into the shop. Mrs Beaven chatted away, amazed at the little car Agnes was driving.

'Not like your lovely one, Mrs Turner.'

'No, it's not, but I didn't want to take mine up to the stables. I wanted to have a quiet look round. I did meet the Lewises' son Bill though. Do you know him, Mrs Beaven?'

The little shopkeeper lowered her voice, although there was no one around. 'No, I didn't know him. But they say, you know, people say, that he and John Merrill were sort of . . .' She paused. 'But I put it like this, Mrs Turner, it takes all sorts and John Merrill was nice enough to me. Moody but generally polite and nice.' She hesitated. 'I mean, people don't mind about men being lovers. It's on the television and in plays, isn't it?'

Agnes agreed. She took her small purchase and made for the door. 'It takes all sorts. You are quite right, Mrs Beaven,' she said.

She was almost out of the shop when Mrs Beaven said something really worth hearing. 'Those other two horses I told you about, Mrs Turner, the ones about a week ago, was it? Other side of Lewes, remember?'

Agnes turned quickly back into the shop. 'Yes, I do. Have you heard anything more about them?'

Mrs Beaven nodded. 'Yes, they cut themselves on some barbed wire. Apparently a dog got into the field and started snapping and barking at them and they took fright and tried to get over this wire.'

'How do you know this, Mrs Beaven?'

'It was in the local paper, about the dog not being properly controlled. The horses' owner reported the dog and the owner to the police.'

'So it wasn't the men who . . . ?'

'No.' Mrs Beaven shook her head. 'So you see, maybe it will stop now. Anyway, I hope so. I thought you would be glad to hear that. I know I was.'

Agnes left the shop feeling a weight had lifted from her mind. Maybe John Merrill's murderer had done some good after all.

She felt she had to talk to Guy Holstein, and yet she couldn't think how to approach him. Ask him for a beer? Hardly the thing. She felt he regarded her as a shy, old maidish bore. Then she had an idea. The Porsche. Why not let him, give him permission to drive the Porsche? But only if she were his passenger. She wondered, with a tinge of apprehension, if he were a good driver. He had been driving Mrs Marshall's car and maybe the dead John Merrill's. Well, it was a risk she felt she must take. The car was well insured but she would hate it to get scratched or dented.

She drove the Mini back to the garage. She was later than she intended but she was glad she had not gone to Jasmine Cottage in her own car. Anyone at the stables would have recognised it immediately, and perhaps have been curious about her making a second visit to Jasmine Cottage.

The girl at the garage first looked slightly put out by Agnes' late arrival, but when Agnes handed her the money she considered reasonable, the girl became all smiles. 'Oh thanks, Mrs Turner,' she said accepting the keys.

'Nice little motor car.'

'Bit different to yours though,' the girl said, motioning towards the clean and gleaming Porsche.

Agnes smiled. 'Oh, I had a Mini once and was very fond and proud of it,' she said, in her turn accepting the keys from the mechanic who had joined them.

'Nothing like a Porsche though,' he said.

'Nothing,' Agnes agreed. 'I've always had one since I could afford one.'

'Seen this year's model, Mrs Turner?'

Agnes shook her head. 'Not yet.' She looked at her own car. It seemed as good as new but she knew it wasn't. The state of her finances at the moment was healthy enough to update it.

'You have it if you want it, darling.' As she stood looking towards her car, she could almost feel and see her dear husband.

'Shall I give you the new brochure, Mrs Turner?' The mechanic's voice broke into her memories.

She looked at him for a second or two, feeling miles away in a different world, in London, Paris, New York. 'Yes, do. I'll have a peep at it,' she said, not wishing to encourage the young man too much. She might decide to keep this one.

She got into the car. The young man came back and handed her the brochure. 'You've made it so shiny and bright again. I don't feel I need to change it now it looks like new,' she said.

'It isn't new though, Mrs Turner,' he said.

Agnes agreed and put the shiny brochure on the seat beside her, raised a hand in farewell and drove smoothly out of the forecourt and on to the road. On the way home her mind was occupied by the way she would approach Guy – perhaps through his sister. She could say something casually. 'If your brother still wants to drive my Porsche, tell him to drop in and have a drink and we will chat about it.' Something like that. She didn't think it would be difficult.

As she put the car away and greeted Mac, the disturbing thought of another Bill came to her. Bill Lewis. If he had been such a mate of John Merrill's and got a kick, a sadistic kick out of hurting horses or donkeys, and he began to feel impatient and disgusted by the way John had apparently dropped him, would he find someone else and start again? Was he or John the leader in those vile escapades? It was hard to tell, but maybe he had looked up to John. The way he had mentioned that he was a 'financial adviser' had rather pointed in that direction. Anyway, her knowledge that there had been no further reports of deliberate injury to horses, only the incident with the barbed wire, was comforting.

How much could she get out of Guy? How much dare she ask? Well, first to get in touch with Amanda, but before that she went into an off-licence and bought a six-pack of lager. Agnes knew little or nothing about beer but she was sure she could dispense some to her angelic plumber or some of the workmen who did or didn't turn up for their respective jobs.

Agnes felt the pace was hotting up a little, the mystery was getting more exciting. She wondered how Pansy would take it, if her son's death was ever found out. Rather more grief from her maybe than her husband had shown. There seemed to be so little concern over his long absence or lack of communication, but then, as Violet Greenham had said, this was John's normal behaviour – though to Agnes what was now four months seemed a little excessive. She wondered, did his work ever take him abroad? Was he perhaps living with another man, having given up all thoughts of Guy Holstein ever returning his feelings? When exactly would the Merrills really start to worry, when would they start to think something might have happened to their son? Never, perhaps. Though Pansy had said nothing derogatory about her son and his father, though dismissing him with a contemptuous remark, had bought him – or at least helped him buy – a decent car that would impress his clients and convince them that he was doing well in the world of money. Agnes decided to do a little research in that direction. She would like to know where Guy had put the body, if it had been Guy who had moved it. It was like a jigsaw puzzle, needing painstaking care to put it together, make it fit. In the end, like all jigsaw puzzles, the picture would emerge clear and self-explanatory.

Next day Agnes drove by the Merrills' garden. Pansy Merrill, who fancied herself as a gardener, was planting a row of Busy Lizzies. The row would not have pleased Agnes' gardener. 'Just like a park,' he would have said, and Agnes rather agreed with him, preferring to see them in thick colourful clumps.

'How are you, Pansy?' she called.

Pansy looked up with her quick, rather timid smile. 'Oh, hello. Aren't these pretty?'

'Yes, and they make such a lovely show,' Agnes replied. She felt she could not herself bring up the subject of John, knowing as much as she did. But Pansy needed no pushing to talk about John's 'naughtiness', as she put it.

'Isn't he a naughty boy, Agnes? It's four months now and not a word, not a telephone call, a letter or even a card.'

Agnes made a tut-tutting noise. 'Has he ever been this naughty in his lack of communication with you before, Pansy?'

Pansy took off one of her gardening gloves and pushed her hair back, thinking. 'Yes, once before he did when he went to the States. Edwin was furious then because he had paid for him to go there.'

'Oh, dear,' was all Agnes could bring herself to say.

'Yes, and this time Edwin did help him buy the car. Children are a trial, Agnes.' Pansy sighed. 'A great trial.'

'Well, perhaps he's not a great letter writer,' was all Agnes was able to say in answer to Pansy's sigh. She felt sorry for her. When, if ever, the body was found she would have to suffer the loss of her son as would her husband. But for John Merrill, she felt not a shred of pity. He had cut and tortured and he had been cut and tortured in return. He had killed a loving innocent animal and in turn had been killed. What he had got, in Agnes' opinion, he had richly deserved. Where the body might be, though – that certainly intrigued her.

Edwin Merrill came out of the door to join his wife. Agnes did not particularly want to hear the story of John's 'naughtiness' again, although she was sure Edwin Merrill would not use that word, so she pretended not to see him and started the car and drove on and into her own driveway.

That night Agnes wandered round her garden. The gardener had mown the lawn. The smell of the newly cut grass, slightly wet now with dew, was very pleasant. It was dark but the polyanthus gleamed, their colours hardly discernible. Summer. Agnes looked forward to it for the first time. Summer in the country, after just sampling it in the London parks, would be a change. The house in the Isle of Wight had at last found a buyer. The contracts had not yet been signed but the estate agents' letter had sounded confident that the buyer would take the house. Agnes was glad to be rid of it. There, in that house, Bill, her husband, had been her next-door neighbour. They had fallen in love there then bought the flat in London. Now all parts of that life were melting away, leaving Rose Cottage. She was glad that the only problems here were domestic ones. Pleased that there was a happening to mystify her, make her think, involve her with other people. Who next? She lent and touched the bluebells in what she liked to call her wild garden. Something scuttled away from amongst the mass of white-flowered wild garlic – a cat, a fox, a badger, a mink? She was glad it was there. She would put out some dog food in case it was a hungry fox. There was no sound from her chicken run as she passed it. The hen-house was strongly built. When she shut them up at night they were safe. She had room to make it bigger, take four more from the concentration camp into her comfortable dwelling place.

Tomorrow she would ring Amanda and ask her to tell her brother that he could drive the Porsche. Perhaps she would ask Amanda to come to coffee, then talk of the drive.

Amanda was pleased to hear from Agnes, as usual. Yes, she would love to come this morning for coffee. Agnes wondered why she didn't seem to have any friends. She was young, passably pretty, yet there were no boyfriends or girlfriends to Agnes' knowledge. She never spoke of any friend. Perhaps it was her rather elderly parents. Perhaps they did not encourage her to bring anyone home. Even poor Magic had been old, older than Amanda, as she had remarked. Agnes decided that when Rose Cottage was straight she would ask Bill's daughter and son-in-law down and introduce them to the girl. They were a young lively couple. Meanwhile Amanda would have to put up with being asked to coffee by herself, well on the way to fifty-seven!

When Agnes suggested that Guy might like to drive the Porsche, the girl's reaction was a bit unexpected. Jealousy, Agnes felt, might have motivated the rather reluctant response. 'Of course Guy would love to drive your car, but why should you let him?' Anyway, she agreed to ask Guy and left, for once, with no reference to Magic or her state of mind. It appeared the shrink had been dismissed or had given up the unequal struggle. Amanda did not mention him, indeed seemed to have little or nothing to say, and went home after a shorter time than usual, leaving Agnes to wait for a telephone call or some message about the proposed drive.

The reply came almost at once.

'Yes, I would love to drive the Porsche. I'd like to see how a car like that feels.' Guy had telephoned. 'I can understand your wanting to come with me. If it were my car I wouldn't let it out of my sight!'

They agreed on a drive the next Wednesday, two days away. Agnes was determined to ask the questions she wanted to and if possible find out the other half of the evil pair who had done things she could never forgive. Maybe Guy knew, maybe he didn't, but if he did know she would perhaps be able to cope in her own way with John Merrill's accomplice.

10

Guy Holstein arrived punctually at Rose Cottage at ten on the Wednesday morning. Agnes had taken her car out of the garage and it stood on the driveway in its gleaming, newly cleaned splendour. Guy put an almost reverent hand on the bonnet of the car.

'It's a beautiful job, Mrs Turner. This is the Carrera, isn't it?'

Agnes nodded.

'I would like a Super Sport!' he laughed. 'Well, I can dream, can't I!'

Guy got into the passenger seat beside Agnes. Mrs Tracy was busy in the cottage so Mac was to be left at home, with her.

Guy had transformed himself. Agnes was not sure whether it was for her benefit or the benefit of the Porsche. The headband had disappeared and his hair was brushed back smoothly and secured into a neat pony tail. A white shirt collar protruded over the neck of a rather hideous multicoloured woolly jumper. His faded jeans were clean and he wore a clean pair of trainers, indeed they looked almost new in their whiteness. Perhaps they too were in honour of the car. His hands, which caressed the leather upholstery, were also clean and his nails almost fastidiously shaped and manicured.

'What a motor, what a motor!' he said.

'We will get on to some straight decent road, then you can drive.'

Agnes started smoothly as she always did, out of the drive and on to the lane. A short drive, and they were on to the Lewes road, a twisty one that would not give her passenger any chance to show his driving skills or sample the delights of driving a Porsche.

'Driving licence clean and current?' she asked as they drove along. 'And having no car, do you drive much?'

'Yes, I've driven more lately.'

'Oh, yes?' There was a question in the remark.

He glanced at her sideways. 'Girlfriend,' he said but did not enlarge on the subject.

'Good.' Agnes left it at that. She wondered if the mentioned 'girlfriend' was Lyn Marshall, or was there someone else? Guy, in spite of – or maybe because of – his eccentricities, might be quite attractive and have several girlfriends.

The whole morning was an undoubted success. Agnes was not sorry to cover the miles they did. The Porsche, since she had been coping with the alterations and adjustments at her new house, had done little enough mileage, only short runs to the village shop or Lewes, and the much longer run it was having today would, she felt, do it good. Guy drove well and obviously enjoyed the car, especially when they were on a motorway and able to reach the allowed seventy miles an hour – sometimes, indeed, a little more. About half-past eleven Agnes suggested they stop for a cup of coffee. They found a wayside restaurant that had already risked putting out chairs and tables so they were able to sit quite comfortably in the spring sunshine.

When the coffee arrived Guy looked around him with satisfaction. 'This is the kind of life I'm looking for, Agnes,' he said. 'Go where you like, do what you like, lovely car, money.'

'What would you like to do for a living to get that kind of life, Guy?' Agnes asked, her question backed by real curiosity.

Guy looked at her, his eyes twinkling with amusement and mischief. 'Marry a very rich, really stinking rich woman,' he said. Then: 'No, Agnes, I promise you I haven't got designs on you, though you are attractive and possibly rich.'

Agnes laughed. 'I'm very offended, Guy,' she said. 'Where do I fall short?'

He traced a pattern with the tip of his finger on the table. 'Probably not quite rich enough, even with a Porsche, and probably because you wouldn't have me.'

'Too true.' Agnes decided to get in a quick question while he was in this disarming mood. 'Tell me about the night Magic was killed, Guy.'

He was leaning back in the chair, balancing on two legs. He leaned forward and gazed at Agnes. 'Why do you want to hear my version, Agnes? Haven't you heard enough from Amanda?'

Agnes stirred her second cup of coffee. 'Amanda seemed very muddled about it all.'

Guy, to her surprise, avoided her gaze, looked out at the passing traffic. 'Perhaps it's just as well she is muddled about it.' Guy's voice was both serious and detached.

Agnes tried once more. 'I think it did her good to talk about it.'

Her companion moved restlessly in his chair. 'That's not what her psychiatrist said when he gave up the case. Let's go, shall we, I'm tired of this place.'

They started out for home. Agnes was aware that the mood was quite different, cooler, distant.

'Is this why you suggested I could drive the Porsche?'

'No. No, of course not.' Agnes was too adamant. She knew it, so she retracted a little. 'Well, partly. I wanted to ask you a few things, Guy.'

He increased the car speed before he replied. 'Well, why didn't you say so?' He stopped the car. 'Here, you can drive.' He sounded like a sulky child.

They changed places. Agnes took a side road.

'Where are we going?' Guy asked.

'Marshall's stables.'

Guy sat up. 'What for?'

Agnes smiled, just a small smile. 'Oh, just a visit,' she said and then turned and looked at him, just a glance. 'You might even see Lyn if you're lucky.'

Guy slumped back in his seat. 'OK. What do you want to know about that bloody night?' he said.

'Just about everything, please, Guy.'

Agnes drew into the side of the road, switched off the engine and turned to her companion.

'Just tell me this first, will you, Agnes?'

Agnes nodded.

'Are you an undercover policewoman, a private detective or just a very nosy person?'

'The last, but added to that, my heart goes out to these animals and I intend to do something to punish whoever is hurting them.'

'OK . . .' Guy settled back. The sun filtered through the trees around them and warmed the car though the windows were open. He drew a deep breath. 'Where to start?' he said. 'Where to start? May I smoke, do you mind?'

Agnes shook her head. 'No, I don't particularly mind and if it makes it easier, go ahead.'

He took a packet out of his pocket and then fumbled around for a lighter, put both on the shelf in front of him as if what he had to tell might require more time than it would take to smoke one cigarette.

'John Merrill was a funny bloke,' he began, and Agnes noted the word 'was'. 'At first I met him in the local. Seemed all right, put on airs a bit, know what I mean? As if he were talking down to us yokels.' He paused. 'Then he seemed to prefer my company to the others. I understood that, or thought I did, found out he lived close to us, said come in for a beer. He did and that started it all.'

'Started what?' Agnes asked.

'The rot, if you can call it that, and I do, that led to poor old Magic pegging out, Amanda going off her trolley and John losing his life.' Agnes waited for him to enlarge on this list of disasters. 'John started coming to the house a lot. He hadn't got his car then. Mum and Dad thought he was keen on Amanda and were chuffed to death. My sister's not much of a . . .' He paused. 'Well, you know what I mean, there's not exactly a great long line of men or boys after her.'

Agnes interrupted him. 'Why do you think that is? She's quite a pretty girl.'

'Yeah, but not the kind . . . Reserved. Animals are her thing, anything needing help and she'll give her all. Birds, mice even. We had a fox cub once she reared. Up at five in the morning to bottle feed the thing. It lived too, went off rejoicing. She cried when it went. Most guys would be bored with that kind of thing. I wouldn't but most guys would.'

Guy lit another cigarette from the end of the one he was finishing and threw the butt out of the window. Agnes disapproved of the chain smoking and the litter of the cigarette end, but she said nothing, just waited patiently for the story to go on.

'This all sounds irrelevant, I know, but I've got to talk to someone, tell someone. Mum and Dad would pass out if they knew. Anyway, enough of all that. I'll get to the nub of it and that is, I killed John Merrill. Stabbed him. I might not have finished him off because he got up, to his feet I mean, and staggered away as if he were making for the gate. Then Amanda got up from her knees, grabbed the knife which I had dropped and ran after John. I've never seen my sister look as she did then, murderous. She plunged the knife into his back, he fell and she ran back to Magic who was doormat dead by this time.'

Agnes drew a long breath.

'It was some scene, man, I mean, Agnes. Blood everywhere, the dead horse, the body. "I'll telephone the police," Amanda said, dropping the bloody knife beside Magic. "No, wait," I told her. Then I dragged John across the wet grass – it was raining buckets by this time – and dumped him in the ditch by the wall.'

'Who do you think killed John Merrill, you or . . . ?' Agnes asked.

'Don't know, don't want to know. But I do know, knew all the time, he was after me not Amanda. I suppose he killed Magic because he thought without the expense of the horse Dad might buy me a car. Poor chap, I suppose he couldn't help what he was, but I can't forgive what he did to Magic.'

'What happened then, I mean when you dragged him . . . ?'

'I left it to Amanda to tell Mum and Dad, and get the police. They would hardly search around for a body when Amanda told them the man had driven off, escaped. They didn't and Amanda kept quiet, just told them about the man running off – me, but she didn't say that, of course. She was quite good really, devastated, but she kept mum about what really happened.'

'I saw the body, Guy, when I was wandering round your garden. I foolishly told Amanda, who I guess already knew, but when we went to look at it, it was gone. Who moved it, Guy?'

He looked at her, almost with amusement. 'I did. I couldn't just let him rot into manure in our garden, could I?'

Agnes was shocked by the way he had put the explanation. 'But . . .' She hesitated. 'Did you bury him?'

He nodded and lit another cigarette. The furious inhaling of the cigarette indicated that he was not as laid back as he would have her believe.

'In some field somewhere?' Agnes was persistent.

He shook his head and there was something almost quizzical in his eyes. 'No, he had a better burial than he deserved.'

'What do you mean, better burial?'

He shook his head. 'Just that. May I drive back?'

'Well, we don't have time to go to Marshall's stables now,' Agnes said as she got out of the car. Guy got out the other side and did not slide across into the driver's seat 'Agnes,' he said, 'that was a terrible night. I drove away. I had to make out he had gone up north to work, as he said. I had to leave Amanda to cope with a lot. Mum and Dad, the police, getting rid of Magic. No wonder she turned a bit odd. That psychiatrist was useless. You have been so good to her.'

They walked a little way up the road, side by side.

'Tell me, Guy, this is important to me.'

They both stopped walking and faced each other.

'What?'

'John Merrill couldn't have done what was done to the other animals alone, could he, if it was he?'

'It was, he boasted about it to Amanda while she was screaming at him to stop stabbing Magic, said it gave him a buzz. He deserved to be put down. Him and his mate enjoyed it, he said. But he didn't tell her the mate's name.'

They walked back to the car.

'Do you know who this man is, his partner?'

'I believe so.'

'Tell me.'

He shook his head. 'No, I want to deal with this myself.'

'Where is the car, John Merrill's car?'

Again he clammed up.

'Maybe I can guess where it is.'

'How?'

Agnes waited a moment before she spoke. 'Marshall's stables?'

'How do you know that?' Guy looked genuinely surprised.

Agnes did not reply. They got into the Porsche, Agnes in the passenger seat and Guy drove back. Hardly a word was exchanged between them. When they arrived at Rose Cottage, Guy drove in and garaged the car. As they were about to leave it, he patted the door. 'Lovely thing,' he said.

Agnes smiled. 'One day you may have one,' she said.

He shrugged. 'Some hopes,' he said.

'What are your ambitions, Guy, apart from having a Porsche?'

He didn't answer, but pulled down the garage door.

'Have you a job, Guy?' Agnes was genuinely interested.

'No, I lost the one I did have, small engineering firm. It folded. I'm not an engineer, I was just sort of dogsbody, not much to lose really.'

'Come in, I've actually got a beer in the refrigerator.'

'Oh, right.' He followed Agnes into the kitchen. Mrs Tracy had left. Mac was sitting in his basket looking doleful. Guy spoke to Mac. 'Hi, fella, all alone?' He lent down and caressed the dog between the ears.

'You like dogs?' Agnes asked.

'All animals. I could kill anyone who tortures or trains them in circuses or cages them. I didn't agree with Amanda about Magic. He was old, not all that fit, the vet said. Never ridden, lonely, not that happy.'

Agnes took a can out of the fridge and put it and a glass in front of her guest. 'I didn't realise you felt like that, Guy.' She watched with some anxiety as he sipped the beer. 'Is that all right? I don't know much about beer.'

'This is a lager and very nice.' He drank some more and half emptied the glass. 'Come to that,' he said suddenly, 'when I said I could kill anyone who tortures an animal, I already have.'

'You, or Amanda,' Agnes corrected him.

'Me, or Amanda.'

'I still will not rest until I find John Merrill's accomplice in the other horrible attacks,' Agnes said.

Just as he was leaving Guy turned to Agnes. 'Could I ask one more favour of you?'

'What favour, Guy? If it's taking out the car by yourself, I'm afraid it's no.'

'It's not that. I wonder if we could drive up to Marshall's stables, there's someone up there I'd really like to see me driving a Porsche.'

Agnes laughed. She felt she could guess who Guy wanted to impress. 'Well, as it happens, I would like to see Maisie, one of the horses who was cut. Not as badly as the others but enough to make her nervous and mistrustful when I approached her.'

They arranged a day and time and Guy left. Agnes felt she had got to know him a great deal better. The show he had put on at High Hurlands was probably reserved for his parents. It worried her a little that he seemed so unconcerned about the fact that he had no job, but that attitude was not uncommon – and indeed not always genuine, she felt, but put on to mask a trace of bitterness at not being needed. She liked the young man, and was curious too. Where had he buried or disposed of John Merrill's body? Where was the green Volvo? What had he meant, 'He had a better burial than he deserved'? It had been an interesting and informative drive. How would the Merrills cope with their son's continued absence?

As Agnes fed her chickens, walked her dog, made telephone calls, did chores, cooked herself a meal and fed Mac, she felt that her life was turning out better than she had expected. She had rather dreaded a quiet secluded time, watching television, reading, loneliness, isolation. It was not turning out like that at all. She had a mission, something to accomplish, and she was acquiring knowledge about a mystery.

11

The angelic plumber finished his jobs, the firm of heating engineers put in the extra two radiators Agnes wanted. The gardener was making quite an impression on the garden and Agnes had really splurged on a large bird feeding table to go next to the pond in the wild part. This was her favourite part of the garden and she planned to have a teak seat put in there so that she could hide herself away and sit quietly and watch the wildlife, the animals, birds and insects she hoped to coax into her little wilderness where they would be safe and fed.

The chickens were a great joy to her. She had ten now and knew each one by name and temperament. Agnes collected enough eggs to be able to occasionally present half a dozen to her neighbours. She planned to rescue two more chickens and for the hen-house to be enlarged by her ever-willing carpenter. One of her pleasures of the day was, as she called it, 'doing the farmer's wife' and scattering food for her busy excited brood. They had no fear of her and she could pick them up. She wondered if there was any memory left in their supposedly small brains of the beastly tortured part of their lives before they were rescued.

Around all these domestic affairs she never forgot the horses. According to Mrs Beaven and the local and national papers no more incidents had happened. She took the trouble to go to the place Mrs Beaven directed her to where the horses had, according to rumour, been accidentally cut on barbed wire. She found the place after motoring through Lewes. There were two horses in the field adjacent to a large and prosperous-looking house. There was the barbed wire stretching down one side of the field and she could see with difficulty, and aided by a pair of binoculars, the scratches on the horses. They could certainly have been caused by the wire and seemed to be healing well. Thankfully, no one appeared to see Agnes from the house so she retreated in good order and felt satisfied as to the two well-kept animals' well-being.

She was aware and afraid, however, that another outburst of sick vandalism might well break out. Meanwhile she was anxious to find out a little more, or perhaps much more, about the happenings on the night of Magic's death. This mystery was to be solved in a rather dramatic and horrifying way when she and Guy Holstein got together for their second drive in the Porsche.

The Sussex lanes were particularly pretty. Summer was getting a firmer hold; the primroses and daffodils were gone, only their untidy leaves now showing where the flowers had bloomed. Lilacs were blossoming mauve, white. Agnes had time, with Guy driving the car, to look around and take in more of the countryside. She rather enjoyed having a chauffeur. She was pleased, too, that Guy himself had suggested that he would love to drive the Porsche once more and visit Marshall's stables. Perhaps he wanted to show himself off to Lyn's husband driving a Porsche.

'You know Mr and Mrs Marshall, then, Guy?' Agnes asked as they drove along.

'Yes. They are an OK couple.'

'You like Mrs Marshall particularly, Guy?'

He looked sideways at her. 'Who told you that?' he asked. Agnes noted that he spoke without guilt but with a certain amount of amusement.

'Oh, I can't remember, Guy, but I thought I saw you with her one day, didn't I?'

'I dunno.'

Guy slowed the car down at the entrance to the stables. The lane was rough and sandy and stretched some way ahead, leading into more lush fields, and then the stable yard where Agnes had been upset by the injured horse.

To the right was a large modern house. Several horses were grazing in the fields. A young child, a girl of about eight, was riding round a smaller field on a chestnut pony at the end of a long leading rein. She was obviously enjoying herself and the young face under the black peaked riding hat was alight and smiling. Just before they reached this field, Guy stopped the car. On the right was another rougher field and about twenty yards from the path was a wide mound of recently dug earth, the grass just beginning to grow on the fairly flat surface. The mound was about the size of a long dining-table.

'See that, Agnes?' Guy opened the window to its fullest extent.

'What is it, Guy?'

'It's a grave. Eric Marshall's favourite horse. Nothing would make him let it go, so he hired a digger and dug a huge deep hole for it, buried it.'

Suddenly Agnes knew exactly what Guy was going to say 'And you . . .'

He nodded and grimaced, drawing his mouth down at the corners and screwing up his eyes. He remained silent for a few seconds, then: 'Well I told you I had found a suitable place to bury him. Lyn told me what her husband was doing. I drove up here. You remember the night you saw him in the garden – well, I knew it couldn't stay there for ever. I didn't know how you'd react either.' He started the engine of the car. 'I got a body bag – never mind how – took him out of that ditch.' He clasped his forehead with his long fingers spread. 'God, it was awful, three months or more. I prayed the horse up here wasn't in the grave yet. It wasn't.' He shivered suddenly. 'I rolled him in, wasn't so bad with the body bag, kicked some earth down, not a lot. Just enough to cover it. That was that.'

'His car, did you use John's car?' Agnes asked.

He nodded. 'Thereby lies my problem. There's a man up there.' He gestured back towards Jasmine Cottage. 'Used to go out on these stabbing sprees, he recognised John's car. He doesn't know he's in the pit there.' He gestured towards the mound. 'Doesn't know he's dead even, but he's suspicious that I've got John's car. It's stored up there, behind what he uses for his garage.'

Agnes could hardly take it all in. 'Do you mean he and John were responsible for stabbing the other horses?'

He nodded again.

'But how are you making him keep quiet about the car?'

'I've given it him to keep him quiet, in case he starts asking where John is. I think he knows. He's getting it resprayed, different colour, new number plates. He's done it all before, knows the drill.'

'Why do you say you think he knows?' Agnes asked.

'Well, all these months and he hasn't heard from John, his mate. Then his nearly new car turns up. What would you think? He'll hold it over me when he wants to, the car won't shut him up.'

'What will he want next, money?' Agnes could see blackmail looming. But Guy Holstein shook his head.

'He's a nutter, so was John Merrill, they're both nutters. He's even suggested I come with him on one of his slashing escapades. I couldn't do it, you know that. I'd die first. Bill Lewis would never get me to hurt a horse or any other animal, not even if he accused me of murder.' He looked at her and his eyes crinkled with amusement. 'Come to that he probably will.'

They arrived at the yard. Lyn Marshall was there petting Maisie. Agnes wondered, perhaps unkindly, if she had seen the Porsche coming with Guy driving and had assumed the attractive posture all ready for his arrival. Her hair, natural gold and long, fell in a cascade in the sunshine. She smiled widely, left Maisie and crossed the yard, greeting Agnes first.

'Mrs Turner, how nice to see you again.' She then turned to Guy. 'And you, Guy. Aren't you lucky driving such a car. I'm surprised you let him, Mrs Turner, but he is a pretty good driver.'

Agnes smiled. 'Very good, or certainly I wouldn't allow him to drive my car.'

The girl looked at Guy. 'Wait till you see Bill Lewis's new car. A baby blue Volvo. Awful, but he loves it.'

Guy cast a look at Agnes as if to say, 'I told you.'

'May I speak to Maisie? I've brought her an apple. I was so worried about her frightened attitude when I was here last.'

'Yes, of course you may.'

Agnes walked across the yard in front of Lyn and Guy. She

could hear whispers, but not decipher the words. Perhaps it was a date they were making, perhaps it was not.

Maisie was much more confident and relaxed. Her bandage was off. Agnes could see the cut marks on the horse's head and neck, thin red scars which would probably disappear in time altogether. Agnes stroked the animal gently and fed her the apple. As with the chickens, she thought as she did so, Do they remember the hurt and fear they have been through once it is over?

A deep man's voice broke in. 'That smart car here again?' He patted the Porsche. Agnes thought what an attractive man he was, but youth attracts youth, she thought. Guy was talking to Lyn who was leading Maisie out into the sunlight. Agnes was delighted to see the animal looking so well.

'May we come back? I'd love to see the other horses.'

Eric Marshall nodded and waved a hand. 'Do. Perhaps we'll get you riding, Mrs Turner.'

Agnes merely smiled and shook her head. She loved horses as she did all animals, but she had never ridden.

'Shall we go and see the pale blue Volvo?' Guy asked.

'Oh do. I haven't seen it yet. Then you can come back and tell me about it.' Lyn sounded enthusiastic. Agnes agreed. Guy turned the car and for the moment they left the stables and motored towards Jasmine Cottage. They drew up outside Jasmine Cottage. Agnes felt a little embarrassed as when she had brought the gift she had intended it to be her last visit. Now here she was again. Luckily, at least for Agnes, Bill Lewis came out of his rickety-looking barn cum garage.

'Ha, Guy, glad to see you. Come and see this little beauty – not a Porsche, not a Rolls, or even a Merc, but the best and newest car I'm ever likely to get, Guysy, old boy.'

He led them both into his garage and there stood the Volvo, sprayed pale blue. 'What about that? She'd done seven thousand. I put the clock on to thirty-eight thousand, changed the number plate to eight years back, took the Volvo name off. Rather sorry to do that. Filed off the security number. What do you think of her, eh?' He was obviously immensely proud of himself. 'I sold the Metro – got a couple of hundred for it.'

He wandered out of the garage; there was no door to shut. 'What are you doing here, anyway?' He looked from Agnes to Guy Holstein.

'Mrs Turner wanted to see Maisie again – you know, Bill, the horse that was cut.'

Bill Lewis looked amused. 'Oh, horse lover, eh? Don't see why they fuss so much. They eat them all the time in France, very tasty. They go to the slaughterhouse like everything else we eat.' He looked as if he enjoyed Agnes' discomfort.

Guy broke in. 'Cut it out, Bill, everyone doesn't like killing things.'

Bill gave Guy a nasty look, his small eyes narrowed, his manner threatening. 'Watch yourself, Buster, you might get yourself in a load of trouble.'

Guy seemed to react. He looked at Agnes as if he would like to leave, go back to the stables.

'I've only got the car after all.' Bill had a nasty habit of wiping the pad of his thumb across his nostrils. Agnes found him repulsive, particularly after his remark about the horses.

'Let's go, Guy,' she said.

They got into the car, Agnes in the driver's seat. Guy did not attempt to indicate he wanted to drive; the talk with Bill seemed to have upset him. The windows were open, Bill leaned on the window, the passenger side.

'Nice car, but not yours, is it, me boy?'

They drove away, back to the stables. Eric Marshall had disappeared. Guy and Lyn, with Agnes feeling rather a gooseberry, introduced the other seven horses. 'Come and have tea.' They walked up to the house. After a rather stiff tea, they left the stables and Guy drove home. He seemed to have recovered a little from the encounter with Bill Lewis.

Agnes could see why he was fearful of the man – he knew too much. Guy had been foolish to hide the car there. But where else could he have done so? It's not easy to hide an almost new car. Bill Lewis had been suspicious. There was a car; where was the driver? Guy had given that awful man complete power over him. What could she, Agnes Turner, do to help him? He had tried to save Magic, protected his sister. Could that dreadful man blackmail Guy into helping him slash more animals? She didn't think Guy would ever be made to knife any animal, but Bill Lewis might make him accompany him on his dreadful sessions. He also had Amanda to protect. Bill Lewis could hurt her too. The papers had said she was there, had chased the man, was covered with blood. What a situation to be in. How involved was he with Lyn Marshall?

All these thoughts filled her mind as they drove home, so it was another silent drive. Then Guy spoke at last.

'I've got myself in a bit of a mess, haven't I, Agnes?'

Agnes glanced sideways at him as he drove. 'I think I'd agree, Guy,' she said without too much emphasis. Then she looked at him again. 'How involved are you with Lyn Marshall?'

He took his eyes off the road for a second to look at her. 'A bit,' he said defensively.

'Well, I shouldn't get any more involved, if you will take my advice.' She said it without malice or being too dogmatic. 'If you do, and Bill Lewis finds out, he won't hesitate to hold that over you as well.'

Guy sighed. 'You're right. It's not a madly in love job, just a bit keen, you know. Anyway, her husband is much older than she is.'

'Well, then...' Agnes left it at that, but she felt her message had probably got through.

When they arrived back at Rose Cottage, Guy asked could he come in for a minute.

'Yes, do, I'll make a cup of tea.'

In the kitchen he did not at first sit down, but stood awkwardly, swinging the car keys in his hand before he put them down on the kitchen table.

'You are right about Lyn, Agnes. I am not that keen. It's stupid with Bill, with his eyes everywhere, only too glad to trip me up on something.'

Agnes merely nodded her agreement. He started again. 'I expect you wonder why I tell you all this, all these dangerous things...'

Agnes poured boiling water into the teapot. 'Are you asking if you can trust me Guy?' she asked calmly.

He shook his head. 'No. I know I can trust you, just as Amanda did, but it's no joke you – I mean us – getting you so involved in all our troubles and worries.'

Agnes set cups and saucers on the table. 'Sit down, Guy,' she said. He suddenly looked young and bewildered, rather as he had when Bill Lewis was talking to him. 'I don't mind you getting me involved, either you or Amanda, but there is one condition I insist on. If that man suggests you help him hurt any horse or any animal, you will tell me.'

Guy looked at her almost helplessly. 'But that would mean that you would tell the police and everything would come out, Agnes, wouldn't it?'

She shook her head. 'No, Guy, I promise you. Whatever you tell me, or let me know is going to happen, I will not, positively not, go to the police. I will sort the matter out in my own way.' He ignored the tea in front of him until Agnes motioned towards it. She smiled her tight rare smile. 'Drink your tea and trust me,' she said. 'Trust me.'

'Suppose someone saw me driving his Volvo and recognised it, Agnes?'

'Probably no one did, and if by some remote chance you were seen, either when you drove it away leaving the body in the garden or when you took the body to Marshall's stables – '

He broke in. 'Yes, that was twice, then I took it to Bill's to hide it. I couldn't think of anywhere else to go.'

Agnes coolly poured out more tea for herself. Guy had not touched his. 'Then you can always say Lyn had lent you hers a couple of times. It's exactly like the one you drove, isn't it, a green Volvo?'

'How did you know that, Agnes, that she had a green Volvo?' Then he relaxed. 'Oh, I expect you saw it at the stables, I didn't see it though.'

Agnes shook her head. 'No, I saw you and Lyn driving out of The Hollies one day.'

He looked at her wide-eyed. 'That's where her parents live, they were away.'

Agnes laughed drily. 'Well, you'd better stop all those little games, Guy. If I saw you, anyone else could, right?'

'I seem to have been letting myself in for trouble all round, Agnes, but I am not sorry John is dead.'

'Neither am I, Guy. Now we have to make sure Bill hurts no more animals in his quest for thrills.'

Guy nodded rather miserably. 'Yes, I know he gets his kicks that way, some people do, don't they?'

Agnes finished her tea and got up. 'Yes, they do, Guy, and they have to be stopped.'

He looked puzzled, anxious. 'But how, Agnes, how?' he asked, also getting up. His chair pushed back by his rising made a harsh noise on the kitchen floor. The noise seemed to startle him. Agnes realised he was in a highly nervous state.

'Leave that to me, Guy, and, as I said before, trust me.'

A plan was already forming in Agnes' mind.

12

Agnes realised she had quite a lot of planning to do. Normally her problems were solved suddenly, spontaneously, no thinking out things beforehand. This time was going to be quite different. First the Porsche: the colour and make of the car would make it recognisable anywhere. This was definitely not a help if she wanted to follow John Merrill's partner in his horrible crime. She wondered, too, if Bill Lewis would ever commit a similar crime. If he did, would he do it alone, or find another partner? John had been missing for over four months now. Would Bill Lewis have already found someone with similar disgusting ideas, or would he go it alone? Agnes shuddered as she thought how probably one man would have to tie the horse up, if it was trusting and would come to them. A job for two people, she would have thought, though Bill Lewis looked a tough, strong, brutal man and people like him might like to torture alone. She shied away from the picture of the two men, or just the one man, enticing the horse or donkey, perhaps with sugar or fruit, grabbing its halter if it had one on, turning it. No, she had to stop herself thinking of that scene – but what she could do to the man or men responsible, that she did not have to stop herself visualising. Agnes had given out punishment before, she could do it again. She suddenly remembered the man who had purposely run over a cat, and she had smashed the man's fingers by slamming the door of the car on his hand. Agnes smiled to herself as that thought went through her mind, it gave her pleasure to think of it.

As she was getting herself supper after giving Mac a walk, she had an idea, born of the day with the garage girl's car. Why not buy a Mini and sell it after she had finished with it? An old Mini, preferably dark in colour – she was bound to be able to pick one up somewhere. Her thoughts, plans wandered on. She couldn't bring it to Rose Cottage though, people would wonder with her lovely Porsche what she wanted with a Mini. Buy it at a garage, leave it there, pay them to garage it, drive out in the Porsche. No, it would look suspicious, it wouldn't do. She would have to park it somewhere, in the street, preferably in a town or village. It all began to make no sense at all. She was used to things happening to help her when she wanted to . . . wanted to what? Well, she didn't know.

Agnes ate her supper, took Mac up the road and back and went to bed without an idea as to what she would do next; tomorrow, maybe, she would get an idea.

Tomorrow certainly brought the idea to her, but it came as Agnes' ideas usually did, from an odd coincidence, almost an accidental happening, when she went to get the Porsche filled with petrol at the garage she used, not far from Lewes. As she approached the garage, she saw that Bill Lewis was there, filling his tank.

She drew to a halt, and as she watched Bill Lewis standing at the pump she realised he had lied. He had said he had sold his car for, what was it? Two hundred pounds. Why say that when here he was, still in possession of the thing and filling the tank with petrol? It might be a clever and, to Agnes, horrifying move. He certainly could not commit any kind of crime in that pale blue Volvo. Anyone would know it for miles around once he had been out in it. But if he told people he had sold the old black car, then, if anyone saw it near a house or field or stable where a horse was kept, they would not associate it with him. As far as Agnes could imagine, it was the only reason for keeping the old car, to commit more horrible injuries. Had he found a new accomplice now he seemed to have accepted the fact that John had, at least as far as he was concerned, for the moment, disappeared from the scene?

As the petrol flowed into Bill Lewis's car from the hand-held help-yourself nozzle Agnes realised she and the Porsche must not be seen. She drove the car forward and parked it at the side of the huge showroom with its plate glass windows. The new cars inside, parked in a shiny diagonal row, concealed her, but gave her a good view of Bill Lewis. At last he put the filling apparatus back in place, screwed on his petrol cap and crossed the forecourt, pushed open the door and went up to the counter to pay for the fuel. Agnes watched him. He swaggered a little as he went back to his old car. It was the first time she had felt the old hatred surging up in her. She could see those podgy hands, with a knife in them, slashing at Maisie, killing the donkey. Well, John Merrill had managed it alone, but that was probably because he had been many times to High Hurlands, maybe had got to know Magic in his efforts to get to know Amanda and so, through her, Guy, and the horse had grown to trust him a little. Agnes' heart quaked and hardened at the thought.

Bill Lewis drove away. Agnes started her own engine. As she followed the other car at a safe distance she felt the resolve growing in her. John Merrill was dead and could do no more harm. Now it remained to deal with the man whose car she was following. Would he hide it, keep it somewhere where no one would associate it with him? The blue Volvo would be his trademark, as it were, if he told everyone he had sold this old car.

She was not wrong. Quite a way before they got to the lane that led to Jasmine Cottage, he turned into an overgrown track that led into a small copse. Within minutes he emerged. Agnes was parked round a convenient corner of trees and bushes. Sitting in the car she could see nothing, but when she got out, being very careful not to slam her door or tread on a snapping twig, she saw him leave the little track. He thrust something in his pocket, probably his keys. The car was completely hidden as far as Agnes could see. She watched him walk down the road, turn up the lane to the cottage with the same fat-bottomed swagger. This proved to Agnes that she was right. He would strike again, otherwise why should he hide the old car from everyone, including his mother and father? She wondered, should she consult with Guy, would she need help to watch, wait and perhaps, if possible, follow? She waited till he was well up the lane then drove back to Rose Cottage, her mind full of fears and uncertainties.

In the morning, after an almost sleepless night, Agnes had sorted out many of her doubts. Guy had told her that Bill Lewis was the other half of the team. John Merrill she knew was guilty. He had been caught, red-handed – blood-red-handed – doing the awful thing to Magic. Alone. If Agnes could catch Bill Lewis red-handed she would have her proof and, being Agnes, deal with things in her own way. The police called in to Magic were looking for John Merrill, but they didn't know this, and anyway he was dead and buried. The other cases were equally difficult for them.

In some cases the horses had not been found until the morning, when all traces of the criminals had long gone. Maybe a tyre mark, a shoe print, a fingerprint, whatever, had been found at the awful scene, but it had been of little help to them. No arrests had been made. Maybe, if she tried, Agnes would catch the evildoer. What she would do then? She would leave it to fate. What occupied her mind, too, was whether she should ask Guy Holstein for help. The other thing she knew she must do was purchase a Mini.

Agnes was glad to have something definite to do. The next day she and Mac set off to find the car she wanted. It wasn't as difficult as she had anticipated. Passing a small garage she spied one Mini, but judged it rather ancient and clapped out; the one thing the little car had to be was reliable.

After that she really began to enjoy her drive. At Ditchling she gave Mac a good walk, which he greatly appreciated, before continuing along the coast to Brighton, which seemed to be the home of the used car, rows and rows, all colours, reflecting the sunlight. Red, yellow, white. Outside garages and just packed in rows and rows in streets. Large signs stuck on their windshields. 'Bargain 60,000 miles, only £500, useful for shopping.' Too many miles, just too many. She could not imagine skulking round that jumble of cars, she was no expert. When she did go in to choose, she intended to park the Porsche somewhere out of sight. No. Brighton was too much. She parked the car in the shade for Mac's sake, had a cup of coffee and studied her map. She decided to motor on to Shoreham-by-Sea: it had a nice sound. This was to be her lucky destination.

She liked the place when she arrived and decided to have lunch there. It was only a small town, if it could be called that, but during her visit Agnes noticed there was a garage. There, parked in the front of two others, was a dark blue Mini. Agnes immediately parked her car out of sight – again in the shade. Mac came first in all her arrangements. She left the back window open about two inches and walked back to the garage. She stood by the car, peering inside, noted the name Neon written on the side. The speedometer, which she could just see, read 4002 miles. That, she argued to herself, could not be right, the registration indicating that the car was nearly three years old. She walked round the little car. A young man approached her. The reason for the low mileage seemed reasonable enough: 'It belonged to an elderly lady who has a new Mini every time the MOT is due. That's why it's rather a high price, for its age and registration.'

Papers were exchanged, the money paid and then Agnes had to make the Mini anonymous as far as her new friends were concerned. She solved the problem quite cleverly. The young man, suitably paid, was to drive it to Shelly's Hotel in Lewes, and put it in the car-park. He could do that tomorrow. Agnes, meanwhile, unknown to the delighted young man, would drive to Shelly's and tell them her niece was coming to stay with her and could she put the Mini in their car-park as she wanted to give it to her niece as a surprise gift. Agnes would be careful to let the manager, or some member of the hotel's staff, see the

Porsche. It still amazed her the doors her expensive car could open.

'How will you get back?' she asked.

'Oh, no probs, miss. I can come on the bus or let one of the lads fetch me.'

A further ten pounds for 'one of the lads' and that little matter was settled. The young man who had sold her the car might well use the bus and pocket the tenner, but she felt that was nothing to do with her. Agnes had, during the first part of her life, been short of money and she well remembered the time when she thought how well she had done to have saved five thousand pounds and have it safely in a building society. Now things were so different, and she was glad of it.

After a light lunch in the garden of a small café that reminded her a little of Rose Cottage, water for Mac and a biscuit, she walked back to the Porsche and started out on her drive home. As she passed green fields she noted horses, grazing quietly. One was cantering round with a little girl on his back, taking very small jumps. A woman, perhaps the child's mother, was following her round the little jumps. When the horse jumped, and landed safely on the other side, the child patted his neck with obvious affection. Agnes wondered if the animal realised that was praise. There was so much to know about animals. How they thought, reacted, suffered. It was a subject that fascinated and worried her. This little tableau of the child and the jumping horse was pleasant. She was pleased too with the little navy blue Mini. If they were going to stalk, it might as well be in a decent little car – Neon. The name was new to her. She realised that she was thinking in the plural. Did that mean that she had finally decided to ask Guy to help her? Yes, she would have a talk to Guy, tell him about the Mini. He would be disappointed not to be using the Porsche, but that did not alter Agnes' decision. She did not want her car involved. The Mini was unknown to anyone. She must stress complete secrecy to Guy.

Then there was Amanda. That was a delicate matter. The poor girl had been hurt and horrified enough. Guy might not agree but Agnes felt she must be sworn to secrecy too, and she must be told of their plans. If they left her out, and then she found out, it would surely send the girl back into her depression again. To be left out, no, that would not do at all. Once long ago, Agnes had spent a short time in a psychiatric hospital for a depressive illness. She would never forget it. 'Fellow feeling makes us wondrous kind,' she whispered to herself, and she meant it. How to go about it, though? Have Guy and Amanda to a meal, take them out to a meal? Amanda did not seem to get many social jauntings. Yes, why not go to Shelly's! First she would move the Mini. No, perhaps not. She could tell them her niece had been delayed, then Guy could make some excuse to call for it. Her arrival in the Porsche with two guests would not hurt her credibility at all. She smiled to herself at this thought. She had never had to use the beautiful car for 'snob' purposes before, but there was a first time for everything! She could perhaps even say her niece had been further delayed and use Shelly's car-park for a few more nights. She would buy Guy and Amanda a really expensive meal.

Agnes decided to have Guy round to Rose Cottage the next day, tell him about the Mini and ask him if he would help stalk, watch and – if they caught him red-handed – eliminate Bill Lewis from the scene of guilt. After all, Agnes was not sure he would want to participate at all.

On the telephone, he seemed keen enough to come and see her and added that he had a bit of interesting news to tell her as well.

They went into the sitting-room. Agnes proffered a can of Heineken and a glass.

'Don't need a glass, Agnes,' he said, the can fizzing as he opened it.

'Yes, you do in my sitting-room,' Agnes insisted.

'Oh, proper behaviour today then.' He poured the liquid into the glass and raised it in a toast. 'Only makes more washing up though,' he said and half drained the glass.

Agnes noted that his smile was attractive. It did not often appear but when it did it was worth waiting for.

She told him about her purchase of the Mini. He immediately recognised the name Neon.

'That's fairly new, but why a Mini, Agnes, when you've got the Porsche?'

'Too familiar to people, Guy.' She gave him another can of beer. 'No drinking while we're doing our detective work and driving.'

'Sure, sure,' he said, pouring out the next can into his glass.

She told him where the garage was delivering the car, the story she had told to enable her to park it there for the moment.

'I see. We drive out there in your car, pick the Mini up?'

Agnes shook her head. 'No, we don't. We take the bus to Lewes and pick up the Mini from wherever it's parked. It can't stay for ever in Shelly's car-park, Guy.'

He shook his head. 'No, I can see your point. I've got a bike, by the way. Bit of exercise will do me good.'

She outlined her plan to him, told him where she had seen Bill Lewis hide the car, the old car.

'Do you remember he told us he'd got two hundred for it? Everything he does makes him look more and more guilty. How could John Merrill team up with a man like that?'

'Who can tell? One thing I must insist on though, Guy. If you want to help me catch this man, I want to bring Amanda into it.'

Guy looked doubtful. 'Is she fit to . . . you know what I mean, Agnes?'

'If we leave her out and do the whole thing without her, make it look as if she can't help, her self-esteem will go crashing again, she's been through enough.'

Guy stroked and twisted one side of his hair. 'You're a nice lady, Agnes. She's got a true friend in you – come to that, we both have, I reckon.'

'I hope so, Guy,' Agnes replied rather primly. Any emotional remark rather embarrassed her, even from Bill. There had been one man who didn't, hadn't ever embarrassed her by an emotional remark. But he was dead and gone. Even now, sitting here with Guy, when she thought of him, her heart leapt and his going seemed the worst thing that had happened to her in her whole life.

She dismissed the thought from her mind and turned again to Guy. 'Well, do you feel you want to be a private detective?'

'Yep. Does Amanda come with us? How do we do it? One night you, one night me?'

Agnes agreed. 'The other horses were attacked about seven in the evening when it was dark. Now it's darker later, so we'll have to adjust our times.'

'So, do you want Amanda to come and stalk?'

Agnes hesitated. 'I'm not quite sure, Guy. I just want her to know what's going on. Remember she did knife John.'

'I will talk to her about it, ask her what she wants to do. She deserves a say.' Guy got up. 'When do we start?'

Agnes did not answer him at once. She had remembered his remark on the telephone. 'You said you had a bit of interesting news to tell me?'

'Oh, yes. Lyn found this by Maisie.' Guy reached into the pocket of his jeans and pulled out a cigarette end in a small plastic bag. The cigarette end had been stubbed out hard so that the filter tip was bent up. However, you could still read the name near the filter – Elco. Not a well-known brand. 'Lyn says she's seen Bill smoking that brand and his father, when he gives him one.' He handed the little bag to Agnes. 'Bright of Lyn to gather it up though, wasn't it?' He spoke rather proudly.

'Yes, indeed. Very purposeful. It's little things like that will bring him down, I hope.'

'Who's doing the first night?' Guy sounded quite enthusiastic.

'Me. I'll do the first night.'

'Porsche?' he asked.

Agnes shook her head, smiling. 'Bus. I've checked the times, hope I don't meet too many people I know, but I can always think up some reason for not using my car.'

'Well, good luck, Agnes.'

'I'll talk to Amanda this afternoon. Will you ask her to come and have a cup of tea with me, if she's got nothing better to do? Don't tell her anything, Guy – let me tell her, will you?'

'Of course, not a word. Don't know how she will take it though.'

'Me neither,' said Agnes and closed the door behind him.

Agnes was surprised that Guy had agreed to co-operate with her schemes. She had got the feeling when she first met him that he was a rebel, a bit work-shy. She supposed he was on the dole. Now that she knew him better, she felt there was potential there, waiting to show itself. Perhaps this adventure might turn him into a private eye, she thought, working freelance. Strange if this set him off on a career he had never thought of.

Amanda arrived at tea-time. Obviously Guy had not filled her in as to anything they were planning. As usual she was pleased to see Agnes and made a fuss of Mac. Agnes had made her rather special sandwiches using very thinly sliced bread; Amanda always remarked on them and called them a celebration tea whenever Agnes produced them. 'Well, we are celebrating something today, Amanda. We are starting a new career as private detectives.'

After a very satisfactory chat with Amanda, Agnes did something she had been wanting to do for some time. She asked them both to dine with her at Shelly's. Amanda was wildly excited and the inevitable question came: 'What shall I wear? What are you going to wear, Agnes?'

'I haven't thought about it yet, Amanda,' she answered.

Amanda looked a little jealous. 'You've got so many lovely clothes, Agnes,' she said. 'Well, I haven't had a new dress for ages. I'll ask Mum and Dad for one.'

'How about you, Guy?'

Guy twinkled at her. 'Tweeds is it?'

Agnes shook her head. 'No, I don't think so, just a dark suit will do.'

'Tell you what, Agnes. I'll come in a Lady Chatterley's lover suit, like a gamekeeper.'

Amanda broke in. 'Guy, don't be awful!' Her cheeks went quite pink.

Agnes was amused. 'You said you couldn't get on with Jane Austen, but you managed to read *Lady Chatterley's Lover*?'

Amanda went pinker. 'Oh, Agnes.' She giggled.

Guy broke in. 'Give over, Agnes. You know all women read that book. It's for the sexy bits.'

The conversation went on with Agnes mentioning the names of one or two books that Amanda might enjoy. They parted with Amanda promising to go straight to the library and take out some of the books that Agnes had suggested. She probably would do it too, Agnes guessed.

Agnes then took herself off to Shelly's Hotel in Lewes. She wanted to choose the table and book it. Agnes was very careful to pick the table she wanted, away from the music, if there were any, not too near the kitchen doors or the entrance foyer. She went to the desk and booked a table for the evening after next. She left the hotel well pleased with her choice.

She had parked the Porsche a little round the side of the hotel. She made her way to the Mini. She took the keys out of her bag, no automatic locks here. She got in the driver's seat and the engine started up immediately as a Mini always did. Agnes smiled with pleasure at sitting in an almost new-looking navy car. She looked around her, noting that the whiplash tops to the front seats were no longer there. She looked over on to the back seat. There was something wooden and shiny wedged down the back seat, well down so that she could not see what it was. It intrigued her. She got out of the car and, with some difficulty, managed to pull the driver's seat forward enough to climb in and, again with some difficulty, pull out the object wedged behind the back seat. It was a well-oiled and well-kept man's cricket bat, not a child's bat. Agnes got out from the rather cramped back of the Mini and stood holding the bat in her hand. She stroked it up and down. Her first thought was that she should take it back to the garage where she had acquired the car, but something said, 'No leave it. No one has rung up. They know your address, therefore your phone number. Keep it. It might be useful.' She put it back in the car but this time she slid it under the two front seats.

She had one more task to do. Drive to that turning where she had seen Bill Lewis hide his old car. She wanted to see if the car was still hidden there, and also the curve she had paused in to watch him leave the car and start to walk back to Jasmine Cottage. She wanted to check it before she introduced Guy to the area they needed to watch, and to measure the curve's ability to conceal the car; she was not sure whether it would hide even the Mini well enough. It had been all right when she had stood there with the Porsche, and the Mini was, of course, smaller –

but perhaps she had not been seen merely because Bill Lewis had been too preoccupied to turn round, to bother. If, however, he was engaged in some terrible deed or was going off to do one, he might be more cautious, more alert, so she wanted the Mini to be well hidden. Indeed, it was vital he did not see it.

She found the place, turned the Mini and drove into the small dip she had concealed herself in before. With the Mini, it seemed perfect, but she must make sure. Having parked the car as close as she could to the mass of shrubs beside her, she got out and looked around with great care and listened for footsteps on the hard surface of the road. Nothing. A crow flew overhead and its noise made her jump. She laughed at herself. 'You're going to be fine if you feel like that when you come to watch and wait and he comes and drives off and you have to follow him!' But she knew what was actually frightening her now. The fear of discovery, while she set up her cover. Agnes had never done anything like this before. Always in solving her problem action had come of its own accord. Quick, spontaneous, to hand. As she thought this, she saw the handle of the cricket bat protruding from under the passenger seat. She looked at it long and she wondered.

Yes, the old black car was still there, that was one thing. She emerged from the little hideaway and stood in the road. All was deserted around her. She couldn't see the Mini at all, even when she looked out or came out frontways. It was well hidden – a great relief. Now, what to do with the Mini? One more night in Shelly's car-park? She felt sure, now she had made herself known to them, they had seen the Porsche and she was giving a little dinner party there ... She had said that she would do the first evening, but now she had another idea. She would take Guy with her that next evening after the dinner party. She would show him where the Mini could be completely hidden. They could discuss what time to get there and – perhaps the most worrying aspect to Agnes – the length of time to stay.

Going through what newspaper reports she could at the library, she found that the malicious woundings seemed to occur between three in the afternoon and seven or eight at night. Now the evenings were lighter, maybe the woundings would be later. With warmer nights, the villains could stay out all night, till dawn. Who would notice an old battered car out at four thirty or five in the morning? Lorries would be driving as fast as they could while other traffic was almost non-existent at that time. What time did the stable men start at the stables? They had found Maisie out of her stable, in the field, padlock of the stable door smashed with a brick. That had been late evening.

She decided to take Amanda home to High Hurlands, then go with Guy in the Mini to show him the hideaway and discuss with him times and communications. She had already invested in two mobile telephones. But this she would tell him after, she hoped, they had enjoyed their dinner.

The dinner, much to Agnes' relief, was a great success. Agnes felt she didn't know much about youngsters and she was uncertain how a formal dinner would go down with them. Most of the young ones she saw on television never seemed to sit round a dinner table any more. They walked about the room clutching and biting at a pizza or munching a half-pounder hamburger jammed between a cut-in-half bun. However, in this case they sat down quietly. Amanda looked around her, rather charmingly shy. She had a habit of looking up at you through quite long thick lashes.

'Soup, fish platter or melon?'

As they looked a little bewildered by this choice, Agnes asked the waiter what the fish platter consisted of. He reeled it off with that faint French accent that many waiters assume.

'Prawn, smoked salmon, a morsel of crab and lobster. With a salad garnish, madam.'

'That sounds nice. Shellfish all right for you two?'

They nodded. Then the main course was chosen. A steak for Guy and roast lamb for Agnes and Amanda. After making their choice they could relax a little. Agnes ordered a bottle of wine. Amanda insisted on a very small amount in her glass and took tiny sips of the wine. Guy downed two glasses before the steak came, so Agnes put herself in the place of 'driver home' and gave up the idea of driving Guy to the hideaway. She ordered another bottle of wine and limited herself to a glass and a half.

She didn't mind the change of plan too much. After all, the next evening would do. Just, please God, let no one be out this evening with a knife raised. She shuddered.

'Lovely beef, Agnes,' Guy said, cutting into what looked like a nice and tender steak. Amanda was loosening up a little too, and by the time the sweet trolley arrived all was very well. Another half-glass of wine had certainly made her blossom. Guy must have noticed too, because suddenly he gave her arm a little poke and said, 'That chap over their fancies you, Amanda.'

Agnes took a quick look and saw a handsome young man, obviously with his family, glancing with interest Amanda's way.

Amanda flushed even pinker and let her head drop forward a little so that her hair draped her face. 'Oh, be quiet, Guy. He's probably looking at Agnes.'

Their host laughed. 'I don't think so, Amanda, you are a pretty girl and look particularly so tonight.' Which was true. The new dress was stunning, in pale lilac with shoulder straps which revealed her shoulders and a very discreet amount of cleavage. At last Guy persuaded his sister to have a quick look too and when she did, her eyes met directly those of the young man. He smiled and Amanda gave a half-smile back.

'It's all right. You're in the protection of your friends, let him have a gander,' said Guy, polishing off another glass of wine with gusto.

The family containing the admiring young man left first, much to Guy's disappointment. Agnes could see that a lot had been done for Amanda's morale in this dinner trip, but any further adventures would have to be taken tomorrow evening with Guy alone involved.

After coffee and the inevitable mints, Agnes paid her bill. They left decorously in the Porsche and the Mini stayed one more night in Shelly's car-park. She felt there was no need even to mention it. The Porsche and the size of her dinner bill for three would well compensate. 'Oh, that lady's left her Mini here for another night. I thought she said one night. Still, she's a good customer.' She could almost hear the manager saying it.

Agnes drove them home and dropped them at their very gate. Profuse in thanks and kisses, they had all enjoyed the little outing and Agnes felt it had sealed something between them that maybe had not been quite as solid before. She turned the car and drove into her own domain. A light welcomed her, left on for Mac, who was sound asleep in his bed in the kitchen and greeted her with stretched legs and a yawn, then a vigorous tail wag. She snapped his lead on, gave him a quick walk round the garden. There was a full moon which lit up the garden and landscape rather eerily. She came in, locked her door and felt pleased with herself – perhaps content would be a better word. She gave Mac a little midnight treat, which he snapped up before returning to his basket as if to say, 'It's all very well, but this high living and the disruption of night hours are too much for me.'

13

The next day dawned dull and wet. Agnes had to don mac and boots for Mac's walk. She was disappointed in one way, because she felt that if this weather continued Bill Lewis was not likely to take his old car out, or bring a mate to the car to set off on an injuring spree. On the other hand it would keep anyone away while she showed Guy where Bill's car was and how she hid the Mini a comparatively short way away from it.

At three o'clock she telephoned Guy and suggested they set off about four thirty. He agreed and seemed excited by the idea. He had to go into Lewes to sign on that morning and asked did she want anything doing. It was a heaven-sent opportunity.

'Yes, Guy. Go to Shelly's car-park and fetch the Mini, bring it as near here as possible, then hide up some little layby if you can find one.' She gave him the registration number. 'I will ring the hotel and tell them you will be fetching it. If you call here on your way to Lewes, I'll give you a note and I will also telephone the hotel.'

He agreed with enthusiasm.

'But be careful.' Agnes voice was sharp. 'Don't let anyone see you driving it if you possibly can help it. We neither of us want to be at all associated with that little car.'

'Right, I've got you. Will do.'

His brisk and businesslike way of replying rather pleased Agnes.

Agnes telephoned Shelly's to tell them that her nephew was picking up the Mini today. By the sound of the receptionist he had already forgotten it was parked there, which was quite comforting to Agnes. Now all she had to do was wait until Guy walked into Rose Cottage and they could walk back to wherever he had hidden Neon. She decided to say nothing about the cricket bat – why, she was not sure.

She wondered how Guy took the signing on and job seeking. Somehow she couldn't imagine him queuing up and answering all the questions that come from behind the counter. His living conditions, how much he paid for his room. Had he made three attempts to get a job in the last so many weeks? Not Guy as she knew him at all. She toyed with the idea of paying him for the job she wanted him to do as she wandered down the garden picking off the dead heads of the polyanthus. An idea jumped into her head. What triggered it was the little Mini. She was thinking to herself that once, by the grace of God, they had caught someone she would have to sell the Mini, probably at a loss, when she stopped in her tracks in the middle of her front garden path. Why not, she thought? Why not?

Agnes was visualising turning herself, Guy and Amanda into a three member detective agency. Part of Rose Cottage or High Hurlands could be made into an office. Did you need a licence? Yes, she was sure you did. Anyone who approched them for help and advice would be charged a fee. Who knew about these things? She could soon find out. The film industry where poor Bill had spent his last years – she remembered they had given her a private eye in New York. He had followed her everywhere. She hadn't liked it much but Bill had said it was safer. She had said it was all nonsense until a director's wife, whose husband was directing a rather controversal film, was gunned down in Times Square and killed.

The whole idea filled her with delighted anticipation. No more tidying the house, coffee mornings, kind little visits. Not any more, but would Guy and Amanda play? Guy had no job and none in prospect. He could work a computer. She would love to learn to. The web, the net, a new vista seemed to be opening up before her. But first . . . and she drew herself firmly back to the job in hand. These devils had to be the first to be caught.

On the way back to the cottage, Mac ambling beside her, she tried to stop herself listing the assets she already had for the imagined firm. Two mobile telephones. Guy had a computer, as had Amanda. A second little car and an office of some sort. She smiled to herself and her step became lighter. Agnes Turner – Private Investigator. Agnes Turner & Partners – Private Investigators. No case too large or too small. Brandy and ginger ale were needed, her 'always' drink in times of crisis or decision. 'It will be wonderful if we are needed again, Mac.' The dog wagged his tail. She got him some hard tack from its box and his tail wagged harder than ever. Agnes felt herself humming a song to herself and realised just how she was saying the words. 'Come on,' she said to herself. 'That is going over the top.' The words and the song sung her way were 'Turner round and you'll find me there.' What a name for an agency! Useless anyway because that would cut the other two out and she certainly would not do that. They were her friends now and once you were Agnes' friend, she would never, never let you down. She knew that much about herself.

Agnes and Guy arrived at her chosen little hiding place at about five thirty. On this, the first evening Agnes had taken Guy to the place so near where the black car was hidden, they were given a shock.

No sooner had Agnes placed the car as much off the road as she possibly could and turned off the engine, than the old black car emerged from its hiding place, its noisy engine disturbing a few crows as it went. The driver was Bill Lewis.

Agnes looked at Guy.

'Let's follow him, Agnes.'

She pulled out into the road and followed at a discreet distance. A little traffic built up and Agnes allowed one car between them. Risky, but she did not want any suspicion drawn to her navy car. If their cover were blown, it would mean either changing the car or, if they were recognised, giving up altogether. Luckily it was made easier for her to follow the black car even if she ventured to get a vehicle in between it and herself because of the almost constant plume of white steam and smoke which came from Bill Lewis's exhaust.

Guy was leaning forward, watching intently. Agnes glanced at him. 'Seat belt, Guy, we don't want to get picked up for not wearing a belt.'

Guy did not take his eyes off the black car, felt around, found the belt and snapped it into place. 'I think there's several chances here, Agnes. He's alone, which may mean he is just doing a recce, or he may be on the way to pick someone up and go somewhere they already know or have already sussed out.'

Agnes shook her head. Her mind was obsessed with the idea that, had he backed his car out and turned right instead of left, he would have seen their car and probably recognised Agnes, seated as she was close to the driver's window. Once they had solved the problem – if it were solvable – another safe hiding place just had to be found. Actually they needed the same kind of hiding place as his. Had he cut down some hedge? It hadn't looked like it. Probably just a natural indent in the shrubs and brambles.

They continued on, Agnes thankful that the garage had filled her tank with petrol. The little car sped along effortlessly and was quite able to overtake if necessary.

'We've done thirteen miles.' Agnes was gratified to see that Guy was noting it down; she had not been even aware that he had been looking at the mileage. 'We need maps, Agnes,' he said suddenly. 'Of this, and perhaps a big larger area, don't you think?'

She nodded. 'You're right. I'll get a selection tomorrow.'

Suddenly, in the middle of four cars, Bill Lewis's left-hand blinker came on. Blink, blink . . . where was the left-hand turning going to lead? Was Bill's the only car to turn up the side road?

It was. Agnes drew up and Guy got out.

'Drive on a bit, Agnes, park by the side of the road and I'll follow him on foot.'

'Can you keep up, do you think?' Agnes asked.

'I don't think the lane can go far, it's bound to end in a farm, or a smallholding or even just a house. At least I can see what he's up to.'

Agnes still felt and looked a bit anxious, so he went on: 'Look, if anything happens, anyone joins him and they start anything, I've got the phone.' He tapped his pocket.

'All right, but be careful, Guy.'

Agnes watched him walk down the lane. He was tall and slouched a little, his leather jacket thrust behind him. She watched him out of sight, then drove on a little way and parked well against the hedge. The traffic was not very heavy, a little convoy of cars passed to and fro now and again.

After about half an hour Guy appeared, covered in grass and dirt. He snatched open the door and got in. He was panting a bit. 'I had to burrow into the undergrowth.' He grinned and wiped some mud off his cheek.

'What happened?'

'Well, he drove right up to a gate, wide open. Lovely house, converted from a barn. Cut off totally but for that little lane.'

He took off his shoes. They were mud-encrusted. Agnes gripped the steering wheel. 'Horses?' she asked, her voice tense.

'Two. Lovely-looking creatures, the stables nice, thatched.'

'What did he do, why are you so covered in mud?'

Guy stretched his back. 'He drove quite slowly up that lane. He didn't go right up to the gate, he got out of the car, went through the gates, crossed the lawns and knocked on the front door. He was having a good look round while he waited for them to answer the door. A man answered, very countryfied-looking. A gent.'

'Did he appear to know Bill Lewis?'

Guy shook his head. 'They talked. I got as close as I could. I thought I heard the word gardener, so perhaps he was after a job there.'

'No sign of anyone joining up with him?'

Guy again shook his head. 'I think he might be . . . He looked at the two horses for a long time, the bastard.'

'Right. At least we know where he's going.'

'We both ought to come tomorrow.'

Agnes shook her head. 'No, we've got to spread this out, there's only two of us. I'll do tomorrow night, you the next. Tonight I think we're safe.'

He was about to remonstrate again.

'I've got a telephone too, you know.'

Guy opened the car door and clapped the shoes together. The mud and grass flew off. 'We'll need wellingtons for this lot,' he said.

Agnes smiled for the first time since they had been out. Her sense of humour, as she knew, was not too well developed, but she suddenly felt happy. Perhaps they could do some good, catch these vile men, and that would be good for Amanda and Guy. Neither of them seemed to have much motivation. The sort of jobs Guy wanted were all probably taken before being advertised, if decently paid. He had no car. One job application he had shown to Agnes – usually he was pretty quiet about his unemployed state. This had been for a hotel receptionist, requiring extensive knowledge of computers. Web, Windows and software generally. Six days a week, time not stated. Own transport. But it was the salary this hotel offered that really startled Agnes. Nine thousand a year. 'Not worth taking,' he had said.

As they drove home, she thought of tomorrow evening. She was not in the least afraid. She was so used to handling situations her own way. Her mobile telephone would not be used to call the police. If they caught them red-handed, a slaughtered or mutilated animal at their feet, would the police, court, jury, judge, deal out adequate and suitable punishment? No, of course not. That was her job. She had always been able to deliver fitting punishment before; she would not alter this time.

When the Mini had been parked and locked up in a Lewes car-park, they walked together to the bus stop. On the bus little was said, but they travelled in a very companionable silence. When they left the bus, which stopped at the end of the lane that led to Rose Cottage, Guy refused to come in because of the mud on his shoes. Mrs Tracy greeted Agnes. She had been in the back of the kitchen, ironing. 'We've been having a game with the

Bally.' She pointed at Mac. He wagged his tail. 'He's had his dinner. I didn't hear the car come in, Mrs Turner.' Lucky, thought Agnes and she went back out into the front garden and threw up the garage doors just to give Mrs Tracy a reassuring glimpse of the Porsche as she left.

The next afternoon Agnes cheated a little. She took the Porsche to Lewes, to the car-park where she had left the Mini and changed cars. As she buckled the Mini's seat belt, she felt the old exhilaration surging through her. Not excitement exactly, but a familiar feeling that at last she was tackling this terrible affair alone, alone as she always did. She appreciated Guy and Amanda and had even contemplated an agency. Agnes realised that to tackle a man, or two men, intent on doing some injury to a horse would be tricky, but she had tackled worse before this and won, or punished, however one phrased it. One thing she would not do was inform the police.

She had come early to the spot where the black car was hidden. She needed to find a new hiding place for the Mini. She cruised a short way up the road, searching the hedgerows for a possible little opening, or path. Nothing on her side, then backing the car slowly along the hedge, she glanced across the road. There, almost opposite where the black car was hidden, was a little drive in. Agnes carefully drove across the road, put the nose of the car between the sparse shrubs. It opened up, while behind and above her the low branches of the trees snapped to again. Ideal place. The small entry ended in a broken-down farm gate. Half open, its edge was embedded in at least six inches of hardened mud. The gate had obviously not been opened or closed for many, many months, so probably the field was not used either. Perfect. If she backed the Mini into this place she would be able to see the black car's ins and outs with ease through the young branches.

It was still early so Agnes took the risk of backing the Mini out into the main road. No traffic at all. She backed in, got out of the car and gently draped the young, almost sapling branches over the bonnet. Now she had the – to her – anxiety-producing recce to see if the black car was still there, or had already departed. That was going to be, she felt, her main worry: how late or how early to arrive.

Agnes crossed the road, looking carefully to right and left, praying that the car was still there. It was. A few leaves had fallen on to the top and bonnet, some lodged in the windshield wipers. Agnes went back across the road, looking in the direction of where Jasmine Cottage was. That was where Bill Lewis would come from if he was taking his old black car out. She got into the Mini, the keys in the ignition, seat belt on, ready for an instant drive out for the chase should it occur. She was more content when she was, as it were, 'in the driving seat'. She had given Guy strict instructions to telephone her if he followed the black car to what he thought might be a stabbing destination. He had, of course, immediately suggested telephoning the police and had seemed very surprised when she had given him an adamant 'No' in reply. 'Just ring me, Guy,' she had said. 'The police didn't catch anyone after poor Magic had been stabbed to death, didn't even discover there was a body not too far away.' No, she was the person to tell and no other.

Agnes sat there patiently. Cars went by, increasing a little in number as the offices and shops let out their captives. Five, five thirty. Then traffic quietened again. Six thirty, seven, seven thirty, no one had come for the black car.

At eight she decided to go home. She motored to Lewes, picked up the Porsche and left the Mini in the car-park. At home her dog sitter, faithful as ever, was watching television, Mac on her lap. He never sat on Agnes' knee, she had always rather discouraged it. Mrs Tracy, however, seemed to take the opposite view. 'Real little lap dog he is,' she said.

Agnes was profuse in her apologies. 'I'm sorry I'm so late, I –'

Mrs Tracy brushed her apologies aside with a wave of her hand. 'I love being here, Mrs Turner, it's never too late for me.'

Agnes thanked her, paid her. Mac brought in a large plastic bone which made a terrible squeak when pinched. Mrs Tracy had left. 'Normal service will be resumed,' Agnes said to herself, but she wondered whether what they would be able to do in the way of watching was, or would be, enough to catch Bill Lewis, if the culprit was indeed he. She felt muddled about it all. What was the most likely time? Should they leave the afternoons? Agnes shuddered suddenly. Supposing they did that, left that particular horse or paddock or stable without their protection, however meagre that protection was. She would take Mac with her next time. How would she time it? How would Guy get on tomorrow night? She thought of a hundred questions as to her procedure, trying to make it comparable with the murders, for she called them that. Murders.

The rest of the evening dwindled away with Agnes constantly thinking of her next move. If it was Bill Lewis and a companion who had killed Magic, she hoped it was she who would catch him. Meanwhile she would have to telephone Guy and tell him about the new and more adequate place to hide the Mini in.

14

The next day Agnes woke with the feeling that she could not bear to be left out, if only for the day. Always before her problems had been dealt with alone. No one else had ever even guessed at the outcome. Now she was feeling increasingly uneasy about having to share. Practically, she realised she could not cover every day, she had to rely on Guy, but having help in a scheme was not in her nature.

As she was making her tea she was surprised, so early in the morning, to see Amanda coming into her front gate. She knocked in her rather timid way. Agnes opened the door with a welcoming smile. 'Just in time to share a cup of tea with me,' she said.

Amanda came in, as usual greeted with enthusiasm and morning barks. Mac was very fond of Amanda, mainly because she was an inexhaustible ball thrower. Amanda sat down at the kitchen table. Mac did his best to jump on her lap, but his rather arthritic back legs failed him, so Amanda picked him up and hugged him, then put him down gently on the kitchen floor. He gave another bark and raced out into the back garden.

'I hope you don't mind my coming, Agnes?' Amanda said at last.

'Of course not, I like you to come when you want.' The girl's relieved look took over at once. 'I want to tell you about what Guy and I have got up to – you know most of it, I expect?'

Amanda nodded. 'Yes, but not being able to drive and . . .'

Agnes nodded. 'Why not have lessons, Amanda? It's always a useful skill.'

Amanda shook her head. 'I couldn't drive, I haven't got the confidence, Agnes.' She traced a little pattern on the table top with her fingernail. 'I wondered . . .' She paused in the rather irritating way she often did.

'You wondered what, Amanda?'

The girl looked up at her through her thick eyelashes. 'I'd love to go and see Maisie and the other horses in that stables.'

'Why?'

'Well, partly because of Magic, but mostly because I don't seem to be helping much.'

Agnes could sympathise. In her early nursing days she had always been the one who was left out, at a party or a dance, at a hockey game, anything, so she knew only too well how this lonely girl felt. So she tried to fill her in on what she and Guy had been doing to try to track down the man or men who were responsible for the carnage.

Amanda listened with interest to every word, some of which Guy had told her. 'I'd loved to see the Mini and where you hide it and where that black car is hidden, just so I feel part of it.'

Agnes suddenly made up her mind. 'Look, Amanda, I've got a free morning. I'll show you the places and then we will go and see Maisie. She's calmed down now, she's not so nervous. Would you like that?'

'Yes, I would, but are you sure you . . . ?'

'Now, just the chickens to feed, come with me, they've nearly all recovered their feathers.'

Down in the chicken coup, Agnes picked up one of her

chickens and placed it in Amanda's arms. There were twelve now.

'That's Henrietta, she was by far the worst, she could barely walk and her neck was raw. You see, she had had her beak cut off.'

'What's that for?' Amanda asked, stroking the bird who was looking up at her with bright beady eyes.

'So they can't peck each other to death with the sheer boredom of being caged in a place not big enough to turn round in.'

Amanda put the hen down and it began to peck away at the layer pellets and corn just as the others did. 'Oh, Agnes, think what you've rescued them from.' She said.

'I'd like to rescue more, I think I can take two more. The battery is still running, under new ownership, I believe.'

After closing up the run, greeting the gardener and loading Mac into the car, they set off. Agnes was determined to show Amanda the Mini in Lewes car-park, the hiding place they had used to watch the black car and the better hiding place she herself had found. Then she promised she would take her to see Maisie. She felt that Amanda had been a little left out, yet she had been and, in a way still was, the one who had suffered most, seen such a horrific death and become so mentally upset it had almost, temporarily at least, robbed her of her memory and reason. It has caused her to strike out in such an agony of rage that she had used a knife on the assailant. Guy might have been the ultimate dispatcher of John Merrill, but she seemed to have suffered much more mental trauma.

As they drove along the lane, Agnes stole a look at the girl beside her. She was very pale. In repose her face looked incredibly sad. Agnes wondered whether she had always been quiet and retiring, perhaps preferring her own company. Agnes was not sure, but the girl sitting beside her certainly did not present a picture of a happy girl in her early twenties. She leant over as she waited for some cars to go by before joining the main Lewes road, and put a large apple on the glove compartment.

'For Maisie,' she said and was pleased to see the girl's face relax a little. Amanda picked up the apple to smell it.

'You think of everything, Agnes.'

'Oh, no, I don't. I've forgotten Mac's bottle of water,' she said, 'so we will have to stop somewhere and have lunch so that he can get a drink.'

'Oh, I didn't tell Mum I'd be out to lunch.'

Agnes got out the mobile phone. 'Have they got one?' she asked.

'No.' Amanda looked quite askance at the idea.

'Well, you can ring them and tell them on this, then they won't worry if we eat out, all right?'

Amanda settled back in her seat, a little of her tension relaxing. 'Lovely,' she said. Mac slept contentedly on the back seat. Occasionally he would sit up, take a look through the window, bark at a passing dog, if there was one, then go back to sleep again. He liked the car and with stops for 'comfort stations' and drinks and the occasional extra meal, he enjoyed a day out.

Agnes stopped the Porsche a good way from where the black car was hidden and they walked along the road, had a peep. The black car was still there, a little more covered with last year's persistent dead leaves, to Agnes' relief – it had obviously not been moved since she had been there. Then she showed Amanda the new place she had found.

'Now on to see the Mini,' she said. Luckily there was room in the Lewes car-park to park the Porsche, then Agnes walked to the navy Mini.

'What a dear little car, Agnes, how I wish I could drive!'

'Why did you never learn?' Agnes asked as they made their way back to the Porsche.

'Oh, Mum and Dad. They said it was no use my driving. I'd never have enough nerve, probably they were right.'

'Rubbish,' Agnes said, rather explosively. She was getting the picture of a not unusual family where the son of the house was all important and the girl not so. It didn't happen so often now, she was sure, but Amanda and Guy's parents were older than most and did appear pretty set in their ways.

Over lunch in a little café with a garden where they were able to eat their meal and even Mac got a snack and a bowl of water, Agnes told Amanda everything. The transformation of John Merrill's car from dark green to light blue, the hiding of the old one when Bill Lewis had told Guy and herself he had sold it for two hundred pounds. The name Bill Lewis had no effect, caused no reaction, but then, why should it. After a leisurely lunch, before which Amanda had telephoned her mother on the mobile telephone, they took Mac for a walk around the deserted field behind the café. Then, back to the Porsche and the pleasant drive to Marshall's stables and a glimpse of Maisie.

They drove up to the stables, Agnes glancing briefly, without a feeling of pity, at the spot where John Merrill was buried, in her opinion rather aptly, under a horse. One of the stable hands, carrying a large bale of hay, dropped it outside a stable and turned, recognising both Agnes and her car. He touched his forehead.

'Hello, miss. Want to see Miss Lyn?'

Agnes shook her head and introduced Amanda. 'This is the young lady whose horse Magic was killed by those vandals. Whoever they were.'

He looked at Amanda with real compassion. 'Sorry, miss. How old was Magic?' he asked.

'Twenty-eight, older than me, but . . .'

'That's a good age and probably he had had a good life, miss.'

Amanda nodded, but mention of her horse had brought the mantle of grief down on her face.

'Well, Maisie's all right. She's got her nerve back. Got an apple there for her?'

He took the apple from Amanda's hands; expertly he broke the fruit into four pieces and handed them back to her. They went to Maisie's stable. She was confident, enjoyed the apple, nuzzled Amanda's arm and generally behaved like an animal with regained confidence in its two-legged friends.

They drove down the lane, Jasmine Cottage a little to the right. The sun was shining and all the way down the lane from the stables Amanada had been thanking Agnes for a lovely day. 'I feel so much more part of what you and Guy are doing. It's just made all the difference.'

'I'm glad, because you are very much part of it, Amanda.'

Agnes turned to the left, on the main road. As she did so, she overtook a man walking towards the barn where she knew the resprayed blue Volvo was housed. He recognised Agnes and the car and waved a cigarette-holding hand. Agnes felt Amanda slide down in the passenger seat as far as she possibly could. She gave a little gasp as she did so. Bill Lewis obviously had not seen the person beside Agnes. She speeded up and left the man well behind. She turned to Amanda. The girl slid back up into her seat. Her face was sheet white.

'That's him. I can remember now. That man was with John. He ran away but I know him, I know him.' She looked wild. 'John called out, "Bill, Bill, help me" but he didn't, he just ran away, and I heard a car. I'm sure I heard a car drive away.'

Agnes pacified the girl as far as she could, but it was difficult. In the end, she had to say rather brusquely that if Amanda was going to behave like this she wasn't going to be much use to Guy and herself in catching him. This helped the girl to regain control.

'I couldn't remember. That psychiatrist and my doctor. Mum and Dad, the police, they all got me so muddled.'

Agnes did remember that Amanda had once mentioned a second man but had then said she was so muddled she may have been wrong and perhaps there had only been John Merrill. Now the sight of this man had jogged her memory into more clarity.

Agnes could not have been more pleased with the revelation. Now they *knew* Bill Lewis had been there when Magic died. She tried to convey this to the girl beside her. 'It's such a help,' she said but Amanda, still shaking and crying, would only say, 'If I had remembered earlier they might have caught him.'

'Well, you didn't but you have now.' They joined the large queue of traffic; it was certainly going-home time.

Once home, Agnes had to ring Guy and tell him about the new hiding place. She was quick to tell him about Amanda recognising Bill Lewis, how she had seemed genuinely horrified to have her memory of a second man jogged into life. They talked about the new hiding place and how long Guy should watch. This was probably their greatest problem. When would he strike, what time? In the early evening before the owners came back from work, later when it was getting dark? Guy was determined to stay till about nine.

'He might be just going for a spin to keep the car battery OK.'

'Hardly,' answered Guy. 'I reckon if he was going just for a drink, he'd take the blue Volvo. I'm off now.'

Agnes wished him well. The rule that he was to ring her and not the police had not gone down well with him. 'We must ring the police, Agnes.' Her answer, 'Well, what good will it do poor Magic?', hardly put him off. She had to wait on tenterhooks till he rang at nine o'clock to say nothing had happened and he was going home.

15

The next morning Agnes woke early. For a moment or two she did not recall there was anything unusual happening today, then she suddenly remembered. Her turn to watch for the emergence of that beastly black car. Mac was still snoring in his bed. Two years ago he would have heard Bill, her husband, or herself stir, but nowadays Agnes suspected he was getting a little deaf. Her thoughts turned to today's task. When should she start the watch? When should she leave for home? She turned on her side and her movement did rouse Mac, who got out of his bed, yawned, gave a quick stretch and managed a leap on to the bed. Agnes gathered him into her arms. If anything happened to her – taking the risks she might be taking even today – what about Mac? Mrs Tracy was probably the one who would adopt Mac, they adored each other. She shook off this thought and turned her mind to Guy's report on his return last evening.

It was 'Nothing had happened.' He didn't sound very pleased; in some ways he sounded bitterly disappointed that Bill Lewis had not got the car out.

'It's early days, Guy,' Agnes had said. 'You couldn't expect him to act quite so conveniently, your first day watching.'

He laughed. 'I want to get him,' he said, 'especially now Amanda has recognised him. He'd taken off before I got there to help Amanda. No wonder she stayed in shock so long, poor kid.'

'Well, my turn today. I shall leave about four thirty, I think.'

'Are you taking Mac, Agnes? He might bark and give the game away.'

'No. Mrs Tracy's looking after him till I get back. Nothing will happen. I don't think he'll do any more damage till he finds another accomplice and such ghastly people can't be too thick on the ground. Besides, what do they get out of it, just kicks? John Merrill had the same kind of nature, I suppose.' Agnes rang off. The mention of John Merrill made her think of his family, surely they must be worrying about him by now?

She decided to call that morning, just to enquire about a cutting Pansy Merrill had suggested she could have from the garden. Pansy was quite interested in her garden in a regimented way, flowers in neat rows, all exactly the same inches apart. Neatly edged lawns. If she thought anything about Agnes' garden, she never showed any reaction when she came to Rose Cottage and looked at Agnes' wild part, full of birds and hanging bits of bacon fat, coconuts and the big bird table. She had only made one comment, ever – 'Aren't they a bit messy, the birds?' – ignoring a robin who, at that moment, was pecking seed, its red chest glowing.

Pansy opened the door and gave her visitor a real welcome.

'Oh, how nice. I'm all by myself this morning, just in time for coffee.'

Pansy never, like Agnes, served coffee in the kitchen. Always the coffee pot and tray were taken into the sitting-room. Agnes, out of habit, walked through. She looked around. It was a pleasant room. Her glance stopped at the baby grand in the corner of the room. On it was something she was sure had not been there before. A silver-framed photograph of a rather good-looking young man – she presumed, their son John Merrill. Pansy walked in with the tray.

'Your son, Pansy?' Agnes asked, indicating the photograph.

'Yes, taken two years ago.' Her voice became a little wistful.

'We were close, John and I, but his father, I believe he hated him.'

Agnes was persistent. 'But he did give him a car, didn't he?'

Pansy nodded. 'Because it meant he wouldn't be at home as much. Anyway, we've not seen him almost since he got it.' She poured the coffee, then took a tissue from her pocket and dabbed her eyes.

'Well, fathers and sons don't always get on, do they?' It's the generation gap, Pansy.'

Her companion looked up at her, her eyes red, the tissue still pressed against her cheek. 'Agnes, it wasn't only that. John was, you know ... how can I put it ... gay. That's what people say, isn't it? He told me and I begged him not to tell his father, but he did.'

'And that upset your husband, I expect?' Agnes asked.

Pansy nodded, a few more tears rolling down her cheeks. 'They quarrelled bitterly. His father told him he never wanted to see him again, he didn't want a son who was not normal.'

Agnes felt a secret rather ironic thought. He's not very likely to see him again. Poor Pansy seemed the one who was suffering most.

'Now it's nearly five months and not even a card or telephone call.' Pansy drank a sip of her coffee. 'I can't understand why he doesn't get in touch with me. I knew he was gay, but it didn't make any difference to me. He was and always will be my son.'

Agnes felt a brief sadness for Pansy, quickly obliterated by her hatred of what John Merrill had done, and had he lived might have done again.

She looked at her watch, she wanted to get herself some lunch before she started on her watch, see that she had what she felt necessary in the car, map, mobile telephone. She thanked Pansy for the coffee, pressed her hand and said, 'Try not to worry too much. I am sure you will hear from John soon.' As she walked back to Rose Cottage she felt her heart quicken a little. How long it was since she had felt stimulated to go and right a wrong, no matter how. She felt for the first time since Bill's death that she was really living fully again.

She was there, she was free to take advantage of her own

impulses. Agnes knew this was how she worked. The involvement with Guy and Amanda had, for the moment, been shaken off. Not that she disliked them. But all the time they were talking about what they would do, or hoped to do, and it was not in accord with what she herself would do, given the opportunity.

As she drove the Porsche into Lewes to pick up the Mini, her heart raced. It always did, like a signal, when something was going to happen. At the car-park she sat for a moment, trying to reason with herself. To tell herself there certainly was no guarantee that Bill Lewis would take out the black car, pick up a maybe a mate, maybe an equally sadistic person, and start out for some field or stable or shed where he knew a horse was kept. Maybe some way from the house. Maybe not even stabled, just old and trusting like Magic had been.

But in her mind, or heart, or wherever the feeling of certainty was generated, she knew, as she sat in the Porsche, that it was to be this evening or early night. What would she do? She had not the faintest idea. Just as she had never had any idea of how she would solve any of her problems before this. Something had always helped her. The punishment had often fitted the crime – but not always.

Agnes locked the Porsche, having put her display ticket on for twelve hours. Then she found her way through the tightly parked cars to Neon, her own little Mini. More car keys this time – not the efficient automatic 'press of a button' as with the Porsche. Agnes' movements became almost automatic. She locked the passenger side door, registering a black mark against Guy, for leaving it unlocked. The engine started smoothly. Not as quiet as the Porsche perhaps, but healthy enough. She sat again, as she had in the bigger car, as she would have put it, to listen to the dictates of her own fatal imagination.

She felt no fear or nervousness at the thought of meeting maybe two men, bent on evil, armed probably with knives. She knew that, as always, something would happen to her advantage. Some quirk of fate.

The lanes leading back to the hiding place were pretty and had that lovely fresh spring look of the opening of young leaves. Several cars passed her when she drew off the main road. There was a large superstore in Lewes, and at this time in the afternoon the shoppers were out, loading their boots with garish carriers and sometimes shouting at their children.

It was when she had almost reached the new, and most useful, hiding place for the Mini that she got a shock. She had to slow down until the road was clear, then cross the road and back Neon into the little path barely wide enough even for this little car. Backed in, she would have no trouble if Bill Lewis did come for his old black car in order either to fetch a helper or to go somewhere on his own. As she waited, two red cars went by, then a white van partially obscuring the car behind it which, when it came into view, was the pale blue Volvo. Bill Lewis was driving it, and there was no passenger in the front. Agnes was certain he had not seen her. Indeed, he had not even glanced in her direction, although she had instinctively lowered her head.

It passed her, obviously on the way to Lewes – but that was not the shock, or rather the greatest shock, for as it passed she saw who was in the back of the car. Lyn Marshall. Agnes could not imagine what she was doing in Bill Lewis's car. The tiny glimpse of the girl gave Agnes the impression that she was distressed. She held a tissue up to her face and was talking to the driver – and why the back seat? If it was just a friendly jaunt out in his new car, why was she seated in the back of the car? What to do now? Agnes wondered. Did the fact that the blue Volvo was taking Lyn Marshall to Lewes mean that Bill Lewis had other things on his mind and would not be walking across the fields once he had got home, and taking out the black car to turn to things sadistic and diabolical?

In any case, Agnes thought, she must get into her hiding place and stay there. Was she wasting her time? Was the blue car a message: 'Not today'? She dared not take her eyes off the road now and her vigilance was at last rewarded. After about three-quarters of an hour a tractor came slowly past her. It was holding up a few cars behind it, one of which was the Volvo. It crept past and Agnes got a really good look. Bill Lewis was shouting and banging his open hands on the steering wheel. Though her open window Agnes could hear his words: 'Oh, for God's sake, shut up. It's your own fault.' Lyn this time was sitting beside him in the passenger seat. Agnes saw her gesticulating, then dab her eyes with a screwed-up tissue. Then the tractor must have turned into a field and released the traffic behind it. The blue car shot forward and disappeared. Agnes felt it was a strange encounter. Three times she had seen Lyn Marshall: the first time, sweeping the stable yard; then driving Guy Holstein out of The Hollies; now, here she was with Bill, the suspect horse mutilator, and obviously not at all happy. What in heaven's name was it all about?

Her mobile phone rang. 'Anything happening, Agnes?' It was Guy. Only he and Amanda knew this number.

Agnes pretended to have a little coughing burst before she replied, to give herself time to try and measure her own feelings. Then: 'No, nothing as yet, Guy. I'm safely tucked in our hidey-hole.'

'How long are you going to stay there?'

'Don't know yet, Guy.' Agnes felt slightly irritated by his questions. This irritation she knew only too well was caused by her wish, whenever a problem looked like coming to a climax, to 'go it alone'.

'OK, take care, Agnes.'

This remark added to her irritation. 'Take care' in such a situation was the last thing she felt should be done; 'Take action' would be a better slogan.

The traffic was growing less on the road in front of her. Seven o'clock. It was not getting any darker yet, but a feeling of evening was in the air. She got out of the car to stretch her legs, just for a moment. As she was about to get back into the Mini she noticed that the driver's seat was a tiny bit thrust forward. She tried to press it back, then realised what was stopping the seat from slotting back into its proper angle – the cricket bat. Agnes had forgotten all about it. She tipped the seat right foward and drew out the bat. She placed it upright on the passenger seat, and got back into the car after checking that the seat now slotted back as far as it was supposed to go.

Two hours passed. Should she go home? Darkness had fallen. Car lights flashed occasionally along the road, lighting it up, then plunging it again into dusk. Agnes had almost determined to give up, to go home; somewhat reluctantly she did up her seat belt and was about to turn on the ignition when she saw him. Bill Lewis, walking towards the place which held his black car. He was carrying a black holdall and he was alone. He looked around him, not particularly furtively, but as if just to check he was not being observed, then he pushed his way into the overgrown track and disappeared. Agnes heard the engine start, cough and then misfire, and stop. He tried again, the starter whined a little, again the engine did not start. A third time, and the engine roared into life, making quite a noise on the now quieter road. Agnes, her heart racing, watching the back of the car emerge on to the road, turn very slightly off a little hump of grass, and swing round into the road. The lights came on. She knew she must let it get a little way away before she started her own car. He drove back the way he had walked from, back the way he had gone when she and Guy had followed him. Was he going to that very house where Guy had watched him? The house with the thatched stable? Could she in some way get there first and warn the occupants that their animals were in danger? No, she remembered Guy saying the little rough lane was the only access to the house. She had to keep a long way back. There were very few cars on the road now. Now and again a car would pass her, then go a little way behind Bill Lewis's car, then overtake it and disappear. Very occasionally a car came the other way, often without dipping its lights, nearly blinding anyone coming towards them, thoughtless, stupid. They came to what Agnes thought she recognised as the stretch of road where the turning he had taken went to the left. Two horses. Beautiful house and stable would not protect them now if this vile man had it in his mind to kill or hurt them. They arrived at the turning, at least the black car did. Agnes was well behind, confident he would turn. He didn't but drove straight on. Where were they going?

The whole situation was becoming more and more mysterious. Why had Bill Lewis shouted those words – what were they? Agnes could almost hear him shout them again in her head: 'Oh, for God's sake, shut up. It's your own fault.' What had he meant, what was her fault? Did he mean her affair with Guy Holstein – if one was going on? He must have some hold over her, to speak to her like that and make her accompany him to Lewes – if that was where they had been. The tractor had in its way been a blessing. As usual, Agnes thought, things often went her way, coincidences happened to help her.

Agnes thought as he passed the turning that maybe he was going to pick up a new partner or a new accomplice. This gave her a quick shiver of fear that she immediately pushed aside. Whether there were one or two men, she would have to follow. The black car went on, not particularly fast. Then suddenly, it pulled to the side of the road. The lights went out and Bill Lewis got out. He did not look to right or left. Agnes passed him, then drew her car to the side of the road, near a house entrance. She put out the Mini lights and followed. He walked a little further back from where he had left the car and turned into a small garden. The gate grated on the ground as he entered. The little garden was heavily overgrown and neglected, the front door badly in need of painting.

Agnes followed him, the flat rubber-soled shoes she had specially worn for this adventure making no sound. She was only about six feet away from him as he rapped on the door. There appeared to be no bell or knocker. There was no answer at first. Bill took out a cigarette and lit it. The lighter illuminated his face. It looked puffy and belligerent to Agnes. The cover given her by the shrubs and brambles was quite adequate.

At last the door opened a crack and a man's voice said, 'What do you want? Oh, it's you.'

'Yes, it's me.'

'Don't you touch Dolly.'

Bill Lewis drew on his cigarette and blew it towards the face showing in the crack of the doorway. The door opened a little further. 'I won't touch Dolly. The old nag is as safe as houses as long as you've got the money, Jack.'

The light from inside the little hallway silhouetted the man inside. He stepped back and Agnes got an even better view. He was fairly old, his back bent, his balding hair wispy round his head, and she could just see his feet thrust into check carpet slippers. 'I'll have it tomorrow, please, please.' The man sounded as if he was almost crying.

'Why tomorrow? What happened to today?' As Bill Lewis stepped forward into the light, Agnes could see he had a knife in his hand.

'I couldn't fetch me pension. I will tomorrow, I promise, I will tomorrow.'

Agnes watched Bill draw his thumb along the knife edge. 'Twenty-five quid? Don't know if that's worth waiting for. Some of my other clients pay twice, three times that to see that their gee-gees come to no harm.'

'Please don't hurt my Dolly. She's all I've got in the world, what harm has she ever done you?'

'None. It's what harm I can do her.' Bill dropped the cigarette on the hall floor and ground it out with his foot. He appeared to relent. 'Right. Day after tomorrow, I'll call again. No lolly, Dolly gets it.' He drew the knife across his neck.

Agnes felt physically sick. It wasn't just horse mutilation and killing that was going on here; there was a protection racket too. The day after tomorrow would be her turn to be on watch again.

To add to her disgust and horror, the old man was thanking Bill for the extra time. 'I'll have it. I'll have it,' he was saying.

Bill called back, as he strode down the little garden path, 'You'd better have, or else.'

He disappeared up the dark road and the house door closed. Agnes waited till she heard the rather rough sound of the engine start up and die away, then she found her way a little further to the back of the front garden and round to the side of the house. She switched on the torch that she had not dared to put on before. It revealed a rough-looking area of grass and a lean-to about twenty yards away. She went over towards it. As she did so she heard movement in the lean-to. She shone her torch in, just for a second. It revealed the tail and rear of a chestnut and white horse. It moved a little more and snorted as if the torch had slightly disturbed it. The horse's coat was as rough as the field. Agnes crept away, not wishing to disturb the animal any more. She made her way, slowly and carefully, back to the road, got into the Mini and drove home. All the way she was debating what exactly to tell Guy Holstein.

Agnes took Mac for a little walk and then gave him his supper. She suddenly realised she herself had not eaten so she fried two eggs and some oven chips with tomatoes and mushrooms. She had not really had time to think how hungry she was and enjoyed her meal. Afterwards she took a cup of coffee through to her sitting-room, pulled the curtains and put on the lights. She switched on the television to watch the late news. She realised she was not taking it all in, but she watched until it was finished and switched off. She made more coffee and sat down again to think, think, get what she had seen and heard into proportion. Not only that, she had to decide what to say to Guy.

Certainly she did not want to tell him about Lyn and the scene in the blue Volvo. Just how serious was Guy's affair with Lyn? Had Bill Lewis found out about it and was he holding it over her head, extracting money from her – or sex? Surely not the latter? She was sure Bill was homosexual. Had he a boyfriend? Was he, as John Merrill had been, keen on Guy? It was all too complicated to share at the moment, and after long careful thought, Agnes decided to keep her own counsel. Let Guy do his watch tomorrow night, and she would do hers the next. How she would handle it she had no idea, but if the past were to be trusted, something would happen to help her.

She telephoned Guy. 'Nothing much to report, Guy,' she said, imparting a little shadow of disappointment into her voice.

'You stayed late, Agnes. I telephoned you at home, it's cheaper than the mobile.'

'Yes, I did, Guy. I kept thinking I would leave, then decided to give it longer, you know how it is.'

Guy agreed. 'Well, my turn tomorrow, perhaps he will come then,' he said quite cheerfully, and rang off.

Agnes hoped and prayed that Bill Lewis would keep away until his promised visit the following night, but you couldn't tell what he would do. He might turn up to go and harass some other poor horse owner tomorrow night when Guy was watching. Still, she would have to take a chance. In some ways she hoped he might turn up and just go and threaten someone else with hurting their animal if they did not pay up. She was afraid if Guy came upon any real action, he might ring the police in desperation. Anyway, she had to let tomorrow take its chances.

Agnes went to bed. She felt very tired yet, perhaps because of the fried supper which she was not used to or perhaps because of the uncertainties surrounding the task she had taken on, she could not sleep. At about two o'clock in the morning she got up, opened the back door and wandered into the garden. Mac growled as they came close to her little wilderness. There was a sudden 'plop' in her little new pool, a frog perhaps. Then Mac sat down, his brown eyes fixed on something in the shrubs, then Agnes saw what he was so interested in. A fox was busily eating the dog food Agnes had put out the night before. The clouds shifted away from the moon and lit up his bushy tail. He turned and looked at Agnes, licked his lips. He had finished his meal. His eyes as brown as Mac's gleamed for a moment in the light of the moon, then he was gone.

Agnes felt so much better for seeing him, satisfied and with no need to commit murder on chickens, not for the moment anyway. 'Come, Mac,' she called and Mac toddled after her. As she reached the grass bank near her back door a hedgehog walked across the path slowly and with dignity. Mac would have interfered with the prickly animal but Agnes picked him up and carried him indoors. She felt a little calmed by her stroll in the garden and filled a hot water bottle to cuddle in bed. She tried to forget what might happen the evening after next and composed herself to sleep, but even when at last she did manage to drop half asleep, her dreams were of horses and she did not have a good night. Sometimes a restless night meant a headache next day. She hoped this wouldn't happen. She wanted to be alert, confident, carry out whatever decision she arrived at with success.

16

The next day Guy called in to see Agnes. She did not regret in any way not telling him of Bill Lewis's double dealing, but she did try to get out of him the extent of his affair with Lyn Marshall. He was not particularly forthcoming. 'Yes, we've been out and about a bit together,' was the extent of the information he would give and Agnes did not press it. But she could not help feeling that there was more to it. Muddled emotions and relationships seemed part of this whole scene. He told her he would be at their hiding place at four thirty and stay either until eight thirty or until, as he hoped would happen, Bill turned up and some action started.

The day passed slowly for Agnes after he had gone. She gardened and did several household jobs, then was interrupted at about tea-time by the figure of Violet, Pansy's sister.

'Hope I'm not interrupting you, Agnes. Just called in to see if you happened to be making a pot of tea?'

Agnes was quite pleased to see her. Violet Greenham was a more laid-back personality than her sister Pansy. 'Yes, do come into the kitchen, I'll make a pot.'

Agnes stripped off her gardening gloves and the two women made their way into the cottage. Violet sat down at the table.

'Phew, it's getting warmer, isn't it?' She took off the cardigan she was wearing over a rather pretty summer dress. 'I've really come to unload a worry on to you, Agnes.'

Agnes switched on the kettle and put out cups and saucers and a plate of biscuits.

'I'm really a bit worried about John. I don't think he's ever gone this long without even a telephone call. Pansy is worried, but of course her dear hubby doesn't want to know.'

Agnes shook her head. 'I don't know how I would feel if it were my son, Violet. You say it hasn't been this long before?'

'So Pansy says.'

Agnes poured boiling water on the tea and sat down opposite Violet. 'What do you think might have happened to him?'

Violet shook her head. 'Nothing, I should think. He's a very thoughtless chap, I always felt.' She sipped her tea with enjoyment.

Violet ceased talking for a moment, as if she were contemplating what to say next, then: 'Your garden is looking pretty, Agnes.'

Agnes smiled. 'I'm doing my best, but I don't know much about plants,' she said.

'It's Pansy I'm worried about, Agnes – she's so worried about John.' She paused and waited while Agnes poured her a second cup of tea. 'She went to one of those card readers. What do you call them? Tarot cards. Stupid, I think. Then the woman persuaded her to have a crystal something or other. I know nothing about it, but she told her some things about John and Pansy believes her – well, half believes her.'

Agnes was slightly interested, but became a good deal more so as Violet went on.

'She told her, first of all, that John was or had been in great danger, then that he was dead. The woman got quite upset in her trance or whatever she was supposed to be in.'

Agnes said, 'Yes, Violet, then what?'

Violet started on her second cup of tea almost as if she didn't want to go on. 'She said he was near a horse – well, that was ridiculous! He wouldn't be near a horse. He always hated horses ever since one threw him, or he fell off one, when he was about twelve. Broke his collar bone and injured his dignity, so that was ridiculous. I told Pansy so.'

Agnes felt a slight shiver run through her. She neither believed nor disbelieved in mediums or Tarot card dealers, but this was a little bit uncanny and too near the truth to be comfortable. She turned away to hide a half-smile. Near a horse, John certainly was, couldn't be nearer! 'Anyway, that's all nonsense, but it certainly is a long time since they have heard from him.' She said this, she realised, purely for something to say.

'Oh,' Pansy immediately thought of Amanda's horse Magic.

'But as I said, when that happened John was already on his way up north.'

Agnes nodded.

'What worries me, Agnes, is that Pansy is crying and carrying on as if John is dead. Edwin is pooh-poohing the whole idea and saying he doesn't want a poof for a son and doesn't care if he gets in touch or not and wishing he hadn't bought him the car.' Suddenly, Violet burst out laughing. 'I can tell you, it's pleasant visiting my dear sister at the moment.'

She got up. 'Thanks for the tea, now I must let you get on with your gardening.'

Agnes was not sorry to see her go. She did not dislike her, but the story of Pansy had been a bit disturbing, even for Agnes. She cleared away and washed up the tea things. Time for Mac's walk. She was rather glad to resume her ordinary duties again. Feeding the chickens, filling up their water cans, watching them running about, crowding round her feet without fear. She collected six eggs and determined to take them round as a present for Pansy. After all, she felt she did owe her something! How could that clairvoyant have ever said such a thing? It was a shot in the dark, surely? Poor Pansy would believe anything she wanted to and Agnes felt she was not in a very 'supportive husband' area. Violet would be good and sympathetic, she was nice, but the only one who really loved John was his mother. Homosexuality, even though it might shock and grieve her, would not, for a moment, stop her loving him. But Agnes was not moved enough to prevent her from feeling that even a mother's love for such a man was ill judged and stupid.

The rest of the day rather dragged by for Agnes. Guy did not telephone, so at last she was curious enough to telephone him. He sounded grumpy and irritable. 'No, nothing. No one has been near the car, not a soul, feel like giving up, it's . . .' A pause, he must be looking at his watch, Agnes guessed. 'Twenty past eight. Well, I'll give it till nine, then pack it in. What do you think?'

Agnes hardly knew what to say. She had stayed later than that, but she remembered she had been thinking of starting home and had only been stopped when Bill Lewis had turned up. 'Well, I agree, Guy. It's getting a bit late. Call into Rose Cottage on your way home and have a beer?'

'OK, will do,' he said.

Agnes was a little undecided about what to say to him. A twenty-four-hour cover was really what was needed, she supposed, but that, with the two of them, was quite impossible. However, she was relying on tomorrow. She knew Bill Lewis would be there. Would the old man have the money? She hoped so. If he hadn't, what would she do to stop Dolly, the 'old nag' as Bill had called her, from getting hurt? Should she tell Guy and take him with her? After all, he had disposed of John Merrill's body. Still the old feeling triumphed in her. She knew about Jack the old man and Dolly the mare, and she knew that Bill was running a protection racket to earn his money. No one else knew but her. Guy might be tempted to have him arrested and she wanted more than that.

Guy arrived at twenty to ten. It was raining, and this had not improved his temper. His hair was wet and he flung himself down on Agnes' settee without taking off his leather coat, which looked pretty rain-bespotted.

'Hot soup, or a beer, Guy?' Agnes asked.

'Oh, hot soup would be great. I stopped for a quick lager on the way home.'

Agnes switched on the television in case he should want to catch the news and went into the kitchen. After a few minutes she came back with a bowl of soup, a piece of French bread, butter and a wedge of Cheddar cheese. He wasn't attending to the television so she picked up the remote control and switched the set off.

'That's good – thanks, Agnes,' he said, spooning up the steaming soup.

When he had finished the soup and was tackling the bread and cheese, Agnes ventured to ask, 'Nothing this evening, Guy?'

He shook his head and swallowed the last of the cheese. 'No, but he'll probably come now I've left. I think we'll only catch him if we're there all the time, Agnes.'

Agnes nodded.

'We could use Amanda, I suppose, if she would do it?' he suggested.

Agnes made herself appear to ponder. 'Well, I suppose if he came to his car she could telephone us, but then we'd have to fetch – '

He interrupted her. 'We could put the Mini there for her, put her in it and just let her watch. At least it would be a pair of eyes.'

Agnes promised to think about it and, after a lager and the food, his temper seemed to have improved quite a bit.

'Thanks, Agnes. All that grub just hit the spot.'

She saw him to the door. 'Well, my turn tomorrow,' she said.

He nodded. 'Wish you better luck than me,' he said, and strode down the path and left, raising a hand in farewell and leaving the gate open behind him. Agnes sighed. How much easier in life, she thought, to deal with things yourself. She went down the path and shut and bolted the little gate.

Agnes had a much better night, in all probability because tomorrow it was her turn. She did not wake until a quarter past eight and then only because Mac, tired of waiting to be let out, had managed to get on to her bed with quite a bump. To sleep this late was unusual for Agnes; she was usually up and dressed by about seven fifteen. She felt better for the extra hour and stretched before she got out of bed, slipped her feet into slippers, put on a dressing-gown, went downstairs and opened the back door for Mac. There was a rap on the door. 'Damn,' Agnes said to herself; she hated being caught not up and dressed. It was the postman with a book she had ordered, a gardening book which she had seen on television and decided might be simple enough to teach her more than the little she felt she knew about plants. Shrubs of all kinds, and various different soils. It was too big to put through the letter box. However, the postman did not look at her and she doubted whether he had even noticed she was in a dressing-gown. She put the book on the hall table, gave Mac some hard tack, his favourite breakfast, and fresh water and went back upstairs to get dressed, resisting the longing for a cup of tea.

As she finished in the bathroom and got dressed, she realised she was dominated by the thought of Dolly, the white and chestnut horse with the rough coat, an animal she had only half seen. Supposing the old man, Jack, as Bill had called him, supposing he had been unable to get the money? Poor old man. It was his pension he had been talking about, little enough to live on, anyway. Supposing he hadn't been able to get to the post office? What would happen to Dolly? Poor creature, at the hands of that brutish hoodlum. She tried to banish the worry from her mind, there was nothing she could do until she was there, at the time and in the place. Then, as always, she would do what she had to do. What that would be, she, as usual, had no idea.

At last, dressed, her hair done, her usual small amount of make-up applied, she allowed herself the longed-for cup of tea and the luxury of opening her parcel. Agnes realised often how the discipline of her nursing life had to some extent remained with her over the years. She was glad of it. Today, or at least this afternoon and evening, was filling her mind with apprehension and yet she was looking forward to it.

After breakfast she took Mac to one of his favourite places for a walk. A small copse about a mile up the road. Agnes loved walking alone with Mac, thinking, planning ideas for Rose Cottage. Her latest idea was for a small conservatory, where she could grow tomatoes or bring on seedlings of her own. The day was warm and sunny but the trees and ferns in the copse made it an ideal place for Mac, who tore about after real and imagined rabbits, barked at noises, cocked his small leg when he wanted to and generally enjoyed himself. After about an hour he had had enough and Agnes put on his lead and they walked back to the Porsche. On the way back, Agnes planned to stop at Mrs Beaven's little shop. She was greeted by dramatic news.

'Oh, Mrs Turner, I'm so glad to see you. Just before you came in an ambulance went toward your place at such a pace, siren going and all. I hope it's not poor Mrs Merrill after all the worry about her son not getting in touch.'

'I hope not too, Mrs Beaven.'

Agnes made her purchases and drove the short way home.

Her first thought was had Bill Lewis attacked anyone, but why should he? He had blackmailed the Volvo out of Guy. If he told of Guy's involvement in John Merrill's disappearance, he himself would be at risk. Even Guy's involvement with Lyn was to his advantage. Did he even know John Merrill was dead? He must suspect, be almost certain, because of the car. However, there was one thing Agnes was pretty certain about – Bill Lewis did not know where John's body was. He had seen Guy in the car and that was all. Had he known where the body was he would almost certainly have confronted Guy with the fact and demanded more of him.

All these thoughts almost made Agnes forget Mrs Beaven's warning about the ambulance. There it was though, sirens no longer sounding, but its light still flashing, the back doors open, the interior empty. It was parked outside High Hurlands. Agnes ran the Porsche into her garage, took Mac out of the car and opened her front door. She put Mac in the kitchen, saw he had water after his long walk, gave him a Bonio and left the cottage, locking the front door behind him. Then she walked rapidly down the road into the tangled garden of her neighbours' house.

Amanda saw her from the front door and she ran down the steps.

'Oh, Agnes, I'm so glad to see you.'

'What has happened, Amanda?'

'We hardly know, Agnes, Dad came downstairs in his dressing-gown, he always fetches the paper and takes the mail in.' She stopped to wipe her eyes. 'He saw Guy walking down the drive and he called out, "Where are you going, Guy?" He was dressed only in his dressing-gown, like Dad. "Thought I saw someone running about in the garden, heard him from upstairs." That's all Guy said. Dad came in with the paper and shut the door. He thought he heard Guy come back in but he couldn't have – he's a bit deaf, you know, Agnes.'

The ambulance men were carrying a stretcher down the stairs. They started through the hall and Agnes had to stand aside to let them pass. On the stretcher was Guy, a bandage round his head and over one eye. One arm outside the red blanket was covered in an arm splint. He saw Agnes and tried to speak but his mother on the other side of the stretcher stopped him. 'Just rest, Guy, dear,' she said. 'You're badly hurt.'

Agnes leant nearer to him, her head almost down to the level of his. Luckily the paramedics had to slow up a little to negotiate the steps. 'It was that bastard Bill Lewis, he was in the garden. I don't know what for, perhaps looking for John's body.'

Agnes was thankful that all he could do was whisper. They carried him carefully down the steps and loaded him into the ambulance. Neither Mr nor Mrs Holstein made a move to go with him and Amanda looked too frightened even to speak.

'I'll go with him, I'm a friend of the family,' Agnes said and, before anyone could offer any other suggestion, she mounted the two metal steps and seated herself beside Guy who looked as if he had passed out. The one uncovered eye was closed, his face pale. The paramedics were busy with blood pressure, heart monitors and oxygen. Agnes was taken back to her nursing days. She thought how efficient they were and how much more they were allowed and also encouraged to do for the patient since her days in hospital.

When they arrived at Lewes hospital she was relegated to the waiting-room. An hour passed then a nurse called her into the department where the young casualty clerk took all the details. Agnes explained that she was only the next-door neighbour and had arrived at Guy Holstein's home only when it was all over and he was being carried out on a stretcher. His parents being rather elderly and his sister in shock, she had offered to come with him, otherwise she could be of little help. 'Apparently he was attacked in his garden, the garden of his house, by some marauder. The police have been called to his home and his parents are being questioned now.'

'How awful.'

'I saw the ambulance pass when I was in the village shop but of course did not know to whom it had been called.'

The girl asked no more questions.

'May I see the casualty sister?' Agnes asked.

When the sister came, Agnes asked, 'How is he, not too badly hurt, I hope?'

The sister was reticent as always when she learned Agnes was only the helpful next-door neighbour. 'He has a head injury so will be kept in for observation.'

'And his arm, I noticed it was splinted?'

'Yes, I'm afraid there is major injury to his arm which will have to be dealt with.'

At that moment a young nurse came up to the casualty sister. 'Mr and Mrs Holstein, the head injury's mother and father, are here, sister,' she said.

'Thank you, Joyce, put them in my office, please.'

The nurse paused, cast a glance at Agnes, then added, 'The police are here too, sister.'

'Do you need me any more, sister?' Agnes asked. 'I've left my house unattended and would like to get back.'

'Yes, of course. Thank you for coming with Mr Holstein, I'm sure his parents will be in touch with you.'

She turned away and Agnes made her escape. Maybe the police would want to get in touch with her later. If they did, so be it, but they would get no information out of her, indeed as far as they were concerned she would appear to have none to give.

This would mean that she was now the sole watcher. Her suspicions were aroused by this attack on Guy. Did it mean that when they had seen Bill Lewis casing the house with the stable and two horses and Guy had had to throw himself in the undergrwoth to escape being seen, Bill had actually spotted him, realised he was being followed? Is that why he had gone to High Hurlands early in the morning and attacked Guy? In either car he could have come and gone with ease. That was what Guy had said to her in that hoarse whisper before he had passed out in the ambulance. 'It was that bastard Bill Lewis,' had been his words. Well, tonight, and all nights, were hers now. She must take the risks, goodness knows how long poor Guy would be incapacitated. If he had a fractured skull they would keep him in the hospital a littler longer but his arm, obviously broken, would keep him from driving for weeks, perhaps longer.

The story she had told Mrs Tracy was that she was visiting a sick friend and it was better not to take Mac. This time when

Mrs Tracy arrived Agnes said she might be a little later back than usual. Mrs Tracy was always delighted to look after Mac and the longer she stayed the better she liked it. Agnes checked her torch, got in the Porsche to drive to Lewes to pick up the Mini, then returned to the hiding place to wait for Bill Lewis to come and collect his car. Then what? She had no idea, but whatever happened she knew, as she always did, that she could and would deal with it.

17

Agnes was seated in the navy blue Mini, screened by tree branches and dead brambles. She had broken off a small branch to make a slightly clearer view of the little track where the black car was hidden. She had toyed with the idea of lurking on the main road near where Dolly's owner lived, but she was afraid that Bill Lewis might decide to go somewhere else before he made his demands on poor old Jack. When he called on the old man, Agnes was determined to be there; her very presence as a witness to the affair might, she hoped, frighten the beastly man off. It might not, but whatever happened, Dolly must be protected. Anyway, she would act as she always did, spontaneously. Let, as she always did, fate take over.

By five o'clock nothing had happened, but it was early yet. Agnes telephoned the Holstein house and got no reply. She tried the hospital to ask after Guy, but got the unsatisfactory answer one always did when one admitted one was not a relative. Goodness knows she herself had given the same answer when she had been a ward sister. She realised now how unsatisfactory it must have been to the enquirer. Poor Guy and poor Amanda. Agnes hardly thought of the boy's parents, they were such an anonymous couple. That was rather cruel, she felt, but they did give that impression. Not like the Merrills, whose emotions – love on Pansy's part and a pretty strong dislike on Edwin's part – were not at all anonymous.

Poor old Pansy. When would it get through to her that she would never see her son again? When the police found out that the car had disappeared off the face of the earth? Or perhaps when time stretched out for years? The police would hardly search for ever for a missing person of John Merrill's age, gay and at odds with his father. After all, if he didn't want to come home ever again no one, not even the police, could force him to. He couldn't even be made to reveal his address. She wondered how Bill Lewis would handle the registration of his car. It probably wouldn't be a problem, false papers about cars were fairly easily come by these days when so many vehicles were stolen, burned, destroyed, or sold for parts.

Twenty to six. No sign of Bill Lewis. The cars flashed by in the rain, lights on long before it was necessary to see, but in obedience to the new 'lights on in inclement weather' rule. Twenty past six. Still overcast, but the rain had stopped. Agnes was glad she had a light macintosh on. It had been raining when she had started out. Five more minutes passed, then she saw him. Bill Lewis at last! No sign of the blue Volvo this time, he had just walked down the road from his parents' cottage. Thrust his way as he had before past the shrubs that hid his old car. As Agnes waited for him to drive out, a bus passed up the road towards Lewes. She thought for a moment of Guy, who had caught that bus and would have gone on catching it to pick up the Mini, to do his turn. She wondered briefly how he was and just how the injuries were that this man, who she was about to follow, had inflicted on him.

Traffic on the road thinned for a moment. She was ready to move out but in the brief silence she wanted the black car to move first. As usual the old engine did not pick up first time; it took three attempts before the starter got to it and the rough sound of the engine took over. Agnes watched him back out. He narrowly missed one oncoming car, who hooted at him. Agnes could clearly see the face Bill made and the two-fingered gesture he directed at the passing motorist who had nearly hit him. She let him drive a little way, then started her engine, came gingerly out into the road, nothing coming either way. It was still daylight, earlier than the visit he had made before to the old pensioner. The sky had lightened quite a bit, so no car lights were needed. She followed at a discreet distance, past the lane leading to the big house where Guy had obviously been seen by Bill and had got the beating up as a result. Agnes wondered for a second, as she approached it, whether Bill would turn up that lane again, either to do damage or to threaten it, but no, he continued on the asphalt to where he had gone before, to the owner of Dolly. This time, in daylight, Agnes felt things were going to be more difficult for her, she would be so easily seen. She needn't have worried. Before he got to where the old man lived he speeded up, passed the house and drew into a very rural-looking pub. He parked the car outside, got out, slammed the door and went in.

Agnes was for a moment at a loss. What could she do? Certainly not follow him in; he would recognise her immediately. Taking a chance, she drove into the little car-park and noticed a place which looked as if it led to the back of the public house. She drove round. A few chickens ran about the car. She reversed, then parked the Mini beside the blank wall at the side of the pub. She could just see the black car, which was parked with its bonnet towards the window of the pub. Bill Lewis would, when he came out, have to reverse. This would allow her – as she had the Mini facing the exit – to take her time in following him out. Maybe towards the old man's place or somewhere else? Wherever, she would have him very safely in her sights, that was what mattered to her. She did not expect him to stay long.

She was wrong. A whole hour went by and still the man did not emerge. Darkness fell. That was, Agnes admitted to herself, well worth waiting for. Car lights now flashed along the road to and fro. A couple of cars and a small lorry drove in and their owners went into the Black Horse, as the place was called. A couple of what looked like older husbands and wives walked off the road and went into the pub, which was now lit up and presented quite a cosy picture. Still Agnes waited. About another quarter of an hour went by, then Bill Lewis reappeared. Agnes could not see him until he reached his car, then she quickly put on her seat belt. She noted a tiny stagger as he stepped back to open the door wide and then he dropped his car keys and was a little bit uncertain when he bent down to pick them up. He got into the car, slammed the door, wound down the window and, after a moment or two, started up his engine. Again, as always, with this old car, making a coughing indecisive start, he reversed and drove out. Agnes waited until he was on the road then started her own engine and followed him out. She was so thankful for the dark, the first step in her favour. It wasn't far to the old man's house and from the way the black car was weaving it was just as well. Bill Lewis had obviously had quite enough to drink, and should not be driving.

He made it to the old man Jack's cottage. Agnes parked her car in the same place she had before, grabbed her torch, thanked goodness again for the cloak of darkness and followed him soundlessly up the path to Jack's front door. She was half-way up the path and Bill Lewis was almost at the front door when Agnes suddenly had an idea. She turned, ran back just as soundlessly to her car, grabbed the only weapon she had – although at that moment she did not think of it as a weapon – the cricket bat. She grabbed it by the handle, then went back the way she had already been, but this time she hid behind a large evergreen bush, its big shiny leaves and dead flowers concealing her nicely.

Bill Lewis rapped loudly on the door. Nothing happened. He rapped again. The lights were on in the downstairs room and hall. The door opened and the old man appeared as he had before, outlined by the light behind him.

'Oh, Bill. I couldn't go, I couldn't go, I couldn't get there, me back seized up.' He was clinging to the door, his back bent so far forward he had to look up at Bill Lewis imploringly. 'I'll get it, I'll get it.' His voice sounded old and quavery.

'Too late, old man, too late. Dolly gets it.' Bill seemed to be getting a real kick out of his threat. He was slightly drunk as Agnes could see. He leant against the wall next to the door and lit a cigarette. As Agnes saw his face, clearly lit up by the brief flame, a wave of hatred went over her that was consuming.

The old man was going on talking, pleading. 'Come in, Bill, I've got a beer, do come in and have a beer.'

'No thanks, I've got other things to do.' Cigarette in mouth, he unzipped the bag he was carrying and took out of the same knife he had before.

'Please, not Dolly. I'll get the money, it was only me back!' He came out of his door, he was begging.

Bill drew on his cigarette, then took it from between his lips and threw it into the bushes. 'Give over, Jack, you know you're too late. You should have got one of your mates to get your pension. I told you what would happen.' He pushed himself away from the wall and started towards where Agnes knew the horse was.

Jack tried to follow him, holding the wall, but he couldn't make it. 'Please, please. I'll give you extra, I will, I promise. Dolly's all I've got, she wouldn't hurt anyone, why should you hurt her?'

No answer from Bill, who walked out of sight. The old man stood there, helpless. He covered his face with his hand. Agnes had seen enough. Taking advantage of the old man's distress, his covered eyes, she ran past him, her rubber-soled shoes making no sound on the rough grass. Bill had reached the makeshift stable. Agnes heard the mare snort and whinny. Then she saw Bill Lewis give her a smart slap on the rump with the handle of the knife. Dolly turned round and ran into the field. The man followed her; the mare only trotted a little way, and stopped, sniffing the night air. Bill had dropped the black bag in which he carried the knife and approached the animal with the weapon only. Agnes drew nearer. Dolly kicked out, frightened perhaps by the man so near her. She struck Bill's shin with her rear hoof. He cursed the mare and raised his knife ready to plunge it into her neck. Agnes was very near now. She raised the cricket bat almost to shoulder height, then backward as if she was about to make a tremendous strike at a cricket ball. With all the force she could muster she bought the cricket bat forward. It struck Bill Lewis on the temple, there was a crunching sound. He toppled like a felled ox, the knife flying from his hand. Dolly cantered away, almost disappearing in the darkness.

Agnes looked down at her victim. She felt nothing at all except fear that he might be still alive. She raised the bat high again and brought it down hard, as he lay, head on one side, his legs spreadagled. The bat struck the same place again. This time the impact was more satisfactory to Agnes because the temple and side of his face was a mangled mess and the jawbone slightly showed through the skin and flesh. His legs twitched once, then he was still. Agnes walked across the rough grass to where Dolly stood. That was that, she thought. The horse killer and protection racketeer was dead. There would be others, of course, but at least this one had been attended to.

She made her way out of the field by another path. Reaching the road, she crept up toward the old man's front door. It was still wide open, the light shining out. As she watched she saw the old man making his way to the field. Well, she would have loved to have been able to help him, he was clutching his back in obvious pain. She would have loved to have gone up to him and said, 'It's all right, you will have no more trouble. Bill Lewis is dead and Dolly is all right.' What would he do, she wondered, ring the police? They would hardly blame him for the death of his enemy. No, she hoped the death would be put down to a kick from Dolly. The knife was there, the hoof mark she hoped would be on the man's calf. Let's hope the marks on the head would also be taken to be a kick from a frightened horse. She examined the bat in her hand. Certainly the end looked hoof-shaped and her latter blow had involved that part of the bat.

She drove the Mini back to Lewes, parked it, then fetched a magazine she remembered was in the Porsche, took it back to the Mini and carefully wrapped up the cricket bat. There was some blood and hair on it. She had been careful not to let any of that touch the inside of the Mini. She put the bat in the Porsche, locked up the Mini, got into the Porsche and drove home. She felt rather tired, but satisfied. She was pleased that whatever helped her when she wanted to inflict a justifable punishment had helped her this time. She thanked Mrs Tracy: Mac had been walked and fed. First things first, though. Always disciplined, before she did anything else she took the bat up to the bathroom, gave it a wash, then ran enough water into the bath to submerge it, added some detergent and left it to soak. Downstairs again, she put away the Porsche, locked the garage and poured herself a rather larger than usual brandy and ginger ale. After all, she felt she deserved it. A good task had been done.

18

Next morning Agnes woke early. She lay for a moment thinking of the good resulting from what she had done. Primarily she had saved the old man Jack from giving part of his money to a wicked cruel creature who deserved to be dead; saved Dolly, that rough-looking old mare, from mutilation, perhaps even death. Saved other horses and their owners who were or had been in Bill Lewis's mind. Rescued Guy from more injury. That attack surely would not have been the last. Saved him from blackmail over John Merrill's stabbing, the car and probably threats to tell of his liaison with Lyn Marshall. Amanda too, although she would not realise it, was revenged in some way for the death of Magic. The death of Bill Lewis would benefit so many people known or unknown. She remembered again the crunch the cricket bat had made when it connected, saw again Bill Lewis lying in the dark field, his face averted, the side of his head smashed in. A shock for the old man, who would call the police, tell of the threats by the man to his beloved mare. The police would find the knife with Bill Lewis's fingerprints on it. On examination the pathologist would find the bruising where Dolly had kicked out and landed her hoof on his shin, then they might, and probably would, think Bill had tried to hold Dolly by her mane, or in some way which had frightened the creature, and she had kicked out again, this time to greater effect. Perfect. Agnes visualised the scene once more, the man spreadeagled, the terrified mare, the pulpy mess which was the side of Bill Lewis's head, the darkened field, the walk back to the car. All over. She got out of bed and padded to the bathroom.

Last night she had telephoned Guy's parents. Guy was better. No fractured skull, though he had had to have nine stitches in his head wound. His arm had been set and he might be discharged in two or three days. Yes, he was allowed visitors and they were sure he would love to see Agnes. To make sure Agnes had rung the hospital and verified that Mr Holstein was now in the Accident and Orthopaedic Ward and was allowed visitors. She decided to go to Lewes before lunch, giving Mac a good walk in his beloved little copse on the way, and purchase a paper, although she doubted if the incident would have had time to reach any of the nationals yet. But she would make sure, and the local newspaper was not due out till the day after tomorrow. She would buy herself a really nice lunch in Lewes, maybe indulge herself with a glass of wine.

Agnes was very strict about drinking and driving, but she felt today she had special cause for celebration; she would leave the Porsche in the hotel car-park and walk to the hospital after her lunch. She felt that so much irritation and so many burdens from other people's lives had been around her. Now they were gone she could do several things she wanted to do, like plan and get built her conservatory, enlarge the chicken run. She did give a passing thought to Pansy and Edwin Merrill who would never see their son again but who, of course, would never be sure, and to Bill Lewis's parents who would be informed of their son's death and would grieve. But what had they brought into the world? A monster who was much better removed from it. They, of course, would not feel like that, but the truth was the truth: their son for a great many people's sakes was much better dead.

Agnes drove to the little copse for Mac's walk. The sun shone warmly and summer really seemed to be starting. Mac had his usual good time with his imaginary and real rabbits, catching nothing but enjoying pretending to. The place was, as usual, deserted. Agnes could never understand why so few people came here to walk their dogs, but was grateful for the fact. She could only remember meeting one man with an ancient, rather fat, grey-muzzled labrador, black and slow, who had regarded Mac's invitation to play with a look of disdain and had lumbered by him. She always carried a dish and a bottle of water for Mac. Once back at the car, she gave him a drink, backed out on to the road and continued her way to Lewes, enjoying the driving as she always did.

The Crown, an expensive and quiet hotel with a very good reputation for its food, was her object, but first she went into a newsagent's and bought the *Daily Mail* and the *Telegraph*. In the car she went fairly carefully through both newspapers, looking for a headline of some sort. HORSE MUTILATOR KICKED TO DEATH BY HIS VICTIM. She found nothing in either. As she refolded the papers and put them on the seat beside her, she concluded that it had happened too late to get into today's papers. With her usual 'Won't be long Mac,' she checked that the window was an inch open, the car was parked in the shade and Mac was comfortable. She knew he watched her as she went into the hotel but, alas, dogs were not allowed, or she would have taken him.

A waiter met her at the dining-room door, escorted her to her table and handed her the menu. He brought her the glass of dry white wine she ordered and left her to choose her meal. Choose it Agnes did, no expense spared, she was so pleased with herself. Smoked salmon as a starter, roast lamb, mint sauce, and her favourite vegetables, followed by crème brulée. She lingered over the coffee, toyed with the idea of having a kümmel, her very favourite liqueur, but decided against it as she had no idea how much alcohol kümmel contained. After enjoying another cup of excellent coffee, she paid her bill, a short walk for Mac before setting out on foot to the hospital, feeling complacent and well fed.

Whenever Agnes approached or entered a hospital her past came rushing back to her. Everything was different, she knew, she was well aware of it. Whether this was for better or worse she was never quite sure. She found the ward. Large posters and a very pleasant young receptionist in the front hall directed her. She asked the nurse who was just passing her, 'Mr Holstein?' For a moment the nurse looked puzzled, then her face cleared. 'Oh, Guy, Guy Holstein. Third bed up on the right,' she replied. She took some flowers from the visitors following Agnes. 'Thank you, I'll put them in water,' she said and disappeared.

Agnes walked up the ward and soon located Guy. He had no bandages on as when she had seen him leaving High Hurlands on the stretcher, but there was a row of stitches on his forehead, covered with some shiny skin dressing. The skin round his eye was purple. His arm was plastered from just below his shoulder to his hand and lay across his midriff. He smiled when he saw Agnes.

'Hello, Guy, how are you feeling?' She came up to the bed, drew out a seat from underneath it and sat down. 'I didn't know what you would feel like eating, so I brought you these.' Agnes put a large box of Melba Fruits on his locker.

'Thanks. I could do with one right now,' he said.

Agnes took off the cellophane wrapper and opened the lid; he put the box in the crook of his plastered arm and, with his good hand, took a sweet out and popped it in his mouth. 'Lovely,' he said.

'They say you will be out in a couple of days, Guy,' Agnes said.

'Yes, but not much use to anyone with this. They say I'll be in plaster for at least six weeks.'

She nodded. 'I'm afraid so, Guy. Tell me what happened. Do you remember telling me it was Bill Lewis before we got into the ambulance?'

Guy put another sweet into his mouth before he replied. Then he made a grimace. 'Yes, I remember seeing your face and telling you who it was, but that's just about all I do remember.'

'Do you remember him beating you up?'

'The police asked me that. I told them all I could remember, but I didn't tell them his name, Agnes. How could I? I knew he'd spill everything if I did.'

'What did he do, Guy?' Agnes put her hand on his, gently touching the fingers protruding from the plaster.

'Well, I heard this noise in the garden, an unusual noise. I heard a car too. I came down and went out of the front door. Dad had come down too, to get the paper, I expect. It was there on the mat. Then, someone came at me. Gave me a wallop on the head then hit me with something, like a thick piece of wood, I don't know. I saw him, then he must have seen Dad because he took off. I think I heard the car, I passed out. Mum and Dad, and Amanda, got me indoors somehow, I suppose, then the ambulance must have come. I was well out of it – all I remember is seeing your face and telling you. After that, blank.'

'Never mind, it's all over now. All you've got to do is get better.'

'That swine may come back, Agnes,' he said, turning his head away from her.

'He won't trouble you again, Guy,' Agnes said, glad to be able to reassure him.

At that moment Mr and Mrs Holstein came into the ward and Agnes got up.

'Don't go, Agnes,' Guy said.

'No, I only dropped in to see you were all right.'

Agnes pulled the seat out a little further to accommodate two people. She greeted Guy's parents. They tried to make her stay too but, when they saw she was determined to leave, they thanked her for coming and for being so helpful when their son was hurt. 'You must come and see us, Agnes.' Mrs Holstein would not leave go of her hand.

At last she managed to release herself, say goodbye and escape. It was then she got one of the greatest shocks of her life, the last thing in the world she had expected.

As she left the ward, in the corridor she met Mr and Mrs Lewis, both looking very old and very worried and upset. She almost collided with them and the nurse or sister who was with them.

'Mrs Turner?' Mrs Lewis looked at Agnes.

Before she could think, Agnes said, 'Mrs Lewis and Mr Lewis, what are you doing here?'

'It's Bill, our son. He is in Intensive Care, they don't think he is going to live.'

The nurse's eyes met Agnes' and she shook her head.

'We've got to go and talk to the surgeon, Mrs Turner, they don't think – '

The nurse stopped her. 'Come along, Mrs Lewis.' She shepherded them away towards a small room, the door of which was partially open. Agnes could see a dark-suited man sitting behind a desk, a stethoscope on the desk beside him. He had the tips of his fingers together and was gazing towards the open door.

Agnes moved away. 'Still alive,' she whispered to herself. He couldn't be, couldn't be. Had he been able to speak, to tell? She thought of the wound she had inflicted, the crunch, that final crunch. She had heard the bone go.

She made her way out of the hospital. Perhaps he was just still breathing, that was all. She felt no pity. That monster was not fit to live, he had to die. If only she had been in charge of him, he would die. Then she remembered in all her days as a nurse, she had always done her best for her patient and she was suddenly glad she was not in charge of this particular Intensive Care Unit. Had she been, she knew that she would have had to do her best for any patient in her care.

To say Agnes felt shattered would be an understatement. She was furious at her own inefficiency. She had intended to stop this dreadful creature in his tracks, stop him just as one day long ago, she had stopped a child abuser. There had been no mistake there. What could she do? She remembered the glimpse she had had of the consultant sitting in his room, looking as if he were waiting to impart bad news, maybe to the rather distracted-looking Mr and Mrs Lewis. Well, she would soon know. All she had to do was wait, wait for the return from Lewes of those two distracted parents, then go to express her sympathy but actually to find out if their son had been able to say anything before – as she hoped – he died. After what she had done to him, he must die!

She felt dead tired. She could not possibly wait around near Jasmine Cottage, she would have to go the next morning or – a better idea occurred to her. Why not offer to fetch Guy Holstein, if he were to be allowed home and find out then from someone if Bill Lewis was still in Intensive Care?

This idea did work out. Guy was to be allowed home tomorrow. Agnes rang his parents to find out.

'Oh, yes, he is to come home tomorrow, we were going to get a taxi.'

'No, please don't. I will fetch him, do you want to come with me?'

Agnes heard Mrs Holstein ask her husband. A whispered conversation went on. Agnes listened patiently, then: 'No. We will get everything ready here, but Amanda would love to come with you. He's to be fetched at three o'clock, after the consultant has seen him. Is that all right?'

'Yes indeed. Tell Amanda to come to Rose Cottage at two thirty, that will give us enough time.'

Many more thanks, and the telephone was at last put down.

Agnes could not eat lunch the next day. She went into the back fields with Mac and walked slowly round, her mind full of thoughts about what she perceived as her failure, the first failure she had ever had in dispensing justice. She felt a little sorrow for his parents, but of course they had little or no knowledge about the cancer on the face of the earth that their son was. They would suffer grief of course, but not as much as the people like poor old Jack, and probably many more victims, who had paid high prices for their animals' safety.

Amanda arrived promptly at two thirty, a suitcase in her hand. She held it up. 'Clean clothes for Guy, Mum packed it,' she said.

Agnes backed the Porsche out into the road. Amanda put the case on the back seat and got in. 'Poor Guy, he'll hate having a broken arm,' she said.

'Yes.' Agnes felt too preoccupied to answer. They drove to Lewes in almost complete silence. Agnes could feel Amanda occasionally glancing at her with curiosity, but Agnes could not dream up any kind of conversation. She could only think of the fate of Bill Lewis. What had happened to him, was he dead or alive?

Amanda seemed a little nervous when they reached the ward. 'I hate hospitals, Agnes,' she said.

A staff nurse came to greet them. 'We've come to fetch Guy Holstein, my brother.' Amanda stammered a little.

'Right, he's all ready except for some clothes, which it looks as if you've brought.' She indicated the suitcase.

They approached Guy's bed. The curtains were drawn round it. Inside the drawn curtains he was sitting on the bed.

'Hello, Amanda and Agnes.' He looked completely put out.

'How am I going to dress with this lot?' He moved his plastered arm.

'We will help you, Guy.' Amanda put the case on the bed, opened it and took out some jeans and a sweatshirt.

'I've no shoes, have I?' Guy sounded petulant and irritable.

Amanda looked at Agnes.

'Men are always like this. Help him get his jeans on, Amanda, I just want a word with sister.'

Amanda looked completely incapable, but Agnes had more pressing things to think of. Through the glass doors and window of the sister's office, she could see the staff nurse sitting at the desk filling in some form or maybe writing a quick report. She crossed the ward, knocked on the glass-topped door and, on the staff nurse's looking up with a 'Come in,' entered the little office.

'I just wanted to ask after a patient, a friend.'

'Oh, yes?'

'Bill, or William, Lewis. He was in Intensive Care when I was last here and I was afraid . . . ?' She paused.

The staff nurse's expression assumed a professional gravity. 'I'm afraid he died yesterday,' she said. 'I'm so sorry.'

Agnes felt her heart leap with relief. 'Thank you for telling me.' She left the office and went back into the ward to help Amanda with Guy. Her inner voice was chanting, 'He is dead, he is dead. I did not fail Dolly or Magic. Poor Magic died but at least he was old and then I didn't know he needed my protection, my help.'

Guy was dressed – well, almost. His temper had not improved. At last they were ready to say goodbye to the staff nurse who gave him his appointment card for the Fracture Clinic and also made an appointment for him to come to casualty to have his stitches out. Agnes felt she was on cloud nine. Once out of the front door, getting Guy into the car was a little problem, then they started for home.

19

The local paper was delivered the next day and its largest headline did much to comfort and reassure Agnes. DOLLY THE MARE KILLS ASSAILANT. Underneath, a very good picture of the mare, with Jack standing beside her, one hand patting her neck, a stick in the other hand, supporting him. The piece written about the incident did not mention any words spoken by the assailant, just stated that Jack Smith had summoned the ambulance and that was about all.

Agnes felt a visit to Dolly and her owner was important. Bill Lewis might have recognised her, who knows? He had after all lived long enough to be transported to hospital. He might have been able to speak. She doubted it, her nursing experience behind her might be wrong, but she doubted that. However, she must do a little checking for her own peace of mind. She did not want to see the police suddenly appearing at her door.

She scanned the two national dailies. One fairly small account of the affair with the headline HORSE MUTILATOR STRIKES AGAIN. No picture here. In the broadsheet she could find no reference. Magic, probably because he had died had been in three of the national papers and, of course, was heavily featured in the local paper although the Holsteins – being so reserved, Agnes felt – had not offered any old photographs or permitted any new ones.

A little happier having read the report, Agnes decided to make two calls, one on the Lewises to offer her condolences and one, because she really wanted to, on the old pensioner Jack. She had felt so much sympathy for his plight but had been unable to even let him know she was there. Now, thanks to the paper giving his picture and describing where he lived, she could go and see him, take him something for Dolly and for himself. She felt he wouldn't be one to receive many presents.

First she rang the Holsteins to ask after Guy. He was recovering, answered the telephone himself, sounded a bit grumpy and asked if he could walk down to Rose Cottage to see her. Agnes said yes, of course, but not today as she had a lot to do. 'Coping with the Mini – and have you seen the papers?' she asked. He hadn't yet, only just woken up.

'It's these beastly painkillers, they work too well, but at least they make my arm less painful.'

'Have a look at them, the news will do you good,' Agnes advised and very gently put the receiver down. She felt that at the moment Guy and Amanda were not priorities on her list.

She started out early in the morning, leaving Mac with Mrs Tracy who was going to do some jobs in Rose Cottage. First she drove to Jasmine Cottage. She half expected the two bereaved parents to be away, perhaps staying with relatives or friends, but they were there and Mrs Lewis opened the door.

'I just called to say how sorry I am, Mrs Lewis.'

'It's nice of you to come, Mrs Turner.' Her face looked stony. 'Do come in.'

Agnes went in, saying as she did so, 'Only for a minute.'

Mr Lewis turned round in his chair; his face too had a stony look about it. 'Who is it?' he asked.

'It's Mrs Turner, dear.'

'Oh.' He turned back. Though the day was warm there was a fire burning in the grate. 'I'm cold all the time,' he explained.

Mrs Lewis gaves Agnes a meaningful look. 'Bill's dead, we had the thing, you know, the support machine turned off. The doctor said his brain was all . . .' She stopped and tears came to her eyes.

'Good thing too, Mrs Turner. He was a bad lot, my son, a bad lot to do that to a horse. He was a poof too, he was no son of mine, he's better dead. The police told us he was demanding money and all sorts of dreadful things.'

Agnes did her best, but in the end she had to ask the question she had come to ask. 'Did he manage to say anything before he died?'

'Say he was sorry, do you mean?'

'No, say anything at all?'

Agnes waited while the handkerchief was got out and Bill's father blew his nose. Agnes wondered was there some feeling there, in spite of everything.

'No, he never spoke, couldn't. That horse had kicked his head in, crushed it. He never spoke to anyone.'

Agnes got up. 'Well, I'm sorry for you both and I felt I had to come and say so.'

Mrs Lewis got up from her chair too. 'That was nice of you, Mrs Turner. He was our son, after all.'

'He was no son of mine!' her husband almost shouted.

Mrs Lewis saw Agnes to the door. 'How could he have been so wicked, he was a nice little boy, good at school, no trouble.'

She broke down and Agnes patted her arm. 'I'm sorry,' she said and escaped. It was obvious the dying man had said nothing to them. Now she must go to see Jack and Dolly.

Agnes felt she had never had to tie up so many loose ends, which irritated her. Had she taken more trouble dealing out justice all this would have been unnecessary. Before she set off to see Jack Smith, she went up to Marshall's stables. Mr Marshall greeted her. She had half hoped to see Lyn but there was no sign of her.

'Ah, Mrs Turner, come to visit Maisie again?'

Agnes had more time to assess Eric Marshall. He was a handsome man, a good deal older than his wife, the sort of man Agnes could admire, a man who could dominate, get things done. Not perhaps the easiest man to deal with or live with.

'No. I've come to ask a favour of you. I know little or nothing about horses, but I believe hay is quite expensive.'

He nodded. 'It is, why?'

'I'm going to pay a visit to the old man pictured in the local paper this morning, with his horse that was responsible for Bill Lewis's death, apparently.'

'Yes, I saw the write-up, kicked his head in. Good for the mare, I say.'

'Well, I wondered, can one buy a bale of hay, get it delivered? Where does one go?'

'A corn merchant perhaps, but I tell you what, it didn't say if the old man stabled the horse, did it, or had some kind of shelter. Our van is bringing some fodder in today. I could get him to deliver a couple of bales to the old chap.'

Agnes was really grateful. She opened her handbag. 'How much, Mr Marshall?' she asked.

'Oh, nothing. Take it as a contribution to the old bloke for what he went through. I'll get them delivered this afternoon. Nice of you to take the trouble.' He walked with Agnes to her car. 'You always had a Porsche?' he asked, patting the car.

'For some years,' Agnes answered evasively.

'Rich widow!' His smile took away the impudence of the remark.

'Maybe,' Agnes answered. She turned the car and left, rather to her surprise thinking Lyn was a lucky girl.

But obviously she didn't think so, or why was she dating or having an affair with Guy? Eric Marshall had been so generous over the hay, she hoped the old man would be pleased. She stopped on the way to the house to buy a bottle of whisky. The old man must be so relieved to hear of Bill Lewis's death, but she had to make sure that he was unaware of who had really crushed his head in. After all, Jack had found him in the field, had realised he was alive and had summoned the ambulance. Had Bill Lewis spoken to him?

Agnes drove home first to see how Mrs Tracy was getting on. She called into the shop on the way. Mrs Beaven was full of news, but none of it was news to Agnes.

'How awful, poor Mr and Mrs Holstein, first poor Magic and now this. Do you think it was the same man, Mrs Turner?'

Agnes was again evasive. 'I really shouldn't think so, Mrs Beaven. I mean, why should he want to go back to the same scene when he had already killed the horse there?'

'I can't imagine. Perhaps it was just a burglar, but at that time in the morning?'

Agnes made one or two purchases.

'And that poor man in the paper this morning and his wonderful horse, kicked the man to death, serve him right, the man I mean. I'm glad he's dead.'

Harsh words from gentle Mrs Beaven, Agnes thought, but she was sure many people who read the big headline in the local paper, or the small piece in any of the national papers, would feel the same. The horse mutilator had met his just deserts.

She left the shop and made for Rose Cottage, Mrs Tracy and Mac. Mrs Tracy as usual had done the jobs set her perfectly and Agnes thought again as always how lucky she was to have her. She offered to stay and look after Mac as Agnes was going out again, but no, Agnes decided Mac would love the drive and maybe, if allowed, a run in the old mare's field for a change from his beloved copse. She paid Mrs Tracy, saw her away, locked up and got into the Porsche with Mac for her next, she hoped reassuring, journey.

Agnes set off. Mac, as a treat, sat on the passenger seat on his special cushion. The day was warm, sunny and one of the first days that really felt like summer. Agnes felt a shade of anxiety as she drove. After all, she was visiting the man who had actually found Bill Lewis, before the ambulance or police had come. The man on the ground must, even to an old man like Jack, have presented a terrible picture. Had he perhaps looked at the man at his feet, then called Dolly or gone to see if she was all right, then returned to his house, and telephoned? He walked slowly because of his back pain.

Agnes could not picture, or imagine, the sequence of events that had taken place that evening. She hoped to get reassurance and peace of mind from whatever Jack said. She was almost sure that the half-dead man, Bill Lewis, would have been incapable of speech, but 'almost' was not good enough! As she drove, she talked to Mac. 'What shall we say, Mac? How can we question him without arousing any suspicions in his mind?' Mac, as could be expected, gave little answer but only cocked his head on one side and stared at her, his brown eyes questioning and perhaps slightly puzzled.

Mac thought it meant a walk when Agnes eventually stopped the car outside the house where Jack Smith lived. The door was shut. Looking to one side, to the left where the field lay, she saw no sign of Dolly. She got out, holding the neatly wrapped bottle of whisky, and went towards the door. It opened almost at once. The old man stood there, slightly differently dressed from the times Agnes had glimpsed him before. He had on an old well-worn, leather waistcoat over a white shirt, from which his neck rose, old and scraggy. His face looked healthy enough, though, and the little white hair he had was mostly distributed in a ring round his head, the top shiny and bald.

'Yes?' He looked at the car, then back to Agnes. Before she could answer a huge tabby cat, fat and obviously affectionate, rubbed round his leg then it looked at Agnes and did the same to her, purring loudly at the same time. 'That's Daffy. You from the press?'

Agnes shook her head. 'No. I just saw the article in the local paper about you and Dolly and wanted to see if Dolly was all right.'

'Why?'

Agnes could quite understand the old man's suspicious attitude. 'Well, the horse belonging to my next-door neighbour was killed some months ago, and I wondered if this awful man had hurt your horse at all?'

Jack Smith relaxed. 'No, he didn't hurt her. She kicked out twice and got him. Once in the leg and then a real hard kick, which landed on his face. I think he must have got hold of her tail. She could never abide that.' He stood aside. 'Come in a minute,' he said.

Agnes entered a tiny little sitting-room. An electric fire was switched on, its bulbs glowing. The tabby cat came in with them and immediately curled up in front of the glow. 'He likes the fire on, thinks it's real, see?' Jack said, smiling for the first time.

Agnes unwrapped the bottle of whisky and placed it on the table. 'I hope you won't be offended, just a little pick-me-up,' she said. He looked at her, almost in amazement. 'I'm Mrs Turner, by the way.' Agnes held out a hand and shook his.

'Will you have one with me?' He looked at the bottle.

'No, I'm driving but I'd really love to see you having one, showing me you don't mind my bringing it to you.'

He twisted off the cap, fetched a surprisingly pretty tumbler from a cupboard and poured himself a small measure.

'Can't afford this, what with paying that beastly man twenty-five pounds a month, just to keep Dolly safe.'

Agnes at last dared to ask the vital question she had come

to ask. 'Did he speak to you at all – when you found him, I mean? It said in the paper you called the ambulance and the police.'

He sipped his whisky with obvious enjoyment. 'No, he couldn't speak. Old Dolly had done a good job on him.' He paused for a moment. 'I suppose I shouldn't say that, should I? But after all, the knife he intended to use on the poor old girl was there. The police picked it up, ever so careful, and put it in a plastic bag, you know, for fingerprints and such.'

'So he didn't speak at all?' Agnes asked.

'Nah, nothing, only gurgles, you know. The ambulance men told me they thought he was a goner.' He poured himself another wee tot of the spirit. 'So did I, and then I heard he died – the next day, wasn't it?'

Agnes nodded. 'Yes, he did, at the hospital.'

Jack shrugged. 'I can't say I care, Mrs . . .' He hesitated.

'Mrs Turner.'

He nodded. 'And the horse next door to you – dead, is it?'

Agnes nodded. 'Yes, though his young owner tried to stop the bleeding. She hasn't got over it yet. She almost had a nervous breakdown, poor thing. She had had Magic all her life, he was older than she was.'

The old man drank the last of his whisky. 'I'm glad you told me that, Mrs Turner. It makes me feel a bit better over what I did.'

Agnes looked at him. 'What you did? What did you do, Jack?' she asked.

He twisted the empty glass round and round on the table. 'Well, when I saw Dolly all upset and the knife, I just went mad. I stamped on his face, hard. I only had bedroom slippers on but I stamped as hard as I could. His face seemed to squash a little more.' He put his head in his hands.

'I don't blame you. People like him are just parasites, like cockroaches, they rot the world.' Agnes covered his old brown spotted hand with her own.

'Thanks,' he said, his eyes reddening with emotion.

Agnes got up. 'I've another confession to make,' she said.

'What about, Mrs Turner?'

'There's two bales of hay coming for Dolly, they should be delivered today.'

Jack looked almost ready to cry. At that moment a car drew up behind the Porsche; the stable owner got out, went round to the rear of his car and threw up the back.

'Here it is now,' said Agnes. 'Your hay, or at least Dolly's hay.'

Jack struggled up. His back was still giving him pain. 'I never knew I had so many friends,' he said.

Outside Eric Marshall was lifting a bale with apparent ease. 'The van wouldn't start, damned thing,' he said, in spite of his words smiling at Agnes. 'Where do you want this?'

'Over here, please.'

'The shed?'

'Dolly's shed isn't all that waterproof.'

Jack opened a door and revealed a cupboard-like space full of spades, garden forks and logs, a real higgledy-piggledy of land implements, all old-fashioned and well worn.

'Can I see Dolly?' Agnes asked, as Eric stacked the hay.

They all then walked a little further and the field became more lush and grassy. Dolly, hearing Jack's voice, came cantering up to them, her mane blowing in the light breeze. Eric Marshall patted the mare's neck. 'Rough Welsh job, aren't you, Dolly?' he said. 'She'll be hot in the summer. Do you have her coat cut?'

Jack shook his head. 'Too expensive to get it done now,' he said. 'But the trees give her plenty of shade.'

Agnes had an idea. The shed which acted as Dolly's stable looked dreadfully the worse for wear. 'Would you let my carpenter, the one who's at the moment enlarging my chicken house, come and repair your roof – the shed roof, I mean?'

Jack looked doubtful. 'Cost too much, thank you, Mrs Turner,' he said.

'No, let me do it in memory of poor Magic, the horse that was killed. We can even use the wood from his stable, because they are pulling it down.'

Jack looked rather as if he could cry again, but pulled himself together. 'I'd like that,' he said. Dolly came up near him and nuzzled his arm.

They returned to the cottage. Eric Marshall fetched the other bale out of his car and stored it in the cupboard in the house wall. He slammed the door shut, then went and closed his car's back hatch.

Agnes came to thank him for bringing the hay. 'How much do I owe you, Mr Marshall?' she said.

'A dinner date will do, Mrs Turner.' Eric Marshall mimicked her, speaking in the same rather prim manner. Agnes felt herself blush. 'I'll ring you, Lyn has your address.'

He reversed the car, speedily and efficiently, gave Agnes a quick smile and was gone. He drove fast and the wheels threw up a little mud as they went.

Jack walked back with her to her car. 'I don't know how to thank you, I just don't – and though perhaps it's wrong, I'm glad he's dead and I won't have to dread that knock on the door again.'

Agnes smiled at him. 'He's got his just deserts and I'm so glad Dolly was not hurt.' She got into the Porsche. 'I'll send Andrew Jones, the carpenter, to have a look at Dolly's house, see if it can be made a bit more waterproof for the winter.'

On the way home she stopped by an inviting field and gave Mac a good run. Walking round, watching Mac to see he didn't go too far astray, she found herself thinking of Eric Marshall. How old was he, late fifties perhaps? Then she called Mac, put on his lead and gave herself a little telling off. 'He's married, for goodness sake!' she said aloud. But as she drove home she could not forget his strong figure, lifting those bales of hay as if they weighed nothing, and then asking her to keep a dinner date. Would he telephone her? Well, time alone would tell that. At a traffic light waiting for green she suddenly leant and gave Mac a kiss on the top of his head. He looked at her surprised, she wasn't one for kissing, but just then she felt like it.

20

Two days went by and Agnes was able to get her domestic chores done. The carpenter made a good job of enlarging her hen run. She motored him over to Jack's and he agreed to fix up the roof of Dolly's makeshift stable. Agnes took Amanda with her and introduced her to Jack and then Dolly. Dolly had been clipped by someone from Marshall's stables and looked quite stylish. Amanda fell in love with the mare and even rode her round the field, bareback. Looking at Jack's face as he watched the carpenter measuring up the wood needed for the roofing and wall of the old shed-like place, Agnes was aware of the difference in the old man's looks from when he had stood confronting Bill Lewis, alone, frightened for his horse, in pain, and wondering where the money was to come from to keep his beloved animal safe. Many people would have been shocked, thought that she was wrong to rid the world of such evil, but not for one moment did she doubt her own judgement. Bill Lewis was gone and he deserved to go. No court could fine him, slap his wrists or even imprison him for a short time and be under the impression that that would quell the evil in him, make him better, teach him to be a good and upright man. No, her method was and always would be the only way to act. Get rid of the evil-doer, preferably caught in the very act.

The third day dawned wet and windy, the flowers in the garden waving and blowing about. Agnes' trip to the chicken run, now recreosoted and larger, had to be made in a mackintosh. Two more chickens had been added to her flock and they were all strutting about seemingly oblivious to the rain. Agnes, having fed them on the wet grass under their run, stood for a moment, wondering was it worth having a perspex roof put on the run. As she stood thinking, a voice said behind her, 'I bet they think the accommodation is the best ever.'

Agnes turned: she was not surprised to see Guy, a mac

carefully draped over his plaster, but she was very surprised to see who was with him – Lyn Marshall. Her hair was bundled into a yellow rain hat, and a yellow mac and wellingtons hid her slim figure and trim ankles. She smiled widely at Agnes.

'Guy tells me you rescued this lot from a battery – what a great thing to do.' She pointed at one of the hens. 'Look, that poor thing is still raw round its neck.'

Agnes nodded. 'Yes, there are two like that, two new inmates, but their feathers grow amazingly quickly.'

'I'd like to do that, I think it's brilliant. May we come in and have a cup of coffee? Guy said you wouldn't mind.'

Guy laughed, putting his head back, the rain falling on his face. 'I never mentioned having the coffee, Agnes, Lyn's making that up.'

Agnes was genuinely pleased to see them and led the way into the house. When Lyn took off the rain hat and mac, her mane of golden hair, straight and silky, fell round her face and on to her shoulders. Both hat and macintosh were dripping with rain water.

'Where shall I put these?'

Agnes took them to the downstairs cloakroom and the girl followed her with Guy's macintosh. Then they all trouped into the kitchen. The golden girl, as Agnes named her in her thoughts, did not sit down, but went towards the dresser where Agnes had a row of pretty flowered mugs hanging.

'Oh, pretty. Can we use these?'

'What cheek, wait till you're asked, bossy cat!' Guy said, and looked at Agnes. 'Can't take her anywhere. She's the most laid-back girl in the south of England,' he said grinning.

'Yes, let's,' Agnes said. It was pleasant having these two young people in the house. She got out her percolator and spooned in coffee.

'Look at that, real coffee – and look at that.' This was directed at Mac who, having had his walk and a meal, had been having a quiet nap, heard the voices in the kitchen and decided to have a look-see. 'A whisky dog, how lovely. I didn't know you had a dog, Agnes.'

Lyn approached Mac in the way Agnes approved, not making a sudden sweep to pat his head, but bending down and offering him her closed hand to smell. Mac approved, licked it and allowed her to pat him.

As she did so, Agnes smelled her perfume. 'Sublime by Patou,' she said.

Lyn nodded. 'How clever of you to recognise it, do you use it?'

Agnes shook her head. 'No, I use Joy, the same perfumers.'

Lyn nodded. 'Yes, that's right. I always think Joy is a bit more suited to the older woman.' Then she realised what she had said.

'Whoops,' Guy said.

'Oh Lord, trust me,' Lyn said ruefully.

Agnes laughed. 'Why whoops? I *am* the older woman.'

'Oh, shut up,' Guy said. 'Concentrate on me. I'm the invalid, I want a pillow for my arm. Someone's bound to use the word well-preserved if we are not careful!'

Agnes fetched him a cushion to put on the kitchen table so that he could rest his arm on it.

'That's better,' he said.

Lyn sat down to take her wellingtons off. 'They squash your toes, wellies do,' she said.

Suddenly Agnes, pouring the coffee, saw a picture of a strong, man lifting a bale of hay out of the back of a car. Lyn's husband. He had not telephoned her for the suggested dinner date and she knew she was disappointed, not severely so, but just a little.

After coffee, Agnes expected them to go. As Lyn slipped back into her wellingtons and crammed her hair under her cute rain hat, Agnes realised she had brought Guy back from somewhere and was now presumably going back to her husband at the stables. Quite naturally and unashamedly having thanked Agnes for the coffee and cuddled Mac goodbye, she came round the table, bent down and kissed Guy on the lips. It was not a long kiss, but a loving one. Guy attempted to get up but she stopped him.

'No, darling, don't get up and don't be silly and refuse to take a couple of those painkillers the hospital gave you, they may give you a better night.' She turned to Agnes. 'He's afraid of getting addicted.' She smiled and made a little face at Agnes. 'I expect they are only paracetamol or something harmless.'

They walked out of the kitchen, leaving Mac sitting next to Guy, leaning on his leg; he approved of him. Lyn turned to Agnes at the door. 'He's such a nice guy, Agnes, he really is. I wish . . . oh hell, it's still raining.'

Agnes was not sure what Lyn had been about to say. She thought it might have been 'I wish I was free,' but of course she could well be wrong; perhaps Lyn was not suited to be a poor man's wife.

She turned suddenly to Agnes and kissed her on the cheek. 'You've made a lot of difference to Guy and Amanda. Poor little Amanda.'

'I'm glad if I really have, but why do you say, "poor little Amanda"?'

Lyn shrugged. Two strands of her blonde hair fell from the hat down the sides of her face, making her look younger and prettier still. She went out to her green Volvo.

As Agnes walked back into the kitchen, she tried to stop herself thinking, She's so young for Eric. He must be at least late fifties. When she walked in, her thoughts were almost echoed by Guy.

'She's too young for Eric, Agnes. Much too young.'

She put the coffee back on the ring for another cup. 'Maybe he's much too old for her, Guy,' she said.

Guy eased his arm on the cushion in front of him on the table and frowned. 'That's what I said.'

Agnes smiled a little secret smile to herself. 'Not quite, you didn't say quite that, Guy,' she said. 'More coffee?'

He pushed his cup across the table towards her. 'Yes, please,' he said. 'I know I told you I didn't love her, but I'm mad about her, Agnes, I really am.'

Agnes poured the coffee but did not answer him. After putting the percolator away, she came back and sat down. 'And is she mad about you, Guy?'

He put sugar in his coffee and stirred and stirred. 'Yes, she is, but she's afraid of her parents. They've very strict Catholics, divorce is absolutely out.'

Agnes nodded. 'I understand, but didn't I see you coming out of their house in the car, you remember I mentioned it?'

'Yes.' He looked slightly ashamed. 'They were away, Lyn was looking after the house and we ... Oh Eric knows, at least I think he does, but he's a strange chap. Loves those horses and his work. She's got to leave him, Agnes. She doesn't love him, never did, she says.' He got up suddenly, supporting his plastered arm. 'This hurts,' he said.

'I've got some paracetamol.'

Agnes left the kitchen and went upstairs. Before she opened her medicine cupboard she looked at herself in the mirror. There were lines at the corner's of her eyes. She touched her throat, did that look scraggy and her eyelids crepey? She opened the cupboard door, blotting out the vision of herself. 'For goodness sake,' she said aloud, took the paracetamol bottle and went downstairs.

At the table she shook two out and put them beside Guy's coffee cup. He swallowed them.

'After all, she married him. Why, if she didn't love him?'

'What?' Guy looked up at her as if in her absence, he had lost track of the conversation, then he picked it up. 'Oh, married him, yes ... well, she wanted to get away from home, I think. He was keen on her, she loved horses. I suppose that all added up.'

Agnes could hear the sarcasm in her voice as she answered. 'All very valid reasons for getting married, I suppose.'

Guy did not catch the sarcasm because he nodded miserably, gently rubbing his hand up and down the plaster cast.

'Those tablets will soon begin to work,' Agnes said kindly – rather, she was aware, to make up for her last remark.

'Yes, they do ease it off a bit.'

Agnes could not resist asking the next question. 'If you and Lyn decided to – how do you call it – become a couple, how would you live, without a job?'

Again he looked a bit sheepish. 'Lyn's got plenty. An uncle

left her a lot of bread when she was eighteen. She's a good one with money too. Eric's pretty loaded. She wouldn't want any of his money if she leaves him for me.'

Agnes suddenly felt sick of the whole conversation. She almost dismissed Guy with an 'I must get on' sentence. Guy finished off the tale with: 'I mean, when Lyn is forty, he'll be seventy-three.'

Agnes walked with him to the door. Mac hated rain, hated getting his coat wet. He went in front of them, cocked his leg on a small camellia and dashed indoors again. He had needed quite a long wee to make himself comfortable. 'That'll do that camellia a world of good,' said Guy, laughing. Agnes was glad the atmosphere had lightened and watched from inside her front door as he walked down the path in the rain, his broken arm carefully covered by the raincoat. He waited at the gate, shut it carefully for a change, and turned towards his own house. Agnes closed her door, went into the kitchen to wash up and tried to marshal her thoughts into some kind of order. You are nearly fifty-seven, for goodness sake, she thought, and anyway he hadn't telephoned.

Agnes asked the Holsteins to drinks, deciding to give them just white wine. They came, Mr Holstein limping very noticeably with a bad knee. Amanda looked rather miserable and, as usual when she was with her parents, said little. On the whole it was a pretty stiff little party, but Agnes felt she could not show an intimacy with Amanda and Guy without occasionally being in touch with their parents.

During the conversation, Agnes thought she would try out an idea. She turned to Mr Holstein. 'I wonder if you could help me, you know the district so well. You don't know anyone who has a vacant garage to let, do you?'

Husband and wife looked at each other, both obviously trying to help, then Mrs Holstein came up with an idea. 'Yes, Mrs Beaven, at the shop. She's got an empty garage. She used to drive but her eyesight failed a little so she got rid of her car, I don't know if she would . . . ?'

Agnes thanked her with real gratitude. She had never noticed the fact that there was a garage at the shop. She needed to fetch the Mini from Lewes and put it somewhere until she decided what to do with the little car.

The next day she drove to the village shop and noticed for the first time a small garage with wooden doors and a lock and padlock, well back from the shop and the road. The run in was clear and consisted of earth and grass, the symmetrical ruts showing where a car had been driven to and fro.

Mrs Beaven, always very pleased to see Agnes, was agreeable. 'Yes indeed, Mrs Turner. I always said I wouldn't let it in case they proved to be unsuitable, but with you . . .'

Agnes smiled. 'I'll try to be a suitable tenant. I may take the car out now and again, my friend wants me to see it remains roadworthy and she may be away many months, she's not sure.'

Agnes named a rent. Mrs Beaven would not accept so much and insisted on a lower amount, something Agnes felt, in this money-grabbing world, was very nice and unusual. So she took a taxi to Lewes, and drove the Mini back to its new home with great enjoyment. She really liked the little car.

Mrs Beaven gave her the key to the old-fashioned padlock. When Agnes arrived home, she telephoned Mrs Holstein to thank her for the success of her suggestion. and then asked to speak to Guy.

'Hello, Agnes. What gives?'

Agnes told him the Mini was garaged.

'Oh yes, Ma told me. That was a good idea "of hers".'

'I want to talk to you about it, Guy.'

'OK, when?'

'Well, we will have to wait until your arm is better, then you can drive it.'

'Brilliant, and thanks, Agnes.'

'There are conditions though, Guy.'

'What? I don't mind any conditions to drive that little baby.'

Agnes smiled to herself. 'Don't be too sure, the conditions are tough ones,' she said, but she said it lightly. 'I'll see you tomorrow sometime, say tea-time – and bring Amanda.'

'Will do.'

Agnes put the telephone down. That little car might be used to make a big difference to how things were at the moment in the Holstein family. She felt happier, too, that the Mini was safely locked up in Mrs Beaven's nearby garage and not at risk, left as it had been in the Lewes public car-park.

The telephone rang again almost immediately.

'You are a very popular lady! I've tried to ring you several times but you're always engaged.'

Agnes recognised the voice at once: it was Eric Marshall.

21

Guy and Amanda arrived in the morning, Guy looking highly expectant and Amanda slightly apprehensive. Agnes made the inevitable coffee, which apparently they didn't get often at their parents' house, except when there were guests. 'Coffee is not good for you,' Amanda had once quoted her mother as saying. 'Too much, I agree.' Agnes had been as diplomatic as she could in her reply, but they always enjoyed the chance to have a cup, or maybe two, in her house.

'Now, a conference,' she said when the steaming cups of her very good coffee were placed in front of them.

'Yes, Agnes?' Guy leaned forward eagerly.

'How is your arm, by the way?'

He moved it. 'Much less pain and I can move my shoulder more easily and my fingers.' He moved them; Agnes noted that the swelling of his fingers had gone down and that they were very nearly back to normal.

'Well, here is the deal.' Agnes stirred her coffee and played out the suspense a little. 'I keep the Mini and pay Mrs Beaven's very reasonable garage fees. Licence and insurance are also my responsibility. Now yours, Guy.'

'Yes, I'll do anything.'

'Well, with a car, or the use of one, you may find it easier to get a job once your arm is back to normal, right?' He nodded. 'The other condition is that you teach your sister to drive!'

Guy looked slightly taken aback by this, Amanda too.

'Oh I don't think I could drive, Agnes, Daddy says...' Agnes put up her hand but it did not quite stop Amanda's protestations. 'He says I'm too nervous and I'm sure Guy would get mad with me.'

Agnes stopped her. 'While Guy's arm is still in plaster, I will do the teaching. We will put L plates on, and off we go.'

Amanda looked slightly pacified at this. 'Do you think I will be able to drive, Ages?'

'Of course I do. Why not?'

Even Guy chipped in. 'I think you will, Am, you're not daft, even if you look it sometimes!'

Amanda smiled and hit out at him quite playfully.

'Then, I have another idea. I wondered whether we could set up an agency, the three of us, give it a name and find, or try to find, missing and strayed animals that people have lost.'

Amanda's face really lit up at this. 'Oh, you mean like a tabby cat missing for a week, or a black dog lost after a walk?' She stopped, her usual shyness getting the better of her.

'That's it exactly, Amanda. Charge a small fee, or take the reward offered.'

Guy did not look as enthusiastic as Amanda. 'Just animals, Agnes?' he asked.

Agnes shook her head. 'No. If we got practised at tracking down animals, why not people? Why not form a real detective agency, the three of us? We've got two cars, mobile telephones, then perhaps we could make a name for ourselves.' Agnes suddenly felt her own enthusiasm rising as she talked about it. It would help Guy, perhaps stop the trek to Lewes to the Job Centre?

'When will you start teaching me, Agnes?'

Agnes laughed. 'Don't look so frightened, Amanda. We'll start on the quietest lanes and I promise I won't beat you up, all right?'

They all stood up, Agnes taking the cups and putting them on the draining board. Mac, who had been sitting on Amanda's knee through most of the talk, brought his lead in. When Amanda visited, Mac always became a lap dog.

'I can take a hint, Mac.' His tail wagged briskly.

'What a lot you've given us to look forward to, Agnes,' Guy said, his face serious. 'A detective agency!'

Agnes remonstrated. 'Now, Guy, it's only, at the moment, a very small pipe dream, that's absolutely all,' she said. 'Amanda, day after tomorrow, if it's fine and sunny, first lesson. Ten in the morning on the dot.'

She had not suggested the next day because she had accepted a dinner date with Eric Marshall and intended to get her hair done, have a manicure and maybe a facial. She wanted to look her best. She was not quite sure if she was making a bad situation worse. But she reasoned, perhaps she had to admit unreasonably, that if Guy and Lyn got together, Eric would be on his own. She also had to admit that if he decided to find someone else, it would probably not be anyone her age. Agnes was surprised at her own thoughts. After Bill's death she had been so determined never to form another relationship and here she was, getting her hair done, tarting herself up. Anyway, she was aware that she was looking forward to the dinner date with a good deal of pleasure and, she argued with herself, why shouldn't one look one's best even out of politeness towards the person, man or woman, who was asking you out? None of this did anything to lesson her awareness that she found Eric Marshall attractive.

Agnes was pleased when Eric Marshall phoned as she had been pleased when he had suggested the dinner date, although she had not been at all sure it was not merely a remark thrown off at the time they were both involved in the same adventure and dealing with the same incident. She had found his way of putting the invitation on the telephone tactful and pleasing.

'I do hope you haven't forgotten my suggestion to have dinner together to celebrate Dolly's new, or rather repaired, makeshift stable?'

'No, I hadn't forgotten and would like to.'

'Good. I thought Jack a nice old fellow and that protection racket disgusting and, I hope, rare.'

'Yes. The man died, I understand,' Agnes said.

'Good thing.'

They went on to arrange the meeting, Eric suggesting a hotel that Agnes did not know. 'Food's good and no music. I'll call for you.' He sounded like a man you did not argue with. 'Look forward to seeing you again.' He ended the conversation almost abruptly.

The day she was to meet him in the evening, Agnes woke with a sense of pleasant anticipation. She curbed the feeling by telling herself that it was to be just a one-off platonic meeting, then she wondered why he had chosen a hotel she had never heard of instead of Shelly's or somewhere well known. Perhaps it was because he did not want anyone to see them together. 'Oh, come on, Agnes,' she said aloud to herself. 'He's just taking you out to dinner to celebrate Dolly's stable being reinforced and because he likes entertaining people.' Why not ask Lyn too, then? Agnes got up and in the bathroom she studied her face again in the small mirror. Mac stood outside the door. He hated the bathroom because sometimes Agnes put him in the bath, and that was not enjoyable to him. In the corner stood the cricket bat, the wood still slightly darkened, not quite dried out since its washing and soaking.

Agnes dressed, let Mac out and made tea. She had an appointment to keep at her hairdresser's. She sat at her dressing-table looking at herself in the mirror. She leaned forward to see her image better and noted the slight lines at the corners of her eyes and again the slighty crepey wrinkles on her eyelids and the almost imperceptible deepening of the lines round her mouth.

She spoke to herself almost sternly. 'Come on, stop this! You are almost fifty-seven years old. Just supposing Lyn does leave him, goes off with someone like Guy, do you think he would want someone your age? No, he would look round for another young, pretty, vivacious girl, maybe a little older than Lyn but...'

She felt annoyed with herself. Rescuing battery chickens, getting Amanda driving and Guy working, these were her aims and objects at the moment. 'Spinster of this parish,' she said to

Mac who had come back in from the garden. 'Come on, Mac, hairdresser's. We must look as good as possible for tonight's date.'

She put him in his accustomed place in the back of her car, and locked the front door. The morning was warm and sunny. Agnes wondered, should she call into that little boutique in Lewes and get something new to wear tonight? No, she decided she would not. She had several dresses to choose from for such a meeting, why worry so much about how she would look when her host would hardly notice what she had on?

'Going somewhere nice, Mrs Turner?' the manicurist asked, smoothing cream into Agnes' hands.

Agnes answered rather shortly, 'No, just dinner with a friend.'

The girl smiled up at her. 'You have very nice-shaped nails, Mrs Turner,' she said tactfully.

Agnes softened a little and mentioned the name of the hotel where she would be dining.

'Oh, very posh, very expensive though.' The girl used the file expertly.

'I've never been there,' Agnes said.

'Oh, it's one of the best hotels. I've never been there either but I've had clients who have. They said it's got one of the best cooks, chefs, in the south of England, one lady said so anyway . . .'

Agnes digested this with some interest. Little did she know it then, but – though the food might be good and the chef a genius – it was what she learned in the conversation with Eric Marshall that was going to be the real feast.

Amanda was waiting at her gate when she got back. Mac bounded out of the car to meet her; he was very fond of Amanda.

'I just came to say . . .' She stopped and looked at Agnes with real admiration. 'Your hair looks really lovely, Agnes.'

'Good, I hoped it would.'

They went into the cottage together. 'I need a cup of coffee, want one?'

Amanda nodded. 'Yes, please,' she said.

'First lesson in the car tomorrow, Amanda,' Agnes said, getting two mugs down from their hooks.

'Yes, that's what I cam to say. I thought I'd be frightened stiff but I'm not. I told Mum and Dad and they tried to put me off, but I didn't let them.'

'Good again, Amanda. You will soon learn and it will make such a difference to your life.'

They drank their coffee and Amanda showed more animation than she had ever done before. The horror of Magic must be fading away. She would, Agnes felt, always remember it, but perhaps that curious blankness that had clouded her mind after the terrible event might mean that she never fully recollected the details.

After she left, Agnes opened her mail. Her bank statement, a very healthy one, pleased her. She was not overfond of money, but being poor for much of her early life meant that she appreciated the fact that she was now able to buy the Mini, spend quite a bit on clothes, take her friends out for a decent meal without leaving a noticeable dent in her current account. When you had always had money she was sure it was different, but money coming suddenly, as hers had, was a surprise and a comfort. She never forgot to thank the old lady and the fluffy white, blind cat who were responsible for her fortune. The photograph of that little cat in a silver frame adorned each mantelpiece as she had moved from house to flat and from flat to cottage, and its blind eyes looking out never ceased to remind her of her good fortune.

The other mail consisted of circulars, one of which she had been waiting for, a catalogue of conservatories. She leafed through it, looking for ideas. She felt that now she owned a cottage, it was time she began to know a little more about cottage gardens. Agnes was always thrilled by learning something new. Her nursing exams had never worried her. Unlike the other nurses, or most of them, she was not often, or really almost never, asked out on dates, so she had plenty of time to study. Rather than admit she was unattractive to men, she had delved into her anatomy and physiology books and passed her exams with ease, sometimes earning praise for her knowledge and high standards. Money had changed that. She had learned that attractiveness could be bought and manufactured if one could afford to pay the right hairdresser, buy the right expensive make-up and, most of all, invest in the tasteful and flattering clothes whose cost had at first appalled her, but to which she had now become accustomed.

Agnes had just a cup of soup for lunch, and gave Mac a good walk, her hair carefully scarved. Guy called, his face lit up with what Agnes felt was some hidden secret. The secret was soon let out – obviously he couldn't keep it in.

'Lyn's going to ask Eric for a divorce, Agnes. Isn't that wonderful news? She wants to marry me.'

'Wonderful news for you, Guy, but not for Eric perhaps?' Agnes tried not to sound reproving, but she wondered what effect Lyn's news would have on her husband and whether she would tell him today.

Guy confirmed her mental question. 'She's gone home to tell him today.'

Agnes hoped this announcement would not upset Eric so much that he would want to cancel their dinner engagement. No such cancellation came, however, much to her relief.

During the early afternoon Pansy Merrill called on Agnes. She brought some begonia plants still in their garden centre box for Agnes.

'I've bought too many and wondered if you could find room for these in your front garden. I know they are very ordinary, but they do flower for a long time.'

Agnes thanked her. 'I don't really know much about plants, Pansy,' she said. 'I'll put them in tomorrow. Thank you very much for thinking of me – come in.'

Pansy came in, but refused tea or coffee. 'I'm still worried, very worried, about John, Agnes. It's five months now.'

Agnes turned away from Pansy, putting the small tray of plants on the kitchen table. 'Come and sit down, Pansy.

She led the way through to the sitting-room. Her guest sat down but did not relax. 'If he didn't get in touch with his father, he always did with me, Agnes,' she said almost tearfully.

Agnes, full of her own affairs, tried hard to show sympathy and understanding. 'Pansy, do you think it's because he is homosexual and realises that fact will never be accepted by his father, and so thinks it is better to stay away, cut himself off completely?'

Pansy gave a little shudder. 'I hate that word "homosexual", Agnes. It's such a disgrace, so horrid I can't bear it.'

Agnes tried to be patient. 'Well, there you are, Pansy, being like that is pretty well accepted by everyone nowadays. Perhaps the fact that you both felt it was, as you put it "horrid", made him stay away.'

Pansy did have a little weep then. 'But I did accept it, Agnes – well, I tried to. I said I didn't mind.'

Agnes nodded. 'But perhaps he saw you did really mind and it upset you so he decided it was better if he stayed away.'

Pansy nodded gloomily. 'Yes, you're probably right, Agnes, and he's all right.'

'I'm sure he is.'

Pansy stood up. 'You are very good to listen to me, Agnes. Violet takes it all so lightly, but she's more a woman of the world than I am.'

Agnes felt really sorry for her, even gave her a light kiss on the cheek as she bade her goodbye at the door, but she felt no sorrow for the son who was dead and had been made unable to do any more harm.

Mac was to be left at home when Agnes went out on her dinner date. Having given him a good long walk and fed him, she felt he was getting a little bit spoilt and expected to have someone with him all the time. She did not want him to turn into a barking nuisance who couldn't be left without making the neighbours complain about his noise. So she gave him one of her little 'talking tos'. 'I won't be long and you are to be a good quiet little boy.' Mac always gave her his full attention, head on one side, ears pricked, brown eyes alert. Did he understand? Agnes always wondered how much animals understood. Their vocabulary was so small. Walk, Dinner, Come, Fetch, not much to live by. Anyway, by the time she had dressed she had given him her little talk three times. Tired out by his walk he had curled up in his bed. Maybe he would stay there; she could only hope so. One thing she did know, there would be a wonderful welcome for her when she came back, and that was worth all the trouble.

By seven fifteen Agnes was ready. She had chosen a favourite dress that she had not worn since Bill's death. A pale, apple green frock. Diaphanous, very suitable for a supper or dinner date and also suitable for a summer night. Permanently pleated skirt, the pleats running over the bodice to a V neck. For jewellery she wore a very thin gold chain, a present from Bill in his poorer days when his books had not yet become television serials or movies. On her wrist a filigree gold and diamond bracelet, also a present from Bill not very long before his untimely death in New York. A piece of jewellery that had figured dramatically and almost fatally in her life not long before the mugger had made her a widow. A spray of Joy followed when she had finished her discreet make-up. Flat shoes the same colour as her frock. She hated high heels and had never been able to walk in them in comfort. She clasped her small gold handbag. Lipstick, powder compact, handkerchief, a tiny gold box containing saccharine and a small purse. By the time she had done this, told Mac once more 'to be a good boy and she wouldn't be long', Eric was there. She heard the car draw up at her gate, the slam of the car door, the slight squeak of her garden gate and the rat-tat of the door knocker. For some reason Eric Marshall had ignored the bell on the door lintel.

In a dark suit instead of his rough tweeds, Eric Marshall looked quite different. As he opened the car door for her, Agnes caught the smell of a very pleasant aftershave that she did not recognise. Once in the car, conscious of the fact that Lyn had probably talked to him about the divorce, Agnes stole a sideways look at him. He looked quite serene, unsmiling, concentrating on his driving. She noticed his hair – he had been wearing a tweed hat both times she had met him before. It was thick and wavy with grey at the sides on his temples.

Once he had driven out on to the main road from the rather

twisty lanes, he turned to her and smiled. His teeth were white and even. 'I was a little early, I believe.' Agnes merely shook her head. 'Yes, I was, I was anxious to get away from the stables.'

Agnes could not ignore that. 'Oh, I'm sorry. Something wrong there? Maisie still all right, I hope?'

'Yes, Maisie's all right, just a few other things gone to pot.'

Agnes did not know how to answer that, or indeed whether to question him any further, so she decided to keep silent. The rest of the drive, which was quite a long way, was conducted in what she felt was quite a companionable silence.

The hotel was, as Agnes' manicurist had termed it, 'quite posh'. The bar was large, airy and tastefully furnished. About half of the small tables were occupied with mixed couples, all well dressed and sipping what looked like gin and tonics or white wine. They looked up as Eric and Agnes entered, then resumed their conversations, presumably having decided the newcomers were not anyone they knew. Eric led Agnes to a vacant table backed by a wall sofa. 'What will you drink, Agnes?' he asked. Agnes chose a white wine, not too dry, and he went off to the bar. Agnes watched him go. He was not handsome, she decided, but 'good-looking' would fit his looks better. As he put down the drinks, Agnes noticed that his eyes were grey and ringed by lashes that any woman would have envied.

'Have you seen Dolly's stable yet?' he asked.

'No, I haven't been back again.'

'It's really much better for the old mare and she looks quite smart now she's been clipped out.'

'I must go and see her,' Agnes said sipping her wine.

'Come with me tomorrow afternoon if you're free,' he said.

Agnes felt a little breathless, his remark was so casual, so matter of fact. She put her glass down on the table. He was gazing across the bar away from her.

'My wife's told me today she wants a divorce so I'm feeling a bit, what should I call it, shattered. I'd like you to come.'

'I'd love to, and I am very sorry about Lyn.'

He turned to her, just for a moment, then took a deep drink from his glass. 'Mineral water, don't worry,' he said, smiling, but the smile was tight and unhappy.

'I wasn't worrying,' Agnes said almost defensively.

'Your table is ready, sir.' A waiter appeared from the restaurant.

'Right.' He held out a hand and took Agnes'. She had finished her wine. They followed the waiter through to their table and sat down. Agnes chose smoked salmon; Eric did too, and a bottle of wine after a careful look at the wine list.

The meal was good, the roast beef perfect. Agnes refused the sweet and, over the restaurant's very good coffee, Eric Marshall seemed to relax a little. She noticed he only drank one glass of wine. She managed two and began to feel slightly more mellow.

'Tell me about Lyn, you only mentioned her briefly. Talk about it if you want to, but if you would rather not, I shall understand.'

He looked down at his coffee cup and then up at her. 'It serves me right, I'm a silly old fool. I'm fifty-nine, fifty-six when I married Lyn. She was twenty-three, thirty-three years younger than me.' He laughed, but not with much humour. 'She's a pretty thing, awful parents – well, perhaps I shouldn't say awful, but very very religious. Roman Catholics. Lyn's an only child, they wanted a young husband for her, children plus...' He paused and looked up at her, slightly anxious. 'You're not a Roman Catholic, I hope?'

'No, atheist,' Agnes replied, letting a little humour into her reply.

'Good,' he went on. 'Of course I'll give her a divorce, parents or not. She's in love with Guy Holstein. I'm sure you know about that, don't you?'

Agnes nodded. 'I guessed it, I'm sorry if it's hurt you.'

Eric put his hand across the table and covered her. 'Thank you.' He made a slight grimace. 'It does hurt a bit, but I think it's mostly my pride. Oh, sex was all right, but youth needs youth, don't you think?'

'Yes, I suppose it does.'

'There's no suppose about it at all, Agnes.'

He ordered more coffee. 'Music, books, experiments with drugs, manners, class, raves, dancing, it's all different. I was a silly fool.' His smile was charming. 'I shall part with her with sorrow, but trust I will know better next time.'

He laughed too. 'Well, you can't waste time at our age can you, or are you much younger than me?'

Agnes hardly knew what to say, whether to be amused or be to scandalised, so she picked 'amused'.

They left the restaurant and drove home to Rose Cottage.

'Do come in, just for a moment,' Agnes said.

He left the car unlocked and followed her in. 'Nice,' he said, greeting a rapturous Mac.

They wandered out into the back garden. It was still moonlight. Mac scampered about. Quite casually again Eric astonished Agnes.

'I hate that drive up to my house since my one and only favourite horse has been buried there. It saddens me, makes me feel lonely.'

'I can imagine that,' Agnes replied.

'And since John Merrill's body's been there . . .' He stopped.

'How did you know that, Eric?'

'Saw him do it. When we came to lift the horse in he hadn't quite covered the body bag so I took a shovelful of earth and threw it down. I told Lyn and the digger machine man that I wanted to put the first earth down over Fenner – that was the name of my horse.'

'Why did you . . . ?' Agnes could hardly ask the question.

'Well, I knew Lyn loved Guy then. If anyone found out, he would have been arrested and they might have been parted for ever.'

'But . . .' Agnes tried to say something, though she hardly knew what she intended to say.

He took her hand and smiled at her. 'Was that bastard worth their happiness?' he said.

Agnes shook her head. 'There are some things that are best left unsaid.'

They stood there for a moment more then he went through the cottage to his car.

Agnes walked back into Rose Cottage. She felt happy, but

rather as if she had been run over by a tank! She remembered his eyes, those long, long lashes. Mac barked and rushed in. 'What to do, Mac, what to do?' she said. Mac as usual cocked his head on one side and said nothing.